Adam Gurowski

Diary March 4, 1861 to November 12, 1862

Adam Gurowski

Diary March 4, 1861 to November 12, 1862

ISBN/EAN: 9783337184544

Printed in Europe, USA, Canada, Australia, Japan

Cover: Foto ©Raphael Reischuk / pixelio.de

More available books at **www.hansebooks.com**

DIARY,

FROM

MARCH 4, 1861, TO NOVEMBER 12, 1862.

BY

ADAM GUROWSKI.

————

BOSTON:

LEE AND SHEPARD,

SUCCESSORS TO PHILLIPS, SAMPSON & CO.

1862.

Dedicated

TO

THE WIDOWED WIVES, THE BEREAVED MOTHERS, SISTERS,

SWEETHEARTS, AND ORPHANS

IN

THE LOYAL STATES.

On doit à son pays sa fortune, sa vie, mais avant tout la Verite.

In this Diary I recorded what I heard and saw myself, and what I heard from others, on whose veracity I can implicitly rely.

I recorded impressions as immediately as I felt them. A life almost wholly spent in the tempests and among the breakers of our times has taught me that the first impressions are the purest and the best.

If they ever peruse these pages, my friends and acquaintances will find therein what, during these horrible national trials, was a subject of our confidential conversations and discussions, what in letters and by mouth was a subject of repeated forebodings and warnings. Perhaps these pages may in some way explain a phenomenon almost unexampled in history, — that twenty millions of people, brave, highly intelligent, and mastering all the wealth of modern civilization, were, if not virtually overpowered, at least so long kept at bay by about five millions of rebels.

GUROWSKI.

WASHINGTON, NOVEMBER, 1862.

CONTENTS.

MARCH, 1861.

APRIL, 1861.

MAY, 1861.

JUNE, 1861.

JULY, 1861.

AUGUST, 1861.

SEPTEMBER, 1861.

OCTOBER, 1861.

NOVEMBER, 1861.

DECEMBER, 1861.

JANUARY, 1862.

FEBRUARY, 1862.

MARCH, 1862.

APRIL, 1862.

MAY, 1862.

JUNE, 1862.

JULY, 1862.

AUGUST, 1862.

SEPTEMBER, 1862.

OCTOBER, 1862.

NOVEMBER, 1862.

DIARY.

MARCH, 1861.

For the first time in my life I assisted at the
simplest and grandest spectacle — the inauguration
of a President. Lincoln's message good, according
to circumstances, but not conclusive ; it is not positive ; it discusses questions, but avoids to assert.
May his mind not be altogether of the same kind.
Events will want and demand more positiveness
and action than the message contains assertions.
The immense majority around me seems to be satisfied. Well, well ; I wait, and prefer to judge and to
admire when actions will speak.

I am sure that a great drama will be played,
equal to any one known in history, and that the
insurrection of the slave-drivers will not end in

smoke. So I now decide to keep a diary in my own way. I scarcely know any of those men who are considered as leaders; the more interesting to observe them, to analyze their mettle, their actions. This insurrection may turn very complicated; if so, it must generate more than one revolutionary manifestation. What will be its march — what stages? Curious; perhaps it may turn out more interesting than anything since that great renovation of humanity by the great French Revolution.

The old, brave warrior, Scott, watched at the door of the Union; his shadow made the infamous rats tremble and crawl off, and so Scott transmitted to Lincoln what was and could be saved during the treachery of Buchanan.

By the most propitious accident, I assisted at the throes among which Mr. Lincoln's Cabinet was born. They were very painful, but of the highest interest for me, and I suppose for others. I participated some little therein.

A pledge bound Mr. Lincoln to make Mr. Seward his Secretary of State. The radical and the puritanic elements in the Republican party were terribly scared. His speeches, or rather demeanor and repeated utterances since the opening of the Congress, his influence on Mr. Adams, who, under Seward's inspiration, made his speech *de lana caprina*, and voted for compromises and concessions, — all this spread and fortified the general and firm belief that Mr. Seward was ready to give up many from among the cardinal articles of the Republican creed of

which he was one of the most ardent apostles.
They, the Republicans, speak of him in a way to
remind me of the dictum, "*omnia serviliter pro
dominatione*," as they accuse him now of subserviency to the slave power.   The radical and puritan•
Republicans likewise dread him on account of his
close intimacy with a Thurlow Weed, a Matteson,
and with similar not over-cautious — as they call
them — lobbyists.

Some days previous to the inauguration, Mr.
Seward brought Mr. Lincoln on the Senate floor, of
course on the Republican side ; but soon Mr. Seward
was busily running among Democrats, begging them
to be introduced to Lincoln.   It was a saddening,
humiliating, and revolting sight for the galleries,
where I was.   Criminal as is Mason, for a minute
I got reconciled to him for the scowl of horror and
contempt with which he shook his head at Seward.
The whole humiliating proceeding foreshadowed the
future policy.   Only two or three Democratic Senators were moved by Seward's humble entreaties.
The criminal Mason has shown true manhood.

The first attempt of sincere Republicans was to
persuade Lincoln to break his connection with Seward.   This failed.   To neutralize what was considered quickly to become a baneful influence in
Mr. Lincoln's councils, the Republicans united on
Gov. Chase.   This Seward opposed with all his
might.   Mr. Lincoln wavered, hesitated, and was
bending rather towards Mr. Seward.   The struggle
was terrific, lasted several days, when Chase was

finally and triumphantly forced into the Cabinet. It was necessary not to leave him there alone against Seward, and perhaps Bates, the old cunning Whig. Again terrible opposition by Seward, but it was overcome by the radicals in the House, in the Senate, and outside of Congress by such men as Curtis, Noyes, J. S. Wadsworth, Opdyke, Barney, &c., &c., and Blair was brought in. Cameron was variously opposed, but wished to be in by Seward; Welles was from the start considered sound and safe in every respect; Smith was considered a Seward man.

From what I witnessed of Cabinet-making in Europe, above all in France under Louis Philippe, I do not forebode anything good in the coming-on shocks and eruptions, and I am sure these must come. This Cabinet as it stands is not a fusion of various shadowings of a party, but it is a violent mixing or putting together of inimical and repulsive forces, which, if they do not devour, at the best will neutralize each other.

Senator Wilson answered Douglass in the Senate, that "when the Republican party took the power, treason was in the army, in the navy, in the administration," etc. Dreadful, but true assertion. It is to be seen how the administration will act to counteract this ramified treason.

What a run, a race for offices. This spectacle likewise new to me.

The Cabinet Ministers, or, as they call them here, the Secretaries, have old party debts to pay, old sores to avenge or to heal, and all this by distributing

offices, or by what they call it here — patronage.
Through patronage and offices everybody is to serve
his friends and his party, and to secure his political
position.   Some of the party leaders seem to me
similar to children enjoying a long-expected and
ardently wished-for toy.   Some of the leaders are
as generals who abandon the troops in a campaign,
and take to travel in foreign parts.   Most of them
act as if they were sure that the battle is over.   It
begins only, but nobody, or at least very few of the
interested, seem to admit that the country is on fire,
that a terrible struggle begins.   (Wrote in this
sense an article for the National Intelligencer ; inser-
tion refused.)   They, the leaders, look to create
engines for their own political security, but no one
seems to look over Mason and Dixon's line to the
terrible and with lightning-like velocity spreading
fire of hellish treason.

The diplomats utterly upset, confused, and do not
know what god to worship.   All their associations
were with Southerners, now traitors.   In Southern
talk, or in that of treacherous Northern Democrats,
the diplomats learned what they know about this
country.   Not one of them is familiar, is acquainted
with the genuine people of the North ; with its true,
noble, grand, and pure character.   It is for them a
terra incognita, as is the moon.   The little they
know of the North is the few money or cotton bags
of New York, Boston, Philadelphia,— these would-be
betters, these dinner-givers, and whist-players.   The

2

diplomats consider Seward as the essence of Northern feeling.

How little the thus-called statesmen know Europe.
Sumner, Seward, etc. already have under consideration if Europe will recognize the secesh.   Europe
recognizes *faits accomplis*, and a great deal of blood
will run before secesh becomes *un fait accompli*.
These Sewards, Sumners, etc. pay too much attention to the silly talk of the European diplomats in
Washington; and by doing this these would-be
statesmen prove how ignorant they are of history in
general, and specially ignorant of the policy of European cabinets.   Before a struggle decides a question a recognition is bosh, and I laugh at it.

The race, the race increases with a fearful rapidity.   No flood does it so quick.   Poor Senators!
Some of them must spend nights and days to decide
on whom to bestow. this or that office.   Secretaries
or Ministers wrangle, *fight* (that is the word used),
as if life and death depended upon it.

Poor (Carlylian-meaning) good-natured Senator
Sumner, in his earnest, honest wish to be just and
of service to everybody, looks as a hare tracked by
hounds; so are at him office-seekers from the whole
country.   This hunting degrades the hounds, and
enervates the patrons.

I am told that the President is wholly absorbed in
adjusting, harmonizing the amount of various sala-
ries bestowed on various States through its office-
holders and office-seekers.

It were better if the President would devote his

time to calculate the forces and resources needed to quench the fire. Over in Montgomery the slave-drivers proceed with the terrible, unrelenting, fearless earnestness of the most unflinching criminals.

After all, these crowds of office-hunters are far from representing the best element of the genuine, laborious, intelligent people, — of its true healthy stamina. This is consoling for me, who know the American people in the background of office-hunters.

Of course an alleviating circumstance is, that the method, the system, the routine, oblige, nay force, everybody to ask, to hunt. As in the Scriptures, "Ask, and you will get; or knock, and it will be opened." Of course, many worthy, honorable, deserving men, who would be ornaments to the office, must run the gauntlet together with the hounds.

It is reported, and I am sure of the truth of the report, that Governor Chase is for recognizing, or giving up the revolted Cotton States, so as to save by it the Border States, and eventually to fight for their remaining in the Union. What logic! If the treasonable revolt is conceded to the Cotton States, on what ground can it be denied to the thus called Border States? I am sorry that Chase has such notions.

It is positively asserted by those who ought to know, that Seward, having secured to himself the Secretaryship of State, offered to the Southern leaders in Congress compromise and concessions, to assure, by such step, his confirmation by the Demo-

cratic vote.   The chiefs refused the bargain, distrusting him.   All this was going on for weeks, nay
months, previous to the inauguration, so it is asserted.
But Seward might have been anxious to preserve
the Union at any price.   His enemies assert that if
Seward's plan had succeeded, virtually the Democrats would have had the power.   Thus the meaning of Lincoln's election would have been destroyed,
and Buchanan's administration would have been
continued in its most dirty features, the name only
being changed.

Old Scott seems to be worried out by his laurels;
he swallows incense, and I do not see that anything
whatever is done to meet the military emergency.   I
see the cloud.

Were it true that Seward and Scott go hand in
hand, and that both, and even Chase, are blunted
axes!

I hear that Mr. Blair is the only one who swears,
demands, asks for action, for getting at them without losing time.   Brave fellow!   I am glad to
have at Willard's many times piloted deputations to
the doors of Lincoln on behalf of Blair's admission
into the Cabinet.   I do not know him, but will try
to become nearer acquainted.

But for the New York radical Republicans,
already named, neither Chase nor Blair would have
entered the Cabinet.   But for them Seward would
have had it totally his own way.   Members of Congress acted less than did the New Yorkers.

The South, or the rebels, slave-drivers, slave-breeders, constitute the most corrosive social decompositions and impurities; what the human race throughout countless ages successively toiled to purify itself from and throw off. Europe continually makes terrible and painful efforts, which at times are marked by bloody destruction. This I asserted in my various writings. This social, putrefied evil, and the accumulated matter in the South, pestilentially and in various ways influenced the North, poisoning its normal healthy condition. This abscess, undermining the national life, has burst now. Somebody, something must die, but this apparent death will generate a fresh and better life.

The month of March closes, but the administration seems to enjoy the most beatific security. I do not see one single sign of foresight, — this cardinal criterion of statesmanship. Chase measures the empty abyss of the treasury. Senator Wilson spoke of treason everywhere, but the administration seems not to go to work and to reconstruct, to fill up what treason has disorganized and emptied. Nothing about reorganizing the army, the navy, refitting the arsenals. No foresight, no foresight! either statesmanlike or administrative. Curious to see these men at work. The whole efforts visible to me and to others, and the only signs given by the administration in concert, are the paltry preparations to send provisions to Fort Sumpter. What is the matter? what are they about?

APRIL, 1861.

COMMISSIONERS from the rebels ; Seward parleying with them through some Judge Campbell. Curious way of treating and dealing with rebellion, with rebels and traitors ; why not arrest them ?

Corcoran, a rich partisan of secession, invited to a dinner the rebel commissioners and the foreign diplomats. If such a thing were done anywhere else, such a pimp would be arrested. The serious diplomats, Lord Lyons, Mercier, and Stoeckl refused the invitation ; some smaller accepted, at least so I hear.

The infamous traitors fire on the Union flag. They treat the garrison of Sumpter as enemies on sufferance, and here their commissioners go about free, and glory in treason. What is this administration about ? Have they no blood ; are they fishes ?

The crime in full blast; *consummatum est*. Sumpter bombarded; Virginia, under the nose of the administration, secedes, and the leaders did not see or·foresee anything : flirted with Virginia.

Now, they, the leaders or the administration, are terribly startled ; so is the brave noble North; the people are taken unawares; but no wonder; the people saw the Cabinet, the President, and the military in complacent security. These watchmen did nothing to give an early sign of alarm, so the people, confiding in them, went about its daily occupation. But it will rise as one man and in terrible wrath. *Vous le verrez mess les Diplomates.*

The President calls on the country for 75,000 men; telegram has spoken, and they rise, they arm, they come. I am not deceived in my faith in the North ; the excitement, the wrath, is terrible. Party lines burn, dissolved by the excitement. Now the people is in fusion as bronze; if Lincoln and the leaders have mettle in themselves, then they can cast such arms, moral, material, and legislative, as will destroy at once this rebellion. But will they have the energy ? They do not look like Demiourgi.

Massachusetts takes the lead ; always so, this first people in the world; first for peace by its civilization and intellectual development, and first to run to the rescue.

The most infamous treachery and murder, by Bal-•timoreans, of the Massachusetts men. Will the cowardly murderers be exemplarily punished ?

The President, under the advice of Scott, seems

to take coolly the treasonable murders of Baltimore ; instead of action, again parleying with these Baltimorean traitors. The rumor says that Seward is for leniency, and goes hand in hand with Scott. Now, if they will handle such murderers in silk gloves as they do, the fire must spread.

The secessionists in Washington — and they are a legion, of all hues and positions — are defiant, arrogant, sure that Washington will be taken. One risks to be murdered here.

I entered the thus called Cassius Clay Company, organized for the defence of Washington until troops came. For several days patrolled, drilled, and lay several nights on the hard floor. Had compensation, that the drill often reproduced that of Falstaff's heroes. But my campaigners would have fought well in case of emergency. Most of them office-seekers. When the alarm was over, the company dissolved, but each got a kind of certificate beautifully written and signed by Lincoln and Cameron. I refused to take such a certificate, we having had no occasion to fight.

The President issued a proclamation for the blockade of the Southern revolted ports. Do they not know better ?

How can the Minister of Foreign Affairs advise the President to resort to such a measure ? Is the Minister of Foreign Affairs so willing to call in foreign nations by this blockade, thus transforming a purely domestic and municipal question into an international, public one ?

The President is to quench the rebellion, a domestic fire, and to do it he takes a weapon, an engine
the most difficult to handle, and in using of which
he depends on foreign nations. Do they not know
better here in the ministry and in the councils?
Russia dealt differently with the revolted Circassians
and with England in the so celebrated case of the
Vixen.

The administration ought to know its rights of
sovereignty and to close the ports of entry. Then
no chance would be left to England to meddle.

Yesterday N—— dined with Lord Lyons, and
during the dinner an anonymous note announced
to the Lord that the proclamation of the blockade
is to be issued on to-morrow. N——, who has a
romantic turn, or rather who seeks for *midi a'* 14¾
heures, speculated what lady would have thus violated a *secret d' Etat.*

I rather think it comes from the Ministry, or, as
they call it here, from the Department. About two
years ago, when the Central Americans were so teased
and maltreated by the fillibusters and Democratic
administration, a Minister of one of these Central
American States told me in New York that in a
Chief of the Departments, or something the like,
the Central Americans have a valuable friend, who,
every time that trouble is brewing against them in
the Department, gives them a secret and anonymous notice of it. This friend may have transferred his kindness to England.

How will foreign nations behave? I wish I may

be misguided by my political anglophobia, but England, envious, rapacious, and the Palmerstons and others, filled with hatred towards the genuine democracy and the American people, will play some bad tricks. They will seize the occasion to avenge many humiliations. Charles Sumner, Howe, and a great many others, rely on England, — on her anti-slavery feeling. I do not. I know English policy. We shall see.

France, Frenchmen, and Louis Napoleon are by far more reliable. The principles and the interest of France, broadly conceived, make the existence of a powerful Union a statesmanlike European and world necessity. The cold, taciturn Louis Napoleon is full of broad and clear conceptions. I am for relying, almost explicitly, on France and on him.

The administration calls in all the men-of-war scattered in all waters. As the commercial interests of the Union will remain unprotected, the administration ought to put them under the protection of France. It is often done so between friendly powers. Louis Napoleon could not refuse ; and accepting, would become pledged to our side.

Germany, great and small, governments and people, will be for the Union. Germans are honest; they love the Union, hate slavery, and understand, to be sure, the question. Russia, safe, very safe, few blackguards excepted ; so Italy. Spain may play double. I do not expect that the Spaniards, goaded to the quick by the former fillibustering administrations, will have judgment enough to find out that the Republicans have been and will be anti-fillibusters, and do not crave Cuba.

Wrote a respectful warning to the President concerning the unvoidable results of his proclamation in regard to the blockade; explained to him that this, his international demonstration, will, and forcibly must evoke a counter proclamation from foreign powers in the interest of their own respective subjects and of their commercial relations. Warned, foretelling that the foreign powers will recognize the rebels as belligerents, he, the President, having done it already in some way, thus applying an international mode of coercion. Warned, that the condition of belligerents, once recognized, the rebel piratical crafts will be recognized as privateers by foreign powers, and as such will be admitted to all ports under the secesh flag, which will thus enjoy a partial recognition.

Foreign powers may grumble, or oppose the closing of the ports of entry as a domestic, administrative decision, because they may not wish to commit themselves to submit to a paper blockade. But if the President will declare that he will enforce the closing of the ports with the whole navy, so as to strictly guard and close the maritime league, then the foreign powers will see that the administration does not intend to humbug them, but that he, the President, will only preserve intact the fullest exercise of sovereignty, and, as said the Roman legist, he, the President, " *nil sibi postulat quod non aliis tribuit.*" And so he, the President, will only execute the laws of his country, and not any arbitrary measure, to say with the Roman Emperor, " *Leges etiam in ipsa arma imperium habere volumus.*" Warned the President that in all matters relating to this country Louis Napoleon has abandoned the initiative to England ; and to throw a small wedge in this alliance, I finally respectfully suggested to the President what is said above about putting the American interests in the Mediterranean under the protection of Louis Napoleon.

Few days thereafter learned that Mr. Seward does not believe that France will follow England. Before long Seward will find it out.

All the coquetting with Virginia, all the presumed influence of General Scott, ended in Virginia's secession, and in the seizure of Norfolk.

Has ever any administration, cabinet, ministry — call it what name you will — given positive, indubitable signs of want and absence of foresight, as did ours in these Virginia, Norfolk, and Harper's Ferry affairs ? Not this or that minister or secretary, but all of them ought to go to the constitutional guillotine.   Blindness — no mere short-sightedness — permeates the whole administration, Blair excepted. And Scott, the politico-military adviser of the President ! What is the matter with Scott, or were the halo and incense surrounding him based on bosh ? Will it be one more illusion to be dispelled ?

The administration understood not how to save or defend Norfolk, nor how to destroy it. No name to be found for such concrete incapacity. The rebels are masters, taking our leaders by the nose. Norfolk gives to them thousands of guns, &c., and nobody cries for shame. They ought to go in sackcloth, those narrow-sighted, blind rulers. How will the people stand this masterly administrative demonstration? In England the people and the Parliament would impeach the whole Cabinet.

Charles Sumner told me that the President and his Minister of Foreign Affairs are to propose to the foreign powers the accession of the Union to the celebrated convention of Paris of 1856. All three considered it a master stroke of policy. They will not catch a fly by it.

Again wrote respectfully to Mr. Lincoln, warning him against a too hasty accession to the Paris convention. Based my warning, —

1st. Not to give up the great principles contained in Marcy's amendment.

2d. Not to believe or suppose for a minute that the accession to the Paris convention at this time can act in a retroactive sense; explained that it will not and cannot prevent the rebel pirates from being recognized by foreign powers as legal privateers, or being treated as such.

3d. For all these reasons the Union will not win anything by such a step, but it will give up principles and chain its own hands in case of any war with England. Supplicated the President not to risk a step which logically must turn wrong.

Baltimore still unpunished, and the President parleying with various deputations, all this under the

guidance of Scott.   I begin to be confused; cannot
find out what is the character of Lincoln, and above
all of Scott.

Governors from whole or half-rebel States refuse
the President's call for troops.   The original call of
75,000, too small in itself, will be reduced by that
refusal.   Why does not the administration call for
more on the North, and on the free States?   In the
temper of this noble people it will be as easy to have
250,000 as 75,000, and then rush on them; sub-
merge Virginia, North Carolina, etc.; it can be now
so easily done.   The Virginians are neither armed
nor organized.   Courage and youth seemingly would
do good in the councils.

The free States undoubtedly will vindicate self-
government.   Whatever may be said by foreign and
domestic croakers, I do not doubt it for a single minute.   The free people will show to the world that the
apparently loose governmental ribbons are the
strongest when everybody carries them in him, and
holds them. The people will show that the intellectual
magnetism of convictions permeating the million is
by far stronger than the commonly called governmental action from above, and it is at the same time
elastic and expansive, even if the official leaders may
turn out to be altogether mediocrities.   The self-
governing free North will show more vitality and
activity than any among the governed European
countries would be able to show in similar emergencies.   This is my creed, and I have faith in the
people.

The infamous slavers of the South would even be
honored if named Barbary States of North America.

Before the inauguration, Seward was telling the
diplomats that no disruption will take place; now
he tells them that it will blow over in from sixty to
ninety days. Does Seward believe it? Or does his
imagination or his patriotism carry him away or
astray? Or, perhaps, he prefers not to look the
danger in the face, and tries to avert the bitter cup.
At any rate, he is incomprehensible, and the more
so when seen at a distance.

Something, nay, even considerable efforts ought to
be made to enlighten the public opinion in Europe,
as on the outside, insurrections, nationalities, etc.,
are favored in Europe. How far the diplomats sent
by the administration are prepared for this task?

Adams has shown in the last Congress his schol-
arly, classical narrow-mindedness. Sanford cannot
favorably impress anybody in Europe, neither in
cabinets, nor in saloons, nor the public at large. He
looks and acts as a *commis voyageur*, will be considered as such at first sight by everybody, and his
features and manners may not impress others as
being distinguished and high-toned.

Every historical, that is, human event, has its
moral and material character and sides. To ignore,
and still worse to blot out, to reject the moral incen-
tives and the moral verdict, is a crime to the public
at large, is a crime towards human reason.

Such action blunts sound feelings and comprehension, increases the arrogance of the evil-doers.

The moral criterion is absolute and unconditional, and ought as such unconditionally to be applied to the events here. Things and actions must be called by their true names. What is true, noble, pure, and lofty, is on the side of the North, and permeates the unnamed millions of the free people; it ought to be separated from what is sham, egotism, lie or assumption. Truth must be told, never mind the outcry. History has not to produce pieces for the stage, or to amuse a tea-party.

Regiments pour in; the Massachusetts men, of course, leading the van, as in the times of the tea-party. My admiration for the Yankees is justified on every step, as is my scorn, my contempt, etc., etc., of the Southern *chivalrous* slaver.

Wrote to Charles Sumner expressing my wonder at the undecided conduct of the administration; at its want of foresight; its eternal parleying with Baltimoreans, Virginians, Missourians, etc., and no step to tread down the head of the young snake. No one among them seems to have the seer's eye. The people alone, who arm, who pour in every day and in large numbers, who transform Washington into a camp, and who crave for fighting, — the people alone have the prophetic inspiration, and are the genuine statesmen for the emergency.

How will the Congress act? The Congress will come here emerging from the innermost of the popular volcano; but the Congress will be manacled by formulas; it will move not in the spirit of the Constitution, but in the dry constitutionalism, and the

Congress will move with difficulty. Still I have faith, although the Congress never will seize upon parliamentary omnipotence. Up to to-day, the administration, instead of boldly crushing, or, at least, attempting to do it; instead of striking at the traitors, the administration is continually on the lookout where the blows come from, scarcely having courage to ward them off. The deputations pouring from the North urge prompt, decided, crushing action. This thunder-voice of the twenty millions of freemen ought to nerve this senile administration. The Southern leaders do not lose one minute's time; they spread the fire, arm, and attack with all the fury of traitors and criminals.

The Northern merchants roar for the offensive; the administration is undecided.

Some individuals, politicians, already speak out that the slaveocratic privileges are only to be curtailed, and slavery preserved as a domestic institution. Not a bit of it. The current and the development of events will run over the heads of the pusillanimous and contemptible conservatives. Slavery must perish, even if the whole North, Lincoln and Seward at its head, should attempt to save it.

Already they speak of the great results of Fabian policy; Seward, I am told, prides in it. Do those Fabiuses know what they talk about? Fabius's tactics — not policy — had in view not to expose young, disheartened levies against Hannibal's unconquered veterans, but further to give time to Rome to restore her exhausted means, to recover political influences

3

with other Italian independent communities, to re-conclude broken alliances with the cities, etc. But is this the condition of the Union? Your Fabian policy will cost lives, time, and money; the people feels it, and roars for action. Events are great, the people is great, but the official leaders may turn out inadequate to both.

What a magnificent chance — scarcely equal in history — to become a great historical personality, to tower over future generations. But I do not see any one pointing out the way. Better so; the principle of self-government as the self-acting, self-preserving force will be asserted by the total eclipse of great or even eminent men.

The administration, under the influence of drill men, tries to form twenty regiments of regulars, and calls for 45,000 three years' volunteers. What a curious appreciation of necessity and of numbers must prevail in the brains of the administration. Twenty regiments of regulars will be a drop in water; will not help anything, but will be sufficient to poison the public spirit. Citizens and people, but not regulars, not hirelings, are to fight the battle of principle. Regulars and their spirit, with few exceptions, is worse here than were the Yanit-schars.

When the principle will be saved and victorious, it will be by the devotion, the spontaneity of the people, and not by Lincoln, Scott, Seward, or any of the like. It is said that Seward rules both Lincoln and Scott. The people, the masses, do not doubt their ability to crush by one blow the traitors, but the administration does. ·

What I hear concerning the Blairs confirms my high opinion of both. Blair alone in the Cabinet represents the spirit of the people.

Something seems not right with Scott. Is he too old, or too much of a Virginian, or a hero on a small scale ?

If, as they say, the President is guided by Scott's advice, such advice, to judge from facts, is not politic, not heroic, not thorough, not comprehensive, and not at all military, that is, not broad and deep, in the military sense. It will be a pity to be disappointed in this national idol.

Scott is against entering Virginia, against taking Baltimore, against punishing traitors. Strange, strange !

Diplomats altogether out of their senses; they are bewildered by the uprising, by the unanimity, by the warlike, earnest, unflinching attitude of the masses of the freemen, of my dear Yankees. The diplomats have lost the compass. They, duty bound, were diplomatically obsequious to the power held so long by the pro-slavery party. They got accustomed to the arrogant assumption and impertinence of the slavers, and, forgetting their European origin, the diplomats tacitly — but for their common sense and honor I hope reluctantly — admitted the assumptions of the Southern banditti to be in America the nearest assimilation to the chivalry and nobility of old Europe. Without taking the cudgel in de-

fence of European nobility, chivalry, and aristocracy, it is sacrilegious to compare those infamous
slavers with the old or even with the modern European higher classes. In the midst of this slave-
driving, slave-worshipping, and slave-breeding society of Washington, the diplomats swallowed,
gulped all the Southern lies about the Constitution,
state-rights, the necessity of slavery, and other like
infamies. The question is, how far the diplomats
in their respective official reports transferred these
pro-slavery common-places to their governments.
But, after all, the governments of Europe will not
be thoroughly influenced by the chat of their diplomats.

Among all diplomats the English (Lord Lyons)
is the most sphinx; he is taciturn, reserved, listens
more than he speaks; the others are more commu-
nicative.

What an idea have those Americans of sending a
secret agent to Canada, and what for? England
will find it out, and must be offended. I would not
have committed such an absurdity, even in my palmy
days, when I conspired with Louis Napoleon, sat in
the councils with Godefroi Cavaignac, or wrote instructions for Mazzini, then only a beginner with
his *Giovina Italia*, and his miscarried Romarino
attempt in Savoy.

Of what earthly use can be such *politique provocatrice* towards England? Or is it only to give some
money to a hungry, noisy, and not over-principled
office-seeker?

MAY, 1861.

The administration tossed by expedients — Seward to Dayton — Spread-eagleism — One phasis of the American Union finished — The fuss about Russell — Pressure on the administration increases — Seward, Wickoff, and the Herald — Lord Lyons menaced with passports — The splendid Northern army — The administration not up to the occasion —'The new men — Andrew, Wadsworth, Boutwell, Noyes, Wade, Trumbull, Walcott, King, Chandler, Wilson — Lyon jumps over formulas — Governor Banks needed — Butler takes Baltimore with two regiments — News from England — The "belligerent" question — Butler and Scott — Seward and the diplomats — "What a Merlin!" — "France not bigger than New York!" — Virginia invaded — Murder of Ellsworth — Harpies at the White House.

RUMORS that the President, the administration, or whoever has it in his hands, is to take the offensive, make a demonstration on Virginia and on Baltimore. But these ups and downs, these vacillations, are daily occurrences, and nothing points to a firm purpose, to a decided policy, or any policy whatever of the administration.

A great principle and a great cause cannot be served and cannot be saved by half measures, and still less by tricks and by paltry expedients. But the administration is tossed by expedients. Nothing is hitherto done, and this denotes a want of any firm decision.

Mr. Seward's letter to Dayton, a first manifesto to foreign nations, and the first document of the new

37

Minister of Foreign Affairs. It is bold, high-toned, and American, but it has dark shadows; shows an inexperienced hand in diplomacy and in dealing with events. The passages about the frequent changes in Europe are unnecessary, and unprovoked by anything whatever. It is especially offensive to France, to the French people, and to Louis Napoleon. It is bosh, but in Europe they will consider it as *une politique provocatrice.*

For the present complications, diplomatic relations ought to be conducted with firmness, with dignity, but not with an arrogant, offensive assumption, not in the spirit of spread-eagleism; no brass, but reason and decision.

Americans will find out how absolute are the laws of history, as stern and as positive as all the other laws of nature. To me it is clear that one phasis of American political growth, development, &c., is gone, is finished. It is the phasis of the Union as created by the Constitution. This war — war it will be, and a terrible one, notwithstanding all the prophecies of Mr. Seward to the contrary — this war will generate new social and constitutional necessities and new formulas. New conceptions and new passions will spring up; in one word, it will bring forth new social, physical, and moral creations: so we are in the period of gestation.

Democracy, the true, the noble, that which constitutes the signification of America in the progress of our race — democracy will not be destroyed. All the inveterate enemies here and in Europe, all who already joyously sing the funeral songs of democracy, all of them will become disgraced. Democracy will emerge more pure, more powerful, more rational; destroyed will be the most infamous oligarchy ever known in history; oligarchy issued neither from the sword, nor the gown, nor the shop, but wombed, generated, cemented, and sustained by traffic in man.

The famous Russell, of the London Times, is what I always thought him to be — a graphic, imaginative writer, with power of description of all he sees, but not the slightest insight in events, in men, in institutions. Russell is not able to find out the epidermis under a shirt. And they make so much fuss about him; Seward brings him to the first cabinet dinner given by the President; Mrs. Lincoln sends him bouquets; and this man, Russell, will heap blunders upon blunders.

The pressure on the administration for decided, energetic action increases from all sides. Seldom, anywhere, an administration receives so many moral kicks as does this one; but it seems to stand them with serenity. Oh, for a clear, firm, well-defined purpose!

The country, the people demands an attack on Virginia, on Richmond, and Baltimore; the country, better than the military authorities, understands the political and military necessities; the people has the consciousness that if fighting is done instantly, it will be done cheaply and thoroughly by a move of its finger. The administration can double the number

of men under arms, but hesitates.   What slow
coaches, and what ignorance of human nature and
of human events.   The knowing ones, the wiseacres,
will be the ruin of this country.   They poison the
sound reason of the people.

What the d—— is Seward with his politicians'
policy?   What can signify his close alliance with
such outlaws as Wikoff and the Herald, and pushing
that sheet to abuse England and Lord Lyons?
Wikoff is, so to speak, an inmate of Seward's house
and office, and Wikoff declared publicly that the
telegram contained in the Herald, and so violent
against England and Lord Lyons, was written under
Seward's dictation.   Wikoff, I am told, showed the
MS. corrected in Seward's handwriting.   Lord
Lyons is menaced with passports.   Is this man mad?
Can Seward for a moment believe that Wikoff knows
Europe, or has any influence?   He may know the
low resorts there.   Can Seward be fool enough to
irritate England, and entangle this country?   Even
my anglophobia cannot stand it.   Wrote about it
warning letters to New York, to Barney, to Opdyke,
to Wadsworth, &c.

The whole District a great camp; the best population from the North in rank and file.   More intelli-
gence, industry, and all good national and intellectual qualities represented in those militia and
volunteer regiments, than in any — not only army,
but society — in Europe.   Artisans, mechanics of
all industries, of trade, merchants, bankers, lawyers;
all pursuits and professions.   Glorious, heart-elevat-

ing sight!   These regiments want only a small touch of military organization.

Weeks run, troops increase, and not the first step made to organize them into an army, to form brigades, not to say divisions; not yet two regiments manœuvring together.   What a strange idea the military chief or chiefs, or department, or somebody, must have of what it is to organize an army.   Not the first letter made. Can it be ignorance of this elementary knowledge with which is familiar every corporal in Europe?   When will they start, when begin to mould an army?

The administration was not composed for this emergency, and is not up to it.   The government hesitates, is inexperienced, and will unavoidably make heaps of mistakes, which may endanger the cause, and for which, at any rate, the people is terribly to pay.   The loss in men and material will be very considerable before the administration will get on the right track.   It is painful to think, nay, to be sure of it.   Then the European anti-Union politicians and diplomats will credit the disasters to the inefficiency of self-government.   The diplomats, accustomed to the rapid, energetic action of a supreme or of a centralized power, laugh at the trepidation of ours.   But the fault is not in the principle of self-government, but in the accident which brought to the helm such an amount of inexperience.   Monarchy with a feeble head is even in a worse predicament.   Louis XV., the Spanish and Neapolitan Bourbons, Gustavus IV., &c., are thereof the historical evidences.

May the shock of events bring out new lights from the people! One day the administration is to take the initiative, that is, the offensive, then it recedes from it. No one understands the organization and handling of such large bodies. They are to make their apprenticeship, if only it may not to be too dearly paid. But they cannot escape the action of that so positive law in nature, in history, and, above all, absolute in war.

Wrote to Charles Sumner, suggesting that the ice magnates send here from Boston ice for hospitals.

The war now waged against the free States is one made by the most hideous *sauvagerie* against a most perfectioned and progressive civilization. History records not a similar event. It is a hideous phenomenon, disgracing our race, and it is so, look on it from whatever side you will.

A new man from the people, like Governor Andrew, of Massachusetts, acts promptly, decisively; feels and speaks ardently, and not as the rhetors. Andrew is the incarnation of the Massachusetts, nay, of the genuine American people. I must become acquainted with Andrew. Thousands of others like Andrew exist in all the States. Can anybody be a more noble incarnation of the American people than J. S. Wadsworth? I become acquainted with numerous men whom I honor as the true American men. So Boutwell, of Massachusetts, Curtis Noyes, Senator Wade, Trumbull, Walcott, from Ohio, Senator King, Chandler, and many, many true patriots.

Senator Wilson, my old friend, is up to the mark ; a man of the people, but too mercurial.

Captain or Major Lyon in St. Louis, the first initiator or revelator of what is the absolute law of necessity in questions of national death or life. · Lyon jumped over formulas, over routine, over clumsy discipline and martinetism, and saved St. Louis and Missouri.·

. It is positively asserted that General Scott's first impression was to court-martial Lyon for this breach of discipline, for having acted on his own patriotic responsibility.

Can Scott be such a dried-up, narrow-minded disciplinarian, and he the Egeria of Lincoln ! Oh ! oh !

Diplomats tell me that Seward uses the dictatorial I, speaking of the government. Three cheers for the new Louis XIV.!

Governor Banks would be excellent for the *Intendant General de l'Armée :* they call it here *General Quartermaster.* Awful disorder and slowness prevail in this cardinal branch of the army. Wrote to Sumner concerning Banks.

Gen. Butler took Baltimore ; did what ought to have been done a long time ago. Butler did it on his own responsibility, without orders. Butler acted upon the same principle as Lyon, and, *horrabile dictu,* astonished, terrified the parleying administration. Scott wishes to put Butler under arrest ; happily Lincoln resisted his boss (so Mr. Lincoln called Scott before a deputation from Baltimore). Scott, Patterson, and Mansfield made a beautiful *strategi-*

cal horror! They began to speak of strategy; plan to approach Baltimore on three different roads, and with about 35,000 men. Butler did it one morning with two regiments, and kicked over the senile strategians in council.

The administration speaks with pride of its forbearing, that is, parleying, policy. The people, the country, requires action. *Congressus impar Achilli:* Achilles, the people, and *Congressus* the forbearing administration.

Music, parades, serenades, receptions, &c., &c., only no genuine military organization. They do it differently on the other side of the Potomac. There the leaders are in earnest.

Met Gov. Sprague and asked him when he would have a brigade; his answer was, soon; but this soon comes very slow.

News from England. Lord John Russell declared in Parliament that the Queen, or the English government, will recognize the rebels in the condition of "belligerents." O England, England! The declaration is too hasty. Lord John cannot have had news of the proclamation of the blockade when he made that declaration. The blockade could have served him as an excuse for the haste. English aristocracy and government show thus their enmity to the North, and their partiality to slavers. What will the anglophiles of Boston say to this?

Neither England or France, or anybody in Europe, recognized the condition of "belligerents" to Poles, when we fought in Russia in 1831. Were the Magyars recognized as such in 1848–'49 ? Lord Palmerston called the German flag hard names in the war with Denmark for Schleswig-Holstein ; and now he bows to the flag of slavers and pirates. If the English statesmen have not some very particular reason for this hasty, uncalled-for condescension to the enemies of humanity, then curse upon the English government. I recollect that European powers recognized the Greeks " belligerents " (Austria opposed) in their glorious struggle against the slavers, the Turks. But then this stretching of positive, international comity, — this stretching was done in the interest of freedom, of right, and of humanity, against savages and slaughterers. On the present occasion England did the reverse. O England, England, thou Judas Iscariot of nations ! Seward said to John Jacob Astor, and to a New York deputation, that this English declaration concerning " belligerents " is a mere formality, having no bearing at all. I told the contrary to Astor and to others, assuring them that Mr. Seward will soon find, to the cost of the people and to his own, how much complication and trouble this *mere formality* will occasion, and occasion it before long. Is Seward so ignorant of international laws, of general or special history, or was it only said to throw dust ?

Wrote about the " belligerents " a warning letter to the President.

Butler, in command of Fortress Monroe, proposes to land in Virginia and to take Norfolk ; Scott, the highest military authority in the land, opposes. Has

Scott used up his energy, his sense, and even his military judgment in defending Washington before the inauguration? He is too old; his brains, *cerebellum*, must be dried up.

Imbecility in a leader is often, nay always, more dangerous than treason; the people can find out — easily, too — treason, but is disarmed against imbecility.

What a thoughtlessness to press on Russia the convention of Paris? Russia has already a treaty with America, but in case of a war with England, the Russian ports on the Pacific, and the only one accessible to Americans, will be closed to them by the convention of Paris.

The governors of the States of Ohio, Illinois, Pennsylvania assure the protection of their respective States to the Union men of the Border States. What a bitter criticism on the slow, forbearing policy of the administration. Mr. Lincoln seems to be a rather slow intellect, with slow powers of perception. However, patience; perhaps the shock of events will arouse and bring in action now latent, but good and energetic qualities. As it stands now, the administration, being the focus of activity, is tepid, if not cold and slow; the circumference, that is, the people, the States, are full of fire and of activity. This condition is altogether the reverse of the physiological and all other natural laws, and this may turn out badly, as nature's laws never can be with impunity reversed or violated.

The diplomats complain that Seward treats them

with a certain rudeness; that he never gives them time to explain and speak, but interrupts by saying, "I know it all," etc. If he had knowledge of things, and of the diplomatic world, he would be aware that the more firmness he has to use, the more politeness, even fastidiousness, he is to display.

Scott does not wish for any bold demonstration, for any offensive movement. The reason may be, that he is too old, too crippled, to be able to take the field in person, and too inflated by conceit to give the glory of the active command to any other man. Wrote to Charles Sumner in Boston to stir up some inventive Yankee to construct a wheelbarrow in which Scott could take the field in person.

In a conversation with Seward, I called his attention to the fact that the government is surrounded by the finest, most complicated, intense, and well-spread web of treason that ever was spun; that almost all that constitutes society and is in a daily, nay hourly, contact with the various branches of the Executive, all this, with soul, mind, and heart is devoted to the rebels. I observed to him that *si licet exemplis in parvo grandibus uti.* Napoleon suffered more from the bitter hostility of the *faubourg St. Germain,* than from the armies of the enemy; and here it is still worse, as this hostility runs out into actual, unrelenting treason. To this Mr. Seward answered with the utmost serenity, " that before long all this will change; that when he became governor of New York, a similar hostility prevailed between the two sections of that State, but soon he pacified everything." What a Merlin! what a sorcerer!

Some simple-minded persons from the interior of the State of New York questioned Mr. Seward, in my presence, about Europe, and "what they will do there?" To this, with a voice of the Delphic oracle, he responded, "that after all France is not bigger than the State of New York." Is it possible to say such trash even as a joke?

Finally, the hesitations of General Scott are overcome. "Virginia's sacred soil is invaded;" Potomac crossed; looks like a beginning of activity; Scott consented to move on Arlington Heights, but during two or three days opposed the seizure of Alexandria. Is that all that he knows of that hateful watchword — strategy — nausea repeated by every ignoramus and imbecile?

Alexandria being a port of entry, and having a railroad, is more a strategic point for the invasion of Virginia than are Arlington Heights.

The brave Ellsworth murdered in Alexandria, and Scott insisted that Alexandria be invaded and occupied by night. In all probability, Ellsworth would not have been murdered if this villanous nest had been entered by broad daylight. As if the troops were committing a crime, or a shameful act! O General Scott! but for you Ellsworth would not have been murdered.

General McDowell made a plan to seize upon Manassas as the centre of railroads, the true defence of Washington, and the firm foothold in Virginia.

Nobody, or only few enemies, were in Manassas. McDowell shows his genuine military insight. Scott, and, as I am told, the whole senile military council, opposed McDowell's plan as being too bold. Do these mummies intend to conduct a war without boldness?

Thick clouds of patriotic, well-intentioned harpies surround all the issues of the executive doors, windows, crevasses, all of them ready to turn an honest, or rather dishonest, penny out of the fatherland. Behind the harpies advance the busy-bodies, the would-be well-informed, and a promiscuous crowd of well-intentioned do-nothings.

4

JUNE, 1861.

THE emancipation of slaves is virtually inaugurated. Gen. Butler, once a hard pro-slavery Democrat, takes the lead. *Tempora mutantur et nos*, &c.
Butler originated the name of *contrabands of war*
for slaves faithful to the Union, who abandon their
rebel masters. A logical Yankee mind operates as
an *accoucheur* to bring that to daylight with which
the events are pregnant.

The enemies of self-government at home and
abroad are untiring in vaticinations that a dictatorship
now, and after the war a strong centralized government, will be inaugurated. I do not believe it.
Perhaps the riddle to be solved will be, to make a
strong administration without modifying the principle of self-government.

The most glorious difference between Americans
and Europeans is, that in cases of national emergencies, every European nation, the Swiss excepted, is
called, stimulated to action, to sacrifices, either by a
chief, or by certain families, or by some high-standing

50

individual, or by the government; here the people
forces upon the administration more of all kinds of
sacrifices than the thus called rulers can grasp, and
the people is in every way ahead of the administration.

Notwithstanding that a part of the army crossed
the Potomac, very little genuine organization is
done. They begin only to organize brigades, but
slowly, very slowly. Gen. Scott unyielding in his
opposition to organizing any artillery, of which the
army has very, very little. This man is incomprehensible. He cannot be a clear-headed general or
organizer, or he cannot be a patriot.

As for the past, single regiments are parading in
honor of the President, of members of the Cabinet,
of married and unmarried *ladies*, but no military
preparatory exercise of men, regiments, or brigades.
It sickens to witness such *incurie*.

Mr. Seward promenading the President from regiment to regiment, from camp to camp, or rather
showing up the President and himself. Do they believe they can awake enthusiasm for their persons?
The troops could be better occupied than to serve for
the aim of a promenade for these two distinguished
personalities.

Gen. Scott refuses the formation of volunteer
artillery and of new cavalry regiments, and the
active army, more than 20,000 men, has a very in-
sufficient number of batteries, and between 600 and
800 cavalry. Lincoln blindly follows his boss.
Seward, of course, sustains Scott, and confuses Lin-

coln. Lincoln, Scott, Seward and Cameron oppose offers pouring from the country. To a Mr. M———, from the State of New York, who demanded permission to form a regiment of cavalry, Mr. Lincoln angrily answered, that (patriotic) offers give more " trouble to him and the administration than do the rebels."

The debates of the English Parliament raise the ire of the people, nay, exasperate even old fogyish Anglo-manes.

Persons very familiar with the domestic relations of Gen. Scott assure me that the vacillations of the old man, and his dread of a serious warfare, result from the all-powerful influence on him of one of his daughters, a rabid secessionist. The old man ought to be among relics in the Patent office, or sent into a nursery.

The published correspondence between Lord Lyons and Lord Russell concerning the blockade furnishes curious revelations.

When the blockade was to be declared, Mr. Seward seems to have been a thorough novice in the whole matter, and in an official interview with Lord Lyons, Mr. Seward was assisted by his chief clerk, who was therefore the quintessence of the wisdom of the foreign affairs, a man not even mastering the red-tape traditions of the department, without any genuine instruction, without ideas. For this chief clerk, all that he knew of a blockade was that it was in use during the Mexican war, that it almost yearly occurred in South American waters, and every tyro knows there exists such a thing as a blockade. But that was all that this chief clerk knew. Lord Lyons asked for some special precedents or former acts of the American government. The chief, and his support, the chief clerk, ignored the existence of any. Lord Lyons went home and sent to the department American precedents and authorities. No Minister of Foreign Affairs in Europe, together with his chief clerk, could ever be caught in such a *flagrante delicto* of ignorance. This chief clerk made Mr. Seward make *un pas de clerc*, and this at the start. As Lord Lyons took a great interest in the solution of the question of blockade, and as the chief clerk was the *oraculum* in this question, these combined facts may give some clue to the anonymous advice sent to Lord Lyons, and mentioned in the month of April.

Suggested to Mr. Seward to at once elevate the American question to a higher region, to represent it to Europe in its true, holy character, as a question of right, freedom, and humanity. Then it will be impossible for England to quibble about technicalities of the international laws; then we can beat England with her own arms and words, as England in 1824, &c., recognized the Greeks as belligerents, on the plea of aiding freedom and humanity. The Southern insurrection is a movement similar to that of the Neapolitan brigands, similar to what partisans of the Grand Dukes of Tuscany or Modena may attempt, similar to any — for argument's sake — supposed insurrection of any Russian bojàrs against the emancipating Czar. Not in one from among the above enumerated cases would England concede to the insurgents the condition of belligerents. If the Deys of Tunis and Tripoli should attempt to throw off their allegiance to the Sultan on the plea that the Porte prohibits the slave traffic, would England hurry to recognize the Deys as belligerents?

Suggested to Mr. Seward, what two months ago I suggested to the President, to put the commercial interests in the Mediterranean, for a time, under the protection of Louis Napoleon.

I maintain the right of closing the ports, against the partisans of blockade. *Qui jure suo utitur neminem lædit*, says the Roman jurisconsult.

The condition of Lincoln has some similarity with that of Pio IX. in 1847–48. Plenty of good-will, but the eagle is not yet breaking out of the egg. And as Pio IX. was surrounded by this or that cardinal, so is Mr. Lincoln by Seward and Scott.

Perhaps it may turn out that Lincoln is honest, but of not transcendent powers. The war may last long, and the military spirit generated by the war may in its turn generate despotic aspirations. Under Lincoln in the White House, the final victory will be due to the people alone, and he, Lincoln, will preserve intact the principle which lifted him to such a height.

The people is in a state of the healthiest and most generous fermentation, but it may become soured

and musty by the admixture of Scott-Seward vacil-
latory powders.

Scott is all in all — Minister or Secretary of War
and Commander-in-chief.   How absurd to unite
those functions, as they are virtually united here,
Scott deciding all the various military questions;
he the incarnation of the dusty, obsolete, everywhere thrown overboard and rotten routine.   They
ought to have for Secretary of War, if not a Carnot, at least a man of great energy, honesty, of strong
will, and of a thorough devotion to the cause.   Senator Wade would be suitable for this duty.   Cameron is devoted, but I doubt his other capacities for
the emergency, and he has on his shoulders General
Scott as a dead weight.

Charles Sumner, Mr. Motley, Dr. Howe, and
many others, consider it as a triumph that the English Cabinet asked Mr. Gregory to postpone his
motion for the recognition of the Southern Confed-
eracy.   Those gentlemen here are not deep, and are
satisfied with a few small crumbs thrown them by
the English aristocracy.   Generally, the thus-called
better Americans eagerly snap at such crumbs.

It is clear that the English Cabinet wished this
postponement for its own sake.   A postponement
spares the necessity to Russells, Palmerstons, Gladstones, and *hoc genus omne,* to show their hands.
Mr. Adams likewise is taken in.

Military organization and *strategic points* are the
watchwords.   *Strategic points,* strategy, are natural
excrescences of brains which thus shamefully con-

ceive and carry out what the abused people believe to be *the* military organization.

Strategy — strategy repeats now every imbecile, and military fuss covers its ignorance by that sacramental word. Scott cannot have in view the destruction of the rebels. Not even the Austrian Aulic Council imagined a strategy combined and stretching through several thousands of miles.

The people's strategy is best : to rush in masses on Richmond ; to take it now, when the enemy is there in comparatively small numbers. Richmond taken, Norfolk and the lost guns at once will be recovered. So speaks the people, and they are right ; here among the wiseacres not one understands the superiority of the people over his own little brains.

Warned Mr. Seward against making contracts for arms with all kinds of German agents from New York and from abroad. They will furnish and bring, at the best, what the German governments throw out as being of no use at the present moment. All the German governments are at work to renovate their fire-arms.

The diplomats more and more confused, — some of them ludicrously so. Here, as always and everywhere, diplomacy, by its essence, is virtually *statu quo;* if not altogether retrograde, is conservative, and often ultra conservative. It is rare to witness diplomacy *in toto*, or even single diplomats, side with progressive efforts and ideas. English diplomacy and

diplomats do it at times ; but then mostly for the
sake of political intrigue.

Even the great events of Italy are not the child
of diplomacy.   It went to work *clopin, clopan*, after
Solferino.

Not one of the diplomats here is intrinsically hostile to the Union.   Not one really wishes its disruption.   Some brag so, but that is for small effect.
All of them are for peace, for *statu quo*, for the
grandeur of the country (as the greatest consumer
of European imports) ; but most of them would
wish slavery to be preserved, and for this reason
they would have been glad to greet Breckinridge or
Jeff. Davis in the White House.

Some among the diplomats are not virtually enemies of freedom and of the North ; but they know
the North from the lies spread by the Southerners,
and by this putrescent heap of refuse, the Washington society.   I am the only Northerner on a footing
of intimacy with the diplomats.   They consider me
an *exalté*.

It must be likewise taken into account, — and
they say so themselves, — that Mr. Seward's oracu-
lar vaticinations about the end of the rebellion from
sixty to ninety days confuse the judgment of diplomats.   Mr. Seward's conversation and words have
an official meaning for the diplomats, are the subject
of their dispatches, and they continually find that
when Mr. Seward says yes the events say no.

Some of the diplomats are Union men out of
obedience to a lawful government, whatever it be ;

others by principle. The few from Central and South American republics are thoroughly sound. The diplomats of the great powers, representing various complicated interests, are the more confused, they have so many things to consider. The diplomatic tail, the smallest, insignificant, fawn to all, and turn as whirlwinds around the great ones.

Scott continually refused the formation of new batteries, and now he roars for them, and hurries the governors to send them. Governor Andrew, of Massachusetts, weeks ago offered one or two rifled batteries, was refused, and now Scott in all hurry asks for them.

The unhappy affair of Big Bethel gave a shock to the nation, and stirred up old Scott, or rather the President.

Aside of strategy, there is a new bugbear to frighten the soldiers; this bugbear is the masked batteries. The inexperience of commanders at Big Bethel makes already *masked batteries* a terror of the country. The stupid press resounds the absurdity. Now everybody begins to believe that the whole of Virginia is covered with masked batteries, constituting, so to speak, a subterranean artillery, which is to explode on every step, under the feet of our army. It seems that this error and humbug is rather welcome to Scott, otherwise he would explain to the nation and to the army that the existence of numerous masked batteries is an absolute material and military impossibility. The terror prevailing now may do great mischief.

Mr. Seward was obliged to explain, exonerate, expostulate, and neutralize before the French Cabinet his famous Dayton letter. I was sure it was to come to this; Mr. Thouvenel politely protested, and Mr. Seward confessed that it was written for the American market (alias, for *bunkum*). All this will make a very unfavorable impression upon European diplomats concerning Mr. Seward's diplomacy and statesmanship, as undoubtedly Mr. Thouvenel will semi-officially confidentially communicate Mr. Seward's *faux pas* to his colleagues.

Mr. Seward emphatically instructs Mr. Adams to exclude the question of slavery from all his sayings and doings as Minister to England. Just to England! That Mr. Adams, once the leader of the constitutional anti-slavery party, submits to this obeisance of a corporal, I am not astonished, as everything can be expected from the man who, in support of the compromise, made a speech *de lana caprina;* but Senator Sumner, Chairman of the Committee of Foreign Affairs, meekly swallowed it.

JULY, 1861.

It seems to me that the destinies of this admirable people are in strange hands. Mr. Lincoln, honest man of nature, perhaps an empiric, doctoring with innocent juices from herbs; but some others around him seem to be quacks of the first order. I wish I may be mistaken.

The press, the thus called good one, is vacillating. Best of all, and almost not vacillating, is the New York Evening Post. I do not speak of principles; but the papers vacillate, speaking of the measures and the slowness of the administration.

The President's message; plenty of good, honest intentions; simple, unaffected wording, but a confession that by the attack on Sumpter, and the uprising of Virginia, the administration was, so to speak, caught napping. Further, up to that day the administration did not take any, the slightest, measure of any kind for any emergency ; in a word, that it expected no attacks, no war, saw no fire, and did not prepare to meet and quench one.

It were, perhaps, better for Lincoln if he could muster courage and act by himself according to his nature, rather than follow so many, or even any single adviser. Less and less I understand Mr. Lincoln, but as his private secretary assures me that Lincoln has great judgment and great energy, I suggested to the secretary to say to Lincoln he should be more himself.

Being *tete-a-tete* with McDowell, I saw him do things of details which in any, even half-way organized army, belong to the speciality of a chief of the staff. I, of course, wondered at it. McDowell, who commands what in Europe would be called a large corps, told me that General Scott allowed him not to form a complete staff, such a one as he, McDowell, wished.

And all this, so to speak, on the eve of a battle, when the army faces the enemy. It seems that genuine staff duties are something altogether unknown to the military senility of the army. McDowell received this corps in the most chaotic state. Almost with his own hands he organized, or rather put together, the artillery. Brigades are scarcely formed ; the commanders of brigades do not know their commands, and the soldiers do not know their generals

—and still they consider Scott to be a great general!

The Congress, well-intentioned, but entangled in formulas, slowly feels its way. The Congress is composed of better elements than is the administration, and it is ludicrous to see how the administration takes airs of hauteur with the Congress. This Congress is in an abnormal condition *for the task of directing a revolution; a formula can be thrown in its face* almost at every bold step. The administration is virtually irresponsible, more so than the government of any constitutional nation whatever. What great things this administration could carry out! Congress will consecrate, legalize, sanction everything. Perhaps no harm would have resulted if the Senate and the House had contained some new, fresher elements directly from the boiling, popular cauldron. Such men would take a *position* at once. Many of the leaders in both Houses were accustomed for many years to make only opposition. But a long opposition influences and disorganizes the judgment, forms not those genuine statesmen able to grasp great events. For such emergencies as are now here, terrible energy is needed, and only a very perfect mind resists the enervating influence of a protracted opposition.

Suggested to Mr. Seward that the best diplomacy was to take possession of Virginia. Doing this, we will find all the cabinets smooth and friendly.

I seldom saw a man with greater facility of labor than Seward. When once he is at work, it runs

torrent-like from his pen. His mind is elastic. His
principal forte is argument on *any* given case. But
the question is how far he masters the variegated
information so necessary in a statesman, and the
more now, when the country earnestly has such
dangerous questions with European cabinets. He is
still cheerful, hopeful, and prophesies a speedy end.

Seward has no Know-Nothingism about him. He
is easy, and may have many genuine generous traits
in his character, were they not compressed by the
habits of the, not lofty, politician. At present,
Seward is a moral dictator; he has Lincoln in his
hand, and is all in all. Very likely he flatters him
and imposes upon his simple mind by his over-bold,
dogmatic, but not over-correct and logical, generalizations. Seward's finger is in all the other departments, but above all in the army.

The opposition made to Seward is not courageous,
not open, not dignified. Such an opposition betrays
the weakness of the opposers, and does not inspire
respect. It is darkly surreptitious. These opponents call Seward hard names, but do this in a
corner, although most of them have their parliamentary chair wherefrom they can speak. If he
is bad and mischievous, then unite your forces and
overthrow him; if he is not bad, or if you are not
strong enough against him, do not cover yourself
with ridicule, making a show of·impotent malice.
When the Senate confirmed him, every one throughout the land knew his vacillating policy; knew him
to be for compromise, for concessions; knew that

he disbelieved in the terrible earnestness of the
struggle, and always prophesied its very speedy end.
The Senate confirmed Seward with open eyes. Perhaps at the start his imagination and his patriotism
made him doubt and disbelieve in the enormity of
treason — he could not realize that the traitors would
go to the bitter end. Seemingly, Seward still hopes
that one day or another they may return as forlorn
sheep. Under the like impressions, he always believed, and perhaps still believes, he shall be able to
patch up the quarrel, and be the savior of the Union.
Very probably his imagination, his ardent wishes,
carry him away, and confuse that clear insight into
events which alone constitutes the statesman.

Suggested to Sumner to demand the reduction of
the tariff on certain merchandises, on the plea of
fraternity of the working American people with their
brethren the operatives all over Europe; by it
principally I wished to alleviate the condition of
French industry, as I have full confidence in Louis
Napoleon, and in the unsophisticated judgment of
the genuine French people. The suggestion did
not take with the Senate.

When the July telegraph brought the news of the
victory at Romney (Western Virginia), it was
about midnight. Mr. Seward warmly congratulated
the President that "*the secession was over.*" What
a far-reaching policy!

When the struggle will be over, England, at least
her Tories, aristocrats, and politicians, will find
themselves baffled in their ardent wishes for the

breaking of the Union. The free States will look tidy and nice, as in the past. But more than one generation will pass before ceases to bleed the wound inflicted by the lies, the taunts, the vituperations, poured in England upon this noble, generous, and high-minded people ; upon the sacred cause defended by the freemen.

These freemen of America, up to the present time, incarnate the loftiest principle in the successive, progressive, and historical development of man. Nations, communities, societies, institutions, stand and fall with that principle, whatever it be, whereof they are the incarnation ; so teaches us history. Woe to these freemen if they will recede from the principle ; if they abandon human rights ; if they do not crush human bondage, this sum of all infamies. Certainly the question paramount to all is, to save and preserve pure self-government in principle and in its direct application. But although the question of slavery seems to be incidental and subordinate to the former, virtually the question of slavery is twin to the former. Slavery serves as a basis, as a nurse, for the most infamous and abject aristocracy or oligarchy that was ever built up in history, and any, even the best, the mildest, and the most honest oligarchy or aristocracy kills and destroys man and self-government.

From the purely administrative point of view, the principle whose incarnation is the American people, the principle begins to be perverted. The embodiment of self-government fills dungeons, suppresses personal liberty, opens letters, and in the reckless saturnalias of despotism it rivals many from among the European despots. Europe, which does not see well the causes, shudders at this *delirium tremens* of despotism in America.

Certainly, treason being in ebullition, the holders of power could not stand by and look. But instead of an energetic action, instead of exercising in full the existing laws, they hesitated, and treason, emboldened, grew over their heads.

The law inflicted the severest capital punishment on the chiefs of the revolt in Baltimore, but all went off unharmed. . The administration one day willingly allows the law to slide from its lap, and the next moment grasps at an unnecessary arbitrary power. Had the traitors of Baltimore been tried by court-martial, as the law allowed, and punished, few, if any, traitors would then have raised their heads in the North.

Englishmen forget that even after a secession, the North, to-day twenty millions, as large as the whole Union eight years ago, will in ten years be thirty millions; a population rich, industrious, and hating England with fury.

Seward, having complete hold of the President, weakens Lincoln's mind by using it up in hunting after comparatively paltry expedients. Seward-Scott's influence neutralizes the energetic cry of the country, of the congressmen, and in the Cabinet that of Blair, who is still a trump.

The emancipation of slaves is spoken of as an

expedient, but not as a sacred duty, even for the maintenance of the Union. To emancipate through the war power is an offence to reason, logic, and humanity; but better even so than not at all. War power is in its nature violent, transient, established for a day; emancipation is the highest social and economical solution to be given by law and reason, and ought to result from a thorough and mature deliberation. When the Constitution was framed, slavery was ashamed of itself, stood in the corner, had no paws.· Now-a-days, slavery has become a traitor, is arrogant, blood-thirsty, worse than a jackal and a hyena ; deliberately slavery is a matricide. And they still talk of slavery as sheltered by the Constitution; and many once anti-slavery men like Seward, etc., are ready to preserve it, to compromise with the crime.

The existence of nations oscillates between epochs when the substance and when the form prevails. The formation of America was the epoch when substance prevailed. Afterward, for more than half a century, the form was paramount; the term of substance again begins. The Constitution is substance and form. The substance in it is perennial; but every form is transient, and must be expanded, changed, re-cast.

Few, if any, Americans are aware of the identity of laws ruling the universe with laws ruling and prevailing in the historical development of man. Rarely has an American patience enough to ascend the long chain from effect to cause, until he reaches

the first cause, the womb wherein was first generated the subsequent distant effect. So, likewise, they
cannot realize that at the start the imperceptible
deviation from the aim by and by widens to a bottomless gap until the aim is missed. Then the
greatest and the most devoted sacrifices are useless.
The legal conductors of the nation, since March 6th,
ignore this law.

The foreign ministers here in Washington were
astonished at the *politeness*, when some time ago the
Department sent to the foreign ministers a circular
announcing to them that armed vessels of the neu-
trals will be allowed to enter at pleasure the rebel
blockaded ports. This favor was not asked, not
hoped for, and was not necessary. It was too late
when I called the attention of the Department to
the fact that such favors were very seldom granted;
that they are dangerous, and can occasion complications. I observed that during the war between
Mexico and France, in 1838, Count Mole, Minister
of Foreign Affairs, and the Premier of Louis Philippe, instructed the admiral commanding the French
navy in the Mexican waters, to oppose, even by
force, any attempt made by a neutral man-of-war to
enter a blockaded port. And it was not so dangerous then as it may be in this civil war. But the
chief clerk adviser of the Department found out
that President Polk's administration during the Mexican war granted a similar permission, and, glad to
have a precedent, his powerful brains could not find
out the difference between *then* and *now*.

The internal routine of the ministry, and the manner in which our ministers are treated abroad by the Chief at home, is very strange, humiliating to our agents in the eyes of foreign Cabinets. Cassius Clay was instructed to propose to Russia our accession to the convention of Paris, but was not informed from Washington that our ministers at Paris, London, etc., were to make the same propositions. When Prince Gortschakoff asked Cassius Clay if similar propositions were made to the other cosigners of the Paris convention, our minister was obliged to confess his utter ignorance about the whole proceeding. Prince Gortschakoff good-naturedly inquired about it from his ministers at Paris and London, and enlightened Cassius Clay.

No ministry of foreign affairs in Europe would treat its agents in such a trifling manner, and, if done, a minister would resent it.

This mistake, or recklessness, is to be credited principally to the internal chief, or director of the department, and not to the minister himself. By and by, the chief clerks, these routinists in the former coarse traditions of the Democratic administrations, will learn and acquire better diplomatic and bureaucratic habits.

If one calls the attention of influential Americans to the mismanagement in the organization of the army; to the extraordinary way in which everything, as organization of brigades, and the inner service, the quartermaster's duty, is done, the general and inevitable answer is, "We are not military; we are young people; we have to learn." Granted; but instead of learning from the best, the latest, and most correct authorities, why stick to an obsolete, senile, musty, rotten, mean, and now-a-days impracticable routine, which is all-powerful in all relating to the army and to the war? The Americans may pay dear for thus reversing the rules of common sense.

. General Scott directs from his sleeping room the movements of the two armies on the Potomac and in the Shenandoah valley. General Scott has given the order to advance. At least a strange way, to have the command of battle at a distance of thirty and one hundred miles, and stretched on his fauteuil. Marshal de Saxe, although deadly sick, was on the field at Fontenoy. What will be the result of this experimentalization, so contrary to sound reason ?

Fighting at Bull Run. One o'clock, P. M. Good news. Gen. Scott says that although we were 40–100 in disadvantage, nevertheless his plans are successful — all goes as he arranged it — all as he foresaw it. Bravo! old man! If so, I make *amende honorable* of all that I said up to this minute. Two o'clock, P. M: General Scott, satisfied with the justness and success of his strategy and tactics — takes a nap.

Evening. Battle lost; rout, panic. The army almost disbanded, in full run. So say the forerunners of the accursed news. Malediction! Malediction !

What a horrible night and day ! rain and cold;

stragglers and disbanded soldiers in every direction, and no order, nobody to gather the soldiers, or to take care of them.

As if there existed not any military or administrative authority in Washington ! Under the eyes of the two commanders-in-chief ! Oh, senility, imbecility, ignominy ! In Europe, a commander of a city, or any other military authority whatever, who should behave in such a way, would be dismissed, nay, expelled, from military service. What I can gather is, that the enemy was in full retreat in the centre and on one flank, when he was reinforced by fresh troops, who outflanked and turned ours. If so, the panic can be explained. Even old veteran troops generally run when they are outflanked.

Johnston, whom Patterson permitted to slip, came to the rescue of Beauregard. So they say. It is *en petit* Waterloo, with Blucher-Johnston, and Grouchy-Patterson. But had Napoleon's power survived after Waterloo, Grouchy, his chief of the staff, and even Ney,* for the fault at Quatre-bras, would have been court-martialed and shot. Here these blind Americans will thank Scott and Patterson.

Others say that a bold charge of cavalry arrived on our rear, and threw in disorder the wagons and the baggage gang. That is nothing new; at the battle of Borodino some Cossacks, pouncing upon the French baggage, created a panic, which for a

---

* That such would have been the presumed fate of Ney at the hands of Napoleon, I was afterwards assured by the old Duke of Bassano, and by the Duchess Abrantes.

moment staggered Napoleon, and prevented him in time from reinforcing Ney and Davoust. But Mc-Dowell committed a fault in putting his baggage train, the ambulances excepted, on a road between the army and its reserves, which, in such a manner, came not in action. By and by I shall learn more about it.

The Congress has made a worse Bull Run than the soldiers. Not a single manly, heroic word to the nation and the army. As if unsuccess always was dishonor. This body groped its way, and was morally stunned by the blow; the would-be leaders more than the mass.

Suggested to Sumner to make, as the Romans did, a few stirring words on account of the defeat.

Some mean fellows in Congress, who never smelt powder, abused the soldiers. Those fellows would have been the first to run. Others, still worse, to show their abject flunkeyism to Scott, and to humbug the public at large about their intimacy with this fetish, make speeches in his defence. Scott broadly prepared the defeat, and now, through the mouths of flunkeys and spit-lickers,* he attempts to throw the fault on the thus called politicians.

The President telegraphed for McClellan, who in

---

* Foremost among them was the editor of the New York Times, publishing a long article wherein he proved that he had been admitted to General Scott's table, and that the General unfolded to him, the editor, the great anaconda strategy. Exactly the thing to be admired and gulped by a man of such *variegated* information as that individual.

That little villianish " article " had a second object : it was to filch subscribers from the Tribune, which broke down, not over courageously.

the West, showed *rapidity of movement*, the first and
most necessary capacity for a commander. Young
blood will be infused, and perhaps senility will be
thrown overboard, or sent to the Museum of the
Smithsonian Institute.

At Bull Run the foreign regiments ran not, but
covered the retreat. And Scott, and worse than he,
Thomas, this black spot in the War Department, both
are averse to, and when they can they humiliate, the
foreigners. A member of Congress, in search of a
friend, went for several miles up the stream of the
fugitive army; great was his astonishment to hear
spoken by the fugitives only the unmixed, pure
Anglo-Saxon.

My friend, J. Wadsworth, behaved cool, brave, on
the field, and was devoted to the wounded. Now,
as always, he is the splendid type of a true man of
the people.

Poor, unhappy McDowell! During the days
when he prepared the army, he was well aware that
an eventual success would be altogether attributed
to Scott; but that he, McDowell, would be the
scapegoat for the defeat. Already, when on Sunday
morning the news of the first successes was known,
Scott swallowed incense, and took the whole credit
of it to himself. Now he accuses the politicians.

Once more. Scott himself prepared the defeat.
Subsequent elucidation will justify this assertion.
One thing is already certain : one of the reasons of
the lost battle is the exhaustion of troops which
fought — and the number here in Washington is

more than 50,000 men. Only an imbecile would
divide the forces in such a way as to throw half of it
to attack a superior and entrenched enemy. But
Scott wished to shape the great events of the coun-.
try in accordance with his narrow, ossified brains,
and with his peculiar patriotism; and he did the
same in the conduct of the war.

I am sure some day or other it will come out that
this immense fortification of Manassas is a similar
humbug to the masked batteries; and Scott was the
first to aggrandize these terrible national nightmares.
Already many soldiers say that they did not see any
fortifications.   Very likely only small earthworks;
if so, Scott ought to have known what was the position and the works of an enemy encamped about
thirty miles from him.   If he, Scott, was ignorant,
then it shows his utter imbecility; if he knew that
the fortifications were insignificant, and did not tell
it to the troops, then he is worse than an incapable
chief.   Up to the present day, all the military
leaders of ancient and modern times told their troops
before a battle that the enemy is not much after all,
and that the difficulties to overcome are rather
insignificant.   After the battle was won, everything
became aggrandized.   Here everybody, beginning
with Scott, ardently rivalled how to scare and
frighten the volunteers, by stories of the masked
batteries of Manassas, with its several tiers of fortifications, the terrible superiority of the Southerners,
etc., etc.   In Europe such behavior would be called
treason.

The administration and the influential men cannot realize that they must give up their old, stupid, musty routine. McClellan ought to be altogether independent of Scott; be untrammelled in his activity; have large powers; have direct action; and not refer to Scott.   What is this wheel within a wheel? Instead of it, Scott, as by concession, cuts for McClellan · a military department of six square miles. Oh, human stupidity, how difficult thou art to lift!

Scott will paralyze McClellan as he did Lyon and Butler.   Scott always pushed on his spit-lickers, or favorites, rotten by old age.   But Scott has pushed aside such men as Wool and Col. Smith; refused the services of many brave as Hooker and others, because they never belonged to his flunkeys.

Send to McClellan a plan for the reorganization of the army.

1st. True mastership consists in creating an army with extant elements, and not in clamoring for what is altogether impossible to obtain.

2d. The idea is preposterous to try to have a large thus-called regular army.   A small number, fifteen to twenty thousand men, divided among several hundreds of thousands of volunteers, would be as a drop of water in a lake.   Besides, this war is to be decided by the great masses of the volunteers, and it is uncivic and unpatriotic to in any way nourish the wickedly-assumed discrimination between regulars and volunteers.

3d. Good non-commissioned officers and corporals constitute the sole, sound, and easy articulations of a regiment. Any one who ever was in action is aware of this truth. With good non-commissioned officers, even ignorant lieutenants do very little harm. The volunteer regiments ought to have as many good sergeants and corporals as possible.

4th. To provide for this want, and for reasons mentioned above, the relics of the regular army ought to be dissolved. Let us have one army, as the enemy has.

5th. All the rank and file of the army ought to be made at once corporals and sergeants, and be distributed as much as possible among the volunteers.

6th. The non-commissioned regulars ought to be made commissioned officers, and with officers of all grades be distributed and merged in the one great army.

For the first time since the armaments, I enjoyed a genuine military view. McClellan, surrounded as a general ought to be, went to see the army. It looks martial. The city, likewise, has a more martial look than it had all the time under Scott. It seems that a young, strong hand holds the ribbons. God grant that McClellan may preserve his western vigor and activity, and may not become softened and dissolved by these Washington evaporations. If he does, if he follows the routine, he will become as impotent as others before him. Young man, beware of Washington's corrupt but flattering influences. To the camp! to the camp! A tent is better for you than a handsome house. The tent, the fumes of bivouacs, inspired the Fredericks, the Napoleons, and Washingtons.

Up to this day they make more history in Secessia than here.   Jeff. Davis overshadows Lincoln. Jeff. Davis and his gang of malefactors are pushed into the whirlpool of action by the nature of their crime; here, our leaders dread action, and grope. The rebels have a clear, decisive, almost palpable aim; but here * *

THE truth about Bull Run will, perhaps, only reach the people when it becomes reduced to an historical use. I gather what I am sure is true.

About three weeks ago General McDowell took upon himself the responsibility to attack the enemy concentrated at Manassas. Deciding upon this step, McDowell showed the determination of a true soldier, and a cool, intelligent courage. According to rumors permeating the whole North; rumors originated by secessionists in and around Washington, and in various parts of the free States; rumors gulped by a part of the press, and never contradicted, but rather nursed, at headquarters, Manassas was a terrible, unknown, mysterious something; a bugbear, between a fortress made by art and a natural fastness, whose approaches were defended for miles by numberless masked batteries, and which

was filled by countless thousands of the most fero-
cious warriors.   Such was Manassas in public opinion when McDowell undertook to attack this formidable American Torres Vedras, and this with the
scanty and almost unorganized means in men and
artillery allotted to him by the senile wisdom of
General Scott.   General McDowell obtained the
promise that Beauregard alone was to be before
him.   To fulfil this promise, General Scott was to
order Patterson to keep Johnston, and a movement
was to be made on the James River, so as to prevent troops coming from Richmond to Manassas.
As it was already said, Patterson, a special favorite
of General Scott, kindly allowed Johnston to save
Beauregard, and Jeff. Davis with troops from Richmond likewise was on the spot.   McDowell planned
his plan very skilfully ; no European general would
have done better, and I am sure that such will be
the verdict hereafter.   Some second-rate mistakes in
the execution did not virtually endanger its success ; but, to say the truth, McDowell and his army
were defeated by the imbecility of the supreme
military authority.   Imbecility stabbed them in the
back.

One part of the press, stultified and stupefied,
staggered under the blow; the other part showed
its utter degradation by fawning on Scott and attacking the Congress, or its best part.   The Evening Post staggered not; its editors are genuine, laborious students, and, above all, students of history.
The editors of the other papers are politicians ;

some of them are little, others are big villains.
All, intellectually, belong to the class called in
America more or less well-read men; information
acquired by reading, but which in itself is not
much.

The brothers Blair, almost alone, receded not, and
put the defeat where it belonged — at the feet of
General Scott.

The *rudis indigestaque moles*, torn away from
Scott's hands, already begins to acquire the shape
of an army.   Thanks to the youth, the vigor, and
the activity of McClellan.

General Scott throws the whole disaster on politicians, and abuses them.   How ungrateful.   His
too lofty pedestal is almost exclusively the work of
politicians.   I heard very, very few military men in
America consider Scott a man of transcendent military capacity.   Years ago, during the Crimean
campaign, I spent some time at West Point in the
society of Cols. Robert Lee, Walker, Hardee, then
in the service of the United States, and now traitors; not one of them classed Scott much higher
above what would be called a respectable capacity;
and of which, as they said, there are many, many in
every European army.

If one analyzes the Mexican campaign, it will be
found that General Scott had, comparatively, more
officers than soldiers; the officers young men, full
of vigor, and in the first gush of youth, who therefore mightily facilitated the task of the commander.
Their names resound to-day in both the camps.   ·

Further, generals from the campaign in Mexico assert that three of the won battles were fought against orders, which signifies that in Mexico youth had the best of cautious senility. It was according to the law of nature, and for it it was crowned with success.

Mr. Seward has a very active intellect, an excellent man for current business, easy and clear-headed for solving any second-rate complications; but as for his initiative, that is another question. Hitherto his initiative does not tell, but rather confuses. Then he sustains Scott, some say, for future political capital. If so it is bad; worse still if Mr. Seward sustains Scott on the ground of high military fitness, as it is impossible to admit that Mr. Seward knows anything about military affairs, or that he ever *studied* the description *of any battle*. At least, I so judge from his conversation.

Mr. Lincoln has already the fumes of greatness, and looks down on the press, reads no paper, that dirty traitor the New York Herald excepted. So, at least, it is generally stated.

The enemies of Seward maintain that he, Seward, drilled Lincoln into it, to make himself more necessary.

Early, even before the inauguration, McDowell suggested to General Scott to concentrate in Washington the small army, the depots scattered in Texas and New Mexico. Scott refused, and this is called a general! God preserve any cause, any people

6

who have for a savior a Scott, together with his civil and military partisans.

If it is not direct, naked treason which prevails among the nurses, and the various advisers of the people, imbecility, narrow-mindedness, do the same work. Further, the way in which many leech, phlebotomize, cheat and steal the people's treasury, is even worse than rampant treason. I heard a Boston shipbuilder complain to Sumner that the ubiquitous lobbyist, Thurlow Weed, was in his, the builder's, way concerning some contracts to be made in the Navy Department, etc., etc. Will it turn out that the same men who are to-day at the head of affairs will be the men who shall bring to an end this revolt or revolution? It ought not to be, as it is contrary to logic, and to human events.

Lincoln alone must forcibly remain, he being one of the incarnated formulas of the Constitution, endowed with a specific, four years' lasting existence.

The Americans are nervous about foreign intervention. It is difficult to make them understand that no intervention is to be, and none can be made. Therein the press is as silly as the public at large. Certainly France does not intend any meddling or intervention; of this I am sure. Neither does England seriously.

Next, if these two powers should even thirst for such an injustice, they have no means to do it. If they break our blockades, we make war, and exclude them from the Northern ports, whose commerce is more valuable to them than that of the

South. I do not believe the foreign powers to be
forgetful of their interest; they know better their
interests than the Americans.

The Congress adjourned, abandoning, with a confidence unparalleled in history, the affairs of the
country in the hands of the not over far-sighted administration. The majority of the Congress are
good, and fully and nobly represent the pure, clear
and sure aspirations, instincts, nay, the clear-sightedness of the people. In the Senate, as in the House,
are many, very many true men, and men of pure
devotion, and of clear insight into the events; men
superior to the administration; such are, above all,
those senators and representatives who do not attempt or aim to sit on a pedestal before the public,
before the people, but wish the thing to be done for
the thing itself. But for *the formula* which chains
their hands, feet, and intellect, the Congress contained several men who, if they could act, would
finish the secession in a double-quick time. But
the whole people move in the treadmill of formulas.
It is a pity that they are not inspired by the axiom
of the Roman legist, *scire leges non est hoc verba
earum tenere, sed vim ac potestatem.* Congress had
positive notions of what ought to be done; the administration, Micawber-like, looks for that something
which may turn up, and by expedients patches all
from day to day.

What may turn up nobody can foresee; matter
alone without mind cannot carry the day. The
people have the mind, but the official legal leaders

a very small portion of it. Come what will, I shall not break down ; I shall not give up the holy principle. If crime, rebellion, *sauvagerie*, triumph, it will be, not because the people failed, but it will be because mediocrities were at the helm. Concessions, compromises, any patched-up peace, will for a century degrade the name of America. Of course, I cannot prevent it ; but events have often broken but not bent me. I may be burned, but I cannot be melted ; so if secesh succeeds, I throw in a cesspool my document of naturalization, and shall return to Europe, even if working my passage.

It is maddening to read all this ignoble clap-trap, written by European wiseacres concerning this country. Not one knows the people, not one knows the accidental agencies which neutralize what is grand and devoted in the people.

Some are praised here as statesmen and leaders. A statesman, a leader of such a people as are the Americans, and in such emergencies, must be a *man* in the fullest and loftiest comprehension. All the noblest criteria of moral and intellectual manhood ought to be vigorously and harmoniously developed in him. He ought to have a deep and lively moral sense, and the moral perception of events and of men around him. He ought to have large brains and a big heart, — an almost all-embracing comprehension of the inside and outside of events, — and when he has those qualities, then only the genius of foresight will dwell on his brow. He ought to forget himself wholly and unconditionally ; his reason, his heart, his soul ought to merge in the principles which lifted him to the elevated station. Who around me approaches this ideal? So far as I know, perhaps Senator Wade.

I wait and wait for the eagle which may break out from the White House. Even the burning fire of the national disaster at Bull Run left the egg unhatched. *Utinam sim falsus,* but it looks as if the slowest brains were to deal with the greatest events of our epoch. Mr. Lincoln is a pure-souled, well-intentioned patriot, and this nobody doubts or contests. But is that all which is needed in these terrible emergencies?

Lyon is killed, — the only man of initiative hitherto generated by events. We have bad luck. I shall put on mourning for at least six weeks. They ought to weep all over the land for the loss of such a man; and he would not have been lost if the administration had put him long ago in command of the West. O General Scott! Lyon's death can be credited to you. Lyon was obnoxious to General Scott, but the General's influence maintains in the service all the doubtful capacities and characters. The War Department, as says Potter, bristles with secessionists, and with them the old, rotten, respectable relics, preserved by General Scott, depress and nip in the bud all the young, patriotic, and genuine capacities.

As the sea corrodes the rocks against which it impinges, so egotism, narrow-mindedness, and immorality corrode the best human institutions. For humanity's sake, Americans, beware!

Always the clouds of harpies around the White House and the Departments, — such a generous ferment in the people, and such impurities coming to the surface!

Patronage is the stumbling stone here to true political action. By patronage the Cabinet keeps in check Congressmen, Senators, etc.

I learn from very good authority that when Russell, with his shadow, Sam. Ward, went South, Mr. Seward told Ward that he, Seward, intends not to force the Union on the Southern people, if it should be positively ascertained that that people does not wish to live in the Union! I am sorry for Seward. Such is not the feeling of the Northern people, and such notions must necessarily confuse and make vacillating Mr. Seward's — that is, Mr. Lincoln's — policy. Seward's patriotism and patriotic wishes and expectations prevent him from seeing things as they are.

The money men of Boston decided the conclusion of the first national loan. Bravo, my beloved Yankees! In finances as in war, as in all, not the financiering capacity of this or that individual, not any special masterly measures, etc., but the stern will of the people to succeed, provides funds and means, prevents bankruptcy, etc. The men who give money send an agent here to ascertain how many traitors are still kept in offices, and what are the prospects of energetic action by the administration.

McClellan is organizing, working hard. It is a pleasure to see him, so devoted and so young. After all, youth is promise. But already adulation begins, and may spoil him. It would be very, very saddening.

Prince Napoleon's visit stirs up all the stupidity of politicians in Europe and here. What a mass of absurdities are written on it in Europe, and even by Americans residing there. All this is more than equalled by the *solemn* and *wise* speculations of the Americans at home. Bar-room and coffee-house politicians are the same all over the world, the same, I am sure, in China and Japan. To suppose Prince Napoleon has any appetite whatever for any kind of American crown! Bah! He is brilliant and intelligent, and to suppose him to have such absurd plans is to offend him. But human and American gullibility are bottomless.

The Prince is a noble friend of the American cause, and freely speaks out his predilection. His sentiments are those of a true Frenchman, and not the sickly free-trade pro-slaveryism of Baroche with which he poisoned here the diplomatic atmosphere. Prince Napoleon's example will purify it.

As I was sure of it, the great Manassas fortifications are a humbug. It is scarcely a half-way fortified camp. So say the companions of the Prince, who, with him, visited Beauregard's army. So much for the great Gen. Scott, whom the companions of the Prince call a *magnificent ruin.*

The Prince spoke with Beauregard, and the Prince's and his companions' opinion is, that Mc-Dowell planned well his attack, but failed in the execution; and Beauregard thought the same. The Prince saw McClellan, and does not prize him so high as we do. These foreign officers say that most probably, on both sides, the officers will make most correct plans, as do pupils in military schools, but the execution will depend upon accident.

Mr. Seward shows every day more and more capacity in dispatching the regular, current, diplomatical business affairs. In all such matters he is now at home, as if he had done it for years and years. He is no more spread-eagle in his diplomatic relations; is easy and prompt in all secondary questions relating to secondary interests, and daily emerging from international complications.

Hitherto the war policy of the administration, as inspired and directed by Scott, was rather to receive blows, and then to try to ward them off. I expect young McClellan to deal blows, and thus to upturn the Micawber policy. Perhaps Gen. Scott believed that his name and example would awe the rebels, and that they would come back after having made a little fuss and done some little mischief. But Scott's greatness was principally built up by the Whigs, and his hold on Democrats was not very great. Witness the events of Polk's and Pierce's administrations. His Mississippi-Atlantic strategy is

a delirium of a softening brain. Seward's enemies
say that he puts up and sustains Scott, because in
the case of success Scott will not be in Seward's
way for the future Presidency.   Mr. Lincoln, an
old Whig, has the Whig-worship for Scott; and as
Mr. Lincoln, in 1851, stumped for Scott, the candi-
date for the Presidency, the many eulogies showered
by Lincoln upon Scott still more strengthened the
worship which, of course, Seward lively entertains
in Lincoln's bosom.   Thus the relics of Whigism
direct now the destinies of the North.   Mr. Lincoln,
Gen. Scott, Mr. Seward, form a triad, with satellites
like Bates and Smith in the Cabinet.   But the
Whigs have not the reputation of governmental
vigor, decision, and promptitude.

The vitiated impulse and direction given by Gen.
Scott at the start, still prevails, and it will be very
difficult to bring it on the right track — to change
the general as well as the war policy from the
defensive, as it is now, to the offensive, as it ought to
have been from the beginning.   The North is five to
one in men, and one hundred to one in material
resources.   Any one with brains and energy could
suppress the rebellion in eight weeks from to-day.

Mr. Lincoln in some way has a slender historical
resemblance to Louis XVI. — similar goodness, honesty, good intentions ; but the size of events seems to
be too much for him.

And so now Mr. Lincoln is wholly overshadowed
by Seward.   If by miracle the revolt may end in a
short time, Mr. Seward will have most of the credit

for it. In the long run the blame for eventual disasters will be put at Mr. Lincoln's door.

Thank heaven! the area for action and the powers of McClellan are extended and increased. The administration seems to understand the exigencies of the day.

I am told that the patriotic and brave Senator Wade, disgusted with the slowness and inanity of the administration, exclaimed, "I do not wonder that people desert to Jeff. Davis, as he shows brains; I may desert myself." And truly, Jeff. Davis and his gang make history.

Young McClellan seems to falter before the Medusa-*ruin* Scott, who is again at his tricks, and refuses officers to volunteers. To carry through in Washington any sensible scheme, more boldness is needed than on the bloodiest battle-field.

If Gen. Scott could have disappeared from the stage of events on the sixth of March, his name would have remained surrounded with that halo to which the people was accustomed; but now, when the smoke will blow over, it may turn differently. I am afraid that at some future time will be applied to Scott * * * *quia turpe ducunt parere minoribus, et quæ imberbi didicere, senes perdenda fateri.*

Not self-government is on trial, and not the genuine principle of democracy. It is not the genuine, virtual democracy which conspired against the republic, and which rebels, but an unprincipled, infamous oligarchy, risen in arms to destroy democracy. From Athens down to to-day, true democracies

never betrayed any country, never leagued themselves with enemies. From the time of Hellas down
to to-day, all over the world, and in all epochs, royalties, oligarchies, aristocracies, conspired against,
betrayed, and sold their respective father-lands. (I
said this years ago in America and Europe.)

Fremont as initiator ; he emancipates the slaves
of the disloyal Missourians. Takes the advance,
but is justified in it by the slowness, nay, by the
stagnancy of the administration.

Gen. Scott opposed to the expedition to Hatteras !

If it be true that Seward and Chase already lay
the tracks for the Presidential succession, then I can
only admire their short-sightedness, nay, utter and
darkest blindness. The terrible events will be a
schooling for the people ; the future President will
not be a schemer already shuffling the cards ; most
probably it will be a man who serves the country,
forgetting himself.

Only two members in the Cabinet drive together,
Blair and Welles, and both on the right side, both
true men, impatient for action, action. Every day
shows on what false principle this Cabinet was constructed, not for the emergency, not in view to suppress the rebellion, but to satisfy various party
wranglings. Now the people's cause sticks in the
mud.

SEPTEMBER, 1861.

What will McClellan do?—Fremont disavowed—The Blairs not in fault—Fremont ignorant and a bungler—Conspiracy to destroy him—Seward rather on his side—McClellan's staff—A Marcy will not do!—McClellan publishes a slave-catching order—The people move onward—Mr. Seward again—West Point—The Washington defences—What a Russian officer thought of them—Oh, for battles!—Fremont wishes to attack Memphis; a bold move!—Seward's influence over Lincoln—The people for Fremont—Col. Romanoff's opinion of the generals—McClellan refuses to move—Manœuvrings—The people uneasy—The staff—The Orleans—Brave boys!—The Potomac closed—Oh, poor nation!—Mexico—McClellan and Scott.

WILL McClellan display unity in conception, and vigor in execution? That is the question. He seems very energetic and active in organizing the army; but he ought to take the field very soon. He ought to leave Washington, and have his headquarters in the camp among the soldiers. The life in the tent will inspire him. It alone inspired Frederick II. and Napoleon. Too much organization may become as mischievous as the no organization under Scott. Time, time is everything. The levies will fight well; may only McClellan not be carried away by the notion and the attempt to create what is called a perfect army on European pattern. Such an attempt would be ruinous to the cause. It is altogether impossible to create such an army on the European model, and no necessity exists for it. The rebel army is no European one. Civil wars have altogether different military exigencies, and the great tactics for a civil war are wholly different from the tactics, etc., needed in a regular war. Napoleon differently fought the Vendeans, and differently the Austrians, and the other coalesced armies. May only McClellan not become intoxicated before he puts the cup to his lips.

Fremont disavowed by Lincoln and the administration. This looks bad. I have no considerable confidence in Fremont's high capacities, and believe that his head is turned a little; but in this question he was right in principle, and right in legality. A commander of an army operating separately has the exercise of full powers of war.

The Blairs are not to be accused; I read the letter from F. Blair to his brother. It is the letter of a patriot, but not of an intriguer. Fremont establishes an absurd rule concerning the breach of military discipline, and shows by it his ignorance and narrow-mindedness. So Fremont, and other bungling martinets, assert that nobody has the right to criticise the actions of his commander.

Fremont is ignorant of history, and those around him who put in his head such absurd notions are a pack of mean and servile spit-lickers. An officer ought to obey orders without hesitation, and if he does not he is to be court-martialed and shot. But it is perfectly allowable to criticise them; it is in human nature — it was, is, and will be done in all armies; see in Curtius and other historians of Alexander of Macedon. It was continually done under Napoleon. In Russia, in 1812, the criticism made by almost all the officers forced Alexander I. to leave the army, and to put Kutousoff over Barclay. In the last Italian campaign Austrian officers criticised loudly Giulay, their commander, etc., etc.

Conspiracy to destroy Fremont on account of his slave proclamation. The conspirators are the Missouri slave-holders : Senator Brodhead, old Bates, Scott, McClellan, and their staffs. Some jealousy against him in the Cabinet, but Seward rather on Fremont's side.

McClellan makes his father-in-law, a man of *very* secondary capacity, the chief of the staff of the army. It seems that McClellan ignores what a highly responsible position it is, and what a special and transcendent capacity must be that of a chief of the staff — the more so when of an army of several hundreds of thousands. I do not look for a Berthier, a Gneisenau, a Diebitsch, or Gortschakoff, but a Marcy will not do.

Colonel Lebedeef, from the staff of the Emperor Alexander II., and professor in the School of the Staff at St. Petersburg, saw here everything, spoke with our generals, and his conclusion is that in military capacity McDowell is by far superior to McClellan. Strange, if true, and foreboding no good.

Mr. Lincoln begins to call a demagogue any one who does not admire all the doings of his administration. Are we already so far ?

McClellan under fatal influences of the rampant

pro-slavery men, and of partisans of the South, as
is a Barlow.   All the former associations of McClellan have been of the worst kind — Breckinridgians.
But perhaps he will throw them off.   He is young,
and the elevation of his position, his standing before
the civilized world, will inspire and purify him, I
hope.   Nay, I ardently wish he may go to the camp,
to the camp.

McClellan published a slave-catching order.   Oh
that he may discard those bad men around him !

Struggles with evils, above all with domestic, internal evils, absorb a great part of every nation's
life.   Such struggles constitute its development,
are the landmarks of its progress and decline.

The like struggles deserve more the attention of
the observer, the philosopher, than all kinds of external wars.   And, besides, most of such external
wars result from the internal condition of a nation.
At any rate, their success or unsuccess almost
wholly depends upon its capacity to overcome internal evils.   A nation even under a despotic rule may
overcome and repel an invasion, as long as the struggle against the internal evils has not broken the
harmony between the ruler and the nation.   Here
the internal evil has torn a part of the constitutional
structure ; may only the necessary harmony between
this high-minded people and the representative of
the transient constitutional formula not be destroyed.
The people move onward, the formula vacillates, and
seems to fear to make any bold step.

If the cause of the freemen of the North succumbs, then humanity is humiliated. This high-spirited exclamation belongs to Tassara, the Minister from Spain. Not the diplomat, but the nobly inspired *man* uttered it.

But for the authoritative influence of General Scott, and the absence of any foresight and energy on the part of the administration, the rebels would be almost wholly without military leaders, without naval officers. The Johnsons, Magruders, Tatnalls, Buchanans, ought to have been arrested for treason the moment they announced their intention to resign.

Mr. Seward has many excellent personal qualities, besides his unquestionable eminent capacity for business and argument; but why is he neutralizing so much good in him by the passion to be all in all, to meddle with everything, to play the knowing one in military affairs, he being in all such matters as innocent as a lamb? It is not a field on which Seward's hazarded generalizations can be of any earthly use; but they must confuse all.

Seward is free from that coarse, semi-barbarous know-nothingism which rules paramount, not the genuine people, but the would-be something, the half-civilized *gentlemen*. Above all, know-nothingism pervades all around Scott, who is himself its grand master, and it nestles there *par excellence* in more than one way. It is, however, to be seen how far this pure American-Scott military wisdom is something real, transcendent. Up to this day, the pure Americanism, West Point schoolboy's conceit, have not produced much.   The defences of Washington, so much clarioned as being the product of a high conception and of engineering skill, — these defences are very questionable when appreciated by a genuine military eye.   A Russian officer of the military engineers, one who was in the Crimea and at Sebastopol, after having surveyed these defences here, told me that the Russian soldiers who defended Sebastopol, and who learned what ought to be defences, would prefer to fight outside than inside of the Washington forts, bastions, defences, etc., etc., etc.

Doubtless many foreigners coming to this country are not much, but the greatest number are soldiers who saw service and fire, and could be of some use at the side of Scott's West Point greenness and presumption.

If we are worsted, then the fate of the men of faith in principles will be that of Sisyphus, and the coming generation for half a century will have uphill work.

If not McClellan himself, some intriguers around him already dream, nay, even attempt to form a pure military, that is, a reckless, unprincipled, unpatriotic party.   These men foment the irritation between the arrogance of the thus-called regular army, and the pure abnegation of the volunteers. Oh, for battles !   Oh, for battles !

Fremont wished at once to attack Fort Pillow and the city of Memphis.   It was a bold move, but the concerted civil and military wisdom grouped around

7

the President opposed this truly great military conception.

Mr. Lincoln is pulled in all directions. His intentions are excellent, and he would have made an excellent President for quiet times. But this civil war imperatively demands a man of foresight, of prompt decision, of Jacksonian will and energy. These qualities may be latent in Lincoln, but do not yet come to daylight. Mr. Lincoln has no experience of men and events, and no knowledge of the past. Seward's influence over Lincoln may be explained by the fact that Lincoln considers Seward as the alpha and omega of every kind of knowledge and information.

I still hope, perhaps against hope, that if Lincoln is what the masses believe him to be, a strong mind, then all may come out well. Strong minds, lifted by events into elevated regions, expand more and more; their "mind's eye" pierces through clouds, and even through rocks; they become inspired, and inspiration compensates the deficiency or want of information acquired by studies. Weak minds, when transported into higher regions, become confused and dizzy. Which of the two will be Mr. Lincoln's fate?

The administration hesitates to give to the struggle a character of emancipation; but the people hesitate not, and take Fremont to their heart.

As the concrete humanity, so single nations have epochs of gestation, and epochs of normal activity,

of growth, of full life, of manhood.   Americans are
now in the stage of manhood.

Col. Romanoff, of the Russian military engineer
corps, who was in the Crimean war, saw here the
men and the army, saw and conversed with the
generals.   Col. R. is of opinion that McDowell is
by far superior to McClellan, and would make a
better commander.

It is said that McClellan refuses to move until he
has an army of 300,000 men and 600 guns.   Has
he not studied Napoleon's wars?   Napoleon scarcely
ever had half such a number in hand; and when at
Wagram, where he had about 180,000 men, himself
in the centre, Davoust and Massena on the flanks,
nevertheless the handling of such a mass was too
heavy even for his, Napoleon's, genius.

The country is — to use an Americanism — in a
pretty fix, if this McClellan turns out to be a mistake.
I hope for the best.   600 guns!   But 100 guns in a
line cover a mile.   What will he do with 600?   Lose
them in forests, marshes, and bad roads; whence it
is unhappily a fact that McClellan read only a little
of military history, misunderstood what he read,
and now attempts to realize hallucinations, as a boy
attempts to imitate the exploits of an Orlando.   It
is dreadful to think of it.   I prefer to trust his
assertion that, once organized, he soon, very soon,
will deal heavy and quick blows to the rebels.

I saw some manœuvrings, and am astonished that
no artillery is distributed among the regiments of
infantry.   When the rank and file see the guns on

their side, the soldiers consider them as a part of
themselves and of the regiment; they fight better
in the company of guns; they stand by them and
defend them as they defend their colors. Such a
distribution of guns would strengthen the body of
the volunteers. But it seems that McClellan has
no confidence in the volunteers. Were this true,
it would denote a small, very small mind. Let us
hope it is not so. One of his generals — a martinet
of the first class — told me that McClellan waits for
the organization of *the regulars*, to have them for
the defence of the guns. If so, it is sheer nonsense.
These narrow-minded West Point martinets will
become the ruin of McClellan.

McClellan could now take the field. Oh, why has
he established his headquarters in the city, among
flunkeys, wiseacres, and spit-lickers? Were he
among the troops, he would be already in Manassas.
The people are uneasy and fretting about this inaction, and the people see what is right and necessary.

Gen. Banks, a true and devoted patriot, is sacrificed by the stupidity of what they call here the
staff of the great army, but which collectively, with
its chief, is only a mass of conceit and ignorance —
few, as General Williams, excepted. Banks is in
the face of the enemy, and has no cavalry and no
artillery; and here are immense reviews to amuse
women and fools.

Mr. Mercier, the French Minister, visited a considerable part of the free States, and his opinions are

now more clear and firm; above all, he is very friendly to our side. He is sagacious and good.

Missouri is in great confusion — three parts of it lost. Fremont is not to be accused of all the mischief, but, from effect to cause, the accusation ascends to General Scott.

Gen. Scott insisted to have Gen. Harney appointed to the command of Missouri, and hated Lyon. If, even after Harney's recall, Lyon had been appointed, Lyon would be alive and Missouri safe. But hatred, anxiety of rank, and stupidity, united their efforts, and prevailed. Oh American people! to depend upon such inveterate blunderers!

Were McClellan in the camp, he would have no flatterers, no antechambers filled with flunkeys; but the rebels would not so easily get news of his plans as they did in the affair on Munson's Hill.

The Orleans are here. I warned the government against admitting the Count de Paris, saying that it would be a *deliberate* breach of good comity towards Louis Napoleon, and towards the Bonapartes, who prove to be our friends; I told that no European government would commit itself in such a manner, not even if connected by ties of blood with the Orleans. At the start, Mr. Seward heeded a little my advice, but finally he could not resist the vanity to display untimely spread-eagleism, and the Orleans are in our service. Brave boys! It is a noble, generous, high-minded, if not an altogether wise, action.

If a mind is not nobly inspired and strong, then

the exercise of power makes it crotchety and dissim-
ulative in contact with men.   To my disgust, I witness this all around me.

The American people, its institutions, the Union
—all have lost their virginity, their political innocence.   A revolution in the institutions, in the mode
of life, in notions begun — it is going on, will grow
and mature, either for good or evil.   Civil war, this
most terrible but most maturing passion, has put an
end to the boyhood and to the youth of the American people.   Whatever may be the end, one thing
is sure — that the substance and the form will be
modified; nay, perhaps, both wholly changed.   A
new generation of citizens will grow and come out
from this smoke of the civil war.

The Potomac closed by the rebels!   Mischief and
shame!   Natural fruits of the dilatory war policy
— Scott's fault.   Months ago the navy wished to
prevent it, to shell out the rebels, to keep our troops
in the principal positions.   Scott opposed; and still
he has almost paramount influence.   McClellan
complains against Scott, and Lincoln and Seward
flatter McClellan, but look up to Scott as to a super-
natural military wisdom.   Oh, poor nation!

In Europe clouds gather over Mexico.   Whatever
it eventually may come to, I suggested to Mr. Seward to lay aside the Monroe doctrine, not to meddle
for or against Mexico, but to earnestly protest
against any eventual European interference in the
internal condition of the political institutions of
Mexico.

Continual secondary, international complications, naturally growing out from the maritime question ; so with the Dutch cheesemongers, with Spain, with England — all easily to be settled ; they generate fuss and trouble, but will make no fire.

Gen. Scott's partisans complain that McClellan is very disrespectful in his dealings with Gen. Scott. I wonder not. McClellan is probably hampered by the narrow routine notions of Scott. McClellan feels that Scott prevents energetic and prompt action ; that he, McClellan, in every step is obliged to fight Gen. Scott's inertia ; and McClellan grows impatient, and shows it to Scott.

As in the mediæval epoch, and some time thereafter, anatomists and physiologists experimented on the living villeins, that is, on peasantry, serfs, and called this process *experientia in anima vili*, so this naïve administration experiments in civil and in military matters on the people's life-blood.

McClellan, stirred up by the fools and peacocks around him, has sent to the War Department a project of a showy uniform for himself and his staff. It would be to laugh at, if it were not insane. McClellan very likely read not what he signed.

The army is in sufficient rig and organization to take the field; but nevertheless McClellan has not yet made a single movement imperatively prescribed by the simplest tactics, and by the simplest common sense, when the enemy is in front. Not a single serious reconnoissance to ascertain the real force

of the enemy, to pierce through the curtain behind
which the rebels hide their real forces.   It must be
conceded to the rebel generals that they show great
skill in humbugging us.   Whenever we try to make
a step we are met by a seemingly strong force (ten-
fold increased by rumors spread by the secessionists
among us, and gulped by our stupidity), which
makes us suppose a deep front, and a still deeper
body behind.   And there is the humbug, I am sure.
If, on such an extensive line as the rebels occupy,
the main body should correspond to what they show
in front, then the rebel force must muster several
hundreds of thousands.   Such large numbers they
have not, and I am sure that four-fifths of their
whole force constitutes their vanguard, and behind
it the main body is chaff.   The rebels treat us as if
we were children.

McClellan fortifies Washington ; Fremont, St.
Louis ; Anderson asks for engineers to fortify some
spots in Kentucky. . This is all a defensive warfare,
and not so will the rebel region be conquered.
We lose time, and time serves the rebels, as it increases their moral force.   Every day of their existence shows their intrinsic vitality.

The theory of starving the rebels out is got up
by imbeciles, wholly ignorant of such matters ;
wholly ignorant of human nature ; wholly ignorant
of the degree of energy, and of abnegation, which
criminals can display when firmly decided upon
their purpose.   This absurdity comes from the
celebrated anaconda Mississippi-Atlantic strategy.

Oh! When in Poland, in 1831, the military chiefs concentrated all the forces in the fortifications of Warsaw, all was gone.   Oh for a dashing general, for a dashing purpose, in the councils of the White House! The constitutional advisers are deaf to the voice of the people, who know more about it than do all the departments and the military wise-acres.   The people look up to find as big brains and hearts as are theirs, and hitherto the people have looked up in vain.   The radical senators, as a King, a Trumbull, a Wade, Wilson, Chandler, Hale, etc., the true Republicans in the last session of Congress — further, men as Wadsworth and the like, are the true exponents of the character, of the clear insight, of the soundness of the people.

McClellan, and even the administration, seem not to realize that pure military considerations cannot fulfil the imperative demands of the political situation.

October 6th. — I met McClellan; had with him a protracted conversation, and could look well into him.   I do not attach any value to physiognomies, and consider phrenology, craniology, and their kindred, to be rather humbugs; but, nevertheless, I was struck with the soft, insignificant inexpressiveness of his eyes and features.   My enthusiasm for him, my faith, is wholly extinct.   All that he said to me and to others present was altogether unmilitary and inexperienced.   It made me sick at heart to hear him, and to think that he is to decide over the destinies and the blood of the people.   And he already an idol, incensed, worshipped, before he did anything whatever. McClellan may have individual courage, so has almost every animal; but he has not the decision and the courage of a military leader and captain. He has no real confidence in the troops; has scarcely any idea how battles are fought; has no confidence in and no notion of the use of the bayonet. I told him that, notwithstanding his opinion, I would take his worst brigade of infantry, and after a fortnight's drill challenge and whip any of the best rebel brigades.

Some time ago it was reported that McClellan considered this war had become a duel of artillery. Fools wondered and applauded. I then protested against putting such an absurdity in McClellan's mouth; now I must believe it. To be sure, every battle is in part a duel of artillery, but ends or is decided by charges of infantry or cavalry. Cannonading alone never constituted and decided a battle. No position can be taken by cannonading alone, and shells alone do not always force an enemy to abandon a position. Napoleon, an artillerist *par excellence*, considered campaigns and battles to be something more than duels of artillery. The great battle of Borodino, and all others, were decided when batteries were stormed and taken. Eylau was a battle of charges by cavalry and by infantry, besides a terrible cannonading, etc., etc. McClellan spoke with pride of the fortifications of Washington, and pointed to one of the forts as having a greater profile than had the world-renowned

Malakoff.   What a confusion of notions, what a misappreciation of relative conditions !

I cannot express my sad, mournful feelings, during this conversation with McClellan.   We spoke about the necessity of dividing his large army into corps.   McClellan took from the table an Army Almanac, and pointed to the names of generals to whom he intended to give the command of corps. He feels the urgency of the case, and said that Gen. Scott prevented him from doing it; but as soon as he, McClellan, shall be free to act, the division will be made.   So General Scott is everywhere to defend senile routine against progress, and the experience of modern times.

The rebels deserve, to the end of time, many curses from outraged humanity.   By their treason they forced upon the free institutions of the North the necessity of curtailing personal liberty and other rights; to make use of depotism for the sake of self-defence.

The enemy concentrates and shortens his lines, and McClellan dares not even tread on the enemy's heels.   Instead of forcing the enemy to do what we want, and upturn his schemes, McClellan seemingly does the bidding of Beauregard.   We advance as much as Beauregard allows us to do.   New tactics, to be sure, but at any rate not Napoleonic.

The fighting in the West and some small successes here are obtained by rough levies; and those imbecile, regular martinets surrounding McClellan still nurse his distrust in the volunteers.   All the wealth, energy, intellect of the country, is concentrated in the hands of McClellan, and he uses it to throw up entrenchments. The partisans of McClellan point to his highly scientific preparations — his science. He may have some little of it, but half-science is worse than thorough ignorance. Oh! for one dare-devil in the Lyon, or in the old-fashioned Yankee style. McClellan is neither a Napoleon, nor a Cabrera, nor a Garibaldi.

Mason and Slidell escaped to Havana on their way to Europe, as commissioners of the rebels. According to all international definitions, we have the full right to seize them in any neutral vessel, they being political contrabands of war going on a publicly avowed errand hostile to their true government. Mason and Slidell are not common passengers, nor are they political refugees invoking the protection of any neutral flag. They are travelling commissioners of war, of bloodshed and rebellion; and it is all the same in whatever seaport they embark. And if the vessel conveying them goes from America to Europe, or *vice versa*, Mr. Seward can let them be seized when they have left Havana, provided he finds it expedient.

We lose time, and time is all in favor of the rebels. Every day consolidates their existence — so to speak, crystallizes them. Further — many so-called Union men in the South, who, at the start, opposed secession, by and by will get accustomed to it. Secession daily takes deeper root, and will so by degrees become *un fait accompli*.

Mr. Adams, in his official relations with the English government, speaks of the rebel pirates as of lawful privateers. Mr. Seward admonished him for it. Bravo!

It is so difficult, not to say impossible, to meet an American who concatenates a long series of effects and causes, or who understands that to explain an isolated fact or phenomenon the chain must be ascended and a general law invoked. Could they do it, various bunglings would be avoided, and much of the people's sacrifices husbanded, instead of being squandered, as it is done now.

Fremont going overboard! His fall will be the triumph of the pro-slavery party, headed by the New York Herald, and supported by military old fogies, by martinets, and by double and triple political and intellectual know-nothings. Pity that Fremont had no brilliant military capacity. Then his fall could not have taken place.

Mr. Seward is too much ruled by his imagination, and too hastily discounts the future. But imagination ruins a statesman. Mr. Seward must lose credit at home and abroad for having prophesied, and having his prophecies end in smoke. When Hatteras was taken (Gen. Scott protested against the expedition), Mr. S. assured me that it was the beginning of the end. A diplomat here made the observation that no minister of a European parliamentary government could remain in power after having been continually contradicted by facts.

Now, Mr. Seward devised these collateral missions to Europe. He very little knows the habit and temper of European cabinets if he believes that such collateral confidential agents can do any good. The European cabinets distrust such irresponsible agents, who, in their turn, weaken the influence and the standing of the genuine diplomatic agents. Mr. S., early in the year, boasted to abolish, even in Europe, the system of passports, and soon afterwards introduced it at home. So his imagination carries him to overhaul the world. He proposes to European powers a united expedition to Japan, and we cannot prevent at home the running of the blockade, and are ourselves blockaded on the Potomac. All such schemes are offsprings of an ambitious imagination. But the worst is, that every such outburst of his imagination Mr. Seward at once transforms into a dogma, and spreads it with all his might. I pity him when I look towards the end of his political career. He writes well, and has put down the insolent English dispatch concerning the *habeas corpus* and the arrests of dubious, if not treacherous, Englishmen. Perhaps Seward imagines himself to be a Cardinal Richelieu, with Lincoln for Louis XIII. (provided he knows as much history), or may be he has the ambition to be considered a Talleyrand or Metternich of diplomacy. But if any, he has some very, very faint similarity with Alberoni. He easily outwits here men around him; most are politicians as he; but he never can outwit the statesmen of Europe. Besides, diplomacy, above all that of great powers, is conceived largely and carried on a grand scale; the present diplomacy has outgrown what is commonly called (but fallaciously) Talleyrandism and Metternichism.

McClellan and the party which fears to make a bold advance on the enemy make so much fuss about the country being cut up and wooded; it proves only that they have no brains and no fertility of expedients. This country is not more cut up than is the Caucasus, and the woods are no great, endless, primitive forests. They are rather groves. In the Caucasus the Russians continually attack great and dense forests; they fire in them several round shots, then grape, and then storm them with the bayonet; and the Circassians are no worse soldiers than are the Southrons.

European papers talk much of mediation, of a peaceful arrangement, of compromise. By intuition of the future the Northern people know very well the utter impossibility of such an arrangement. A peace could not stand; any such peace will establish the military superiority of the arrogant, reckless, piratical South. The South would teem with hundreds of thousands of men ready for any piratical, fillibustering raid, enterprise, or excursion, of which the free States north and west would become the principal theatres. Such a marauding community as the South would become, in case of success, will be unexampled in history. The Cylician pirates, the Barbary robbers, nay, the Tar-

tars of the 12th, 13th, and 14th centuries, were virtuous and civilized in comparison with what would be an independent, man-stealing, and man-whipping Southern agglomeration of lawless men. The free States could have no security, even if *all* the thus *called* gentlemen and men of honor were to sign a treaty or a compromise. The Southern pestilential influence would poison not only the North, but this whole hemisphere. The history of the past has nothing to be compared with organized, legal piracy, as would become the thus-called Southern chivalry on land and on sea; and soon European maritime powers would be obliged to make costly expeditions for the sake of extirpating, crushing, uprooting the nest of pirates, which then will embrace about twelve millions, — *every* Southern gentleman being a pirate at heart.

This is what the Northern people know by experience and by intuition, and what makes the people so uneasy about the inertia of the administration.

Mr. Lincoln, Mr. Seward, Gen. Scott, and other great men, are soured against the people and public opinion for distrusting, or rather for criticising their little display of statesmanlike activity. How unjust! As a general rule, of all human sentiments, confidence is the most scrutinizing one. If *confidence* is bestowed, it wants to perfectly know the *why*. But from the outset of this war the American people gave and give to everybody full, unsuspecting confidence, without asking the why, without even scrutinizing the actions which were to justify the claim.

Up to this day Secesh is the positive pole; the Union is the negative, — it is the blow recipient. When, oh, when will come the opposite? When will we deal blows? Not under McClellan, I suspect.

THE season is excellent for military operations, such as any Napoleon could wish it. And we, lying not on our oars or arms, but in our beds, as our *spes patriæ* is warmly and cosily established in a large house, receiving there the incense and salutations of all flunkeys. Even cabinet ministers crowd McClellan's antechambers !

The massacre at Ball's Bluff is the work either of treason, or of stupidity, or of cowardice, or most probably of all three united.

No European government and no European nation would thus coolly bear it. Any commander culpable of such stupidity would be forever disgraced, and dismissed from the army. Here the administration, the Cabinet, and all the Scotts, the McClellans, the Thomases, etc., strain their brains and muscles to whitewash themselves or the culprit — to represent this massacre as something very innocent.

Victoria ! Victoria ! Old Scott, Old Mischief, gone

overboard! So vanished one of the two evil genii
keeping guard over Mr. Lincoln's brains. But it
will not be so easy to redress the evil done by
Scott. He nailed the country's cause to such a
turnpike that any of his successors will perhaps be.
unable to undo what Old Mischief has done. Scott
might have had certain, even eminent, military
capacity; but, all things considered, he had it only
on a small scale. Scott never had in his hand
large numbers, and hundreds of European generals
of divisions would do the same that Scott did, even
in Mexico. Any one in Europe, who in some way
or other participated in the events of the last forty
years, has had occasion to see or participate in one
single day in more and better fighting, to hear more
firing, and smell more powder, than has General
Scott in his whole life.

Scott's fatal influence palsied, stiffened, and poisoned every noble or higher impulse, and every aspiration of the people. Scott diligently sowed the
first seeds of antagonism between volunteers and
regulars, and diligently nursed them. Around his
person in the War Department, and in the army,
General Scott kept and maintained officers, who,
already before the inauguration, declared, and daily
asserted, that if it comes to a war, few officers of the
army will unite with the North and remain loyal to
the Union.

He never forgot to be a Virginian, and was filled
with all a Virginian's conceit. To the last hour he
warded off blows aimed at Virginia. To this hour

he never believed in a serious war, and now *requiescat in pace* until the curse of coming generations.

McClellan is invested with all the powers of Scott. McClellan has more on his shoulders than any man — a Napoleon not excepted — can stand; and with his very limited capacity McClellan must necessarily break under it. Now McClellan will be still more idolized. He is already a kind of dictator, as Lincoln, Seward, etc., turn around him.

In a conversation with Cameron, I warned him against bestowing such powers on McClellan. "What shall we do?" was Cameron's answer; "neither the President nor I know anything about military affairs." Well, it is true; but McClellan is scarcely an apprentice.

Again the intermittent fear, or fever, of foreign intervention. How absurd! Americans belittle themselves talking and thinking about it. The European powers will not, and cannot. That is my creed and my answer; but some of our agents, diplomats, and statesmen, try to made capital for themselves from this fever which they evoke to establish before the public that their skill preserves the country from foreign intervention. Bosh!

All the good and useful produced in the life and in the economy of nations, all the just and the right in their institutions, all the ups and downs, misfortunes and disasters befalling them, all this was, is, and forever will be the result of logical deductions from pre-existing dates and facts.   And here almost everybody forgets the yesterday.

A revolution imposes obligations.   A revolution makes imperative the development and the practical application of those social principles which are its basis.

The American Revolution of 1776 proclaimed self-government, equality before all, happiness of all, etc. ; it is therefore the peremptory duty of the American people to uproot domestic oligarchy, based upon living on the labor of an enslaved man ; it has to put a stop to the moral, intellectual, and physical servitude of both, of whites and of colored.

Eminent men in America are taunted with the ambition to reach the White House.   In itself it is not condemnable ; it is a noble or an ignoble ambition, according to the ways and means used to reach that aim.   It is great and stirring to see one's name recorded in the list of Presidents of the United States ; but there is still a record far shorter, but by far more to be envied — a record venerated by our race — it is the record of truly *great men*.   The actually inscribed runners for the White House do not think of this.

No one around me here seems to understand (and no one is familiar enough with general history) that protracted wars consolidate a nationality.   Every day of Southern existence shapes it out more and more into a *nation*, with all the necessary moral and material conditions of existence.

Seeing these repeated reviews, I cannot get rid of

the idea that by such shows and displays McClellan tries to frighten the rebels in the Chinaman fashion.

The collateral missions to England, France, and Spain, are to add force to our cause before the public opinion as well as before the rulers. But what a curious choice of men! It would be called even an unhappy one. Thurlow Weed, with his off-hand, apparently sincere, if not polished ways, may not be too repulsive to English refinement, provided he does not buttonhole his interlocutionists, or does not pat them on the shoulder. So Thurlow Weed will be dined, wined, etc. But doubtless the London press will show him up, or some "Secesh" in London will do it. I am sure that Lord Lyons, as it is his paramount duty, has sent to Earl Russell a full and detailed biography of this Seward's *alter ego*, sent *ad latus* to Mr. Adams. Thurlow Weed will be considered an agreeable fellow; but he never can acquire much weight and consideration, neither with the statesmen, nor with the members of the government, nor in saloons, nor with the public at large.

Edward Everett begged to be excused from such a false position offered to him in London. Not fish, not flesh. It was rather an offence to proffer it to Everett. The old patriot better knows Europe, its cabinets, and exigencies, than those who attempted to intricate him in this ludicrous position. He is right, and he will do more good here than he could do in London — there on a level with Thurlow Weed!

Archbishop Hughes is to influence Paris and France,—but whom? The public opinion, which is on our side, is anti-Roman, and Hughes is an Ultra Montane — an opinion not over friendly to Louis Napoleon. The French clergy in every way, in culture, wisdom, instruction, theology, manners, deportment, etc., is superior to Hughes in incalculable proportions, and the French clergy are already generally anti-slavery. Hughes to act on Louis Napoleon! Why! the French Emperor can outwit a legion of Hugheses, and do this without the slightest effort. Besides, for more than a century European sovereigns, governments, and cabinets, have generally given up the use of bishops, etc., for political, public, or confidential missions. Mr. Seward stirs up old dust. All the liberal party in Europe or France will look astonished, if not worse, at this absurdity.

All things considered, it looks like one of Seward's personal tricks, and Seward outwitted Chase, took him in by proffering a similar mission to Chase's friend, Bishop McIlvaine. But I pity Dayton. He is a high-toned man, and the mission of Hughes is a humiliation to Dayton.

Whatever may be the objects of these missions, they look like petty expedients, unworthy a minister of a great government.

Mason and Slidell caught. England will roar, but here the people are satisfied. Some of the diplomats make curious faces. Lord Lyons behaves

with dignity.   The small Bremen flatter right and
left, and do it like little lap-dogs.

Governor Andrew of Massachusetts, ex-Governor
Boutwell; are tip-top men — men of the people.   The
Blairs are too heinous, too violent, in their persecu-
tion of Fremont.   Warned M. Blair not to protect
one whom Fremont deservedly expelled.   But M.
Blair, in his spite against Fremont, took a mean
adventurer by the hand, and entangled therein the
President.

The vessel and the crew are excellent, and would
easily obey the hand of a helmsman, but there is the
rub, where to find him ?   Lincoln is a simple man
of the prairie, and his eyes penetrate not the fog,
the tempest.   They do not perceive the signs of the
times — cannot embrace the horizon of the nation.
And thus his small intellectual insight is dimmed
by those around him.   Lincoln begins now already
to believe that he is infallible ; that he is ahead of
the people, and frets that the people may remain
behind.   Oh simplicity or conceit !

Again, Lincoln is frightened with the success in
South Carolina, as in his opinion this success will
complicate the question of slavery.   He is frightened as to what he shall do with Charleston and
Augusta, provided these cities are taken.

It is disgusting to hear with what supercilious-
ness the different members of the Cabinet speak of
the approaching Congress — and not one of them is
in any way the superior of many congressmen.

When Congress meets, the true national balance

account will be struck. The commercial and piratical flag of the secesh is virtually in all waters and ports. (The little cheese-eater, the Hollander, was the first to raise a fuss against the United States concerning the piratical flag. This is not to be forgotten.) 2d. Prestige, to a great extent, lost. ·3d. Millions upon millions wasted. Washington besieged and blockaded, and more than 200,000 men kept in check by an enemy not by half as strong. 4th. Every initiative which our diplomacy tried abroad was wholly unsuccessful, and we are obliged to submit to new international principles inaugurated at our cost; and, summing up, instead of a broad, decided, general policy, we have vacillation, inaction, tricks, and expedients. The people fret, and so will the Congress. Nations are as individuals ; any partial disturbance in a part of the body occasions a general chill. Nature makes efforts to check the beginning of disease, and so do nations. In the human organism nature does not submit willingly to the loss of health, or of a limb, or of life. Nature struggles against death. So the people of the Union will not submit to an amputation, and is uneasy to see how unskilfully its own family doctors treat the national disease.

Port Royal, South Carolina, taken. Great and general rejoicing. It is a brilliant feat of arms, but a questionable military and war policy. Those attacks on the circumference, or on extremities, never can become a death-blow to secesh. The rebels must be crushed in the focus; they ought to receive a blow at the heart. This new strategy seems to indicate that McClellan has not heart enough to attack the fastnesses of rebeldom, but expects that something may turn up from these small expeditions. He expects to weaken the rebels in their focus. I wish McClellan may be right in his expectations, but I doubt it.

Officers of McClellan's staff tell that Mr. Lincoln almost daily comes into McClellan's library, and sits there rather unnoticed. On several occasions McClellan let the President wait in the room, together with other common mortals.

The English statesmen and the English press have the notion deeply rooted in their brains that the American people fight for empire. The rebels do it, but not the free men.

Mr. Seward's emphatical prohibition to Mr. Adams to mention the question of slavery may have contributed to strengthen in England the above-mentioned fallacy. This is a blunder, which before long or short Seward will repent. It looks like astuteness — *ruse;* but if so, it is the resource of a rather limited mind. In great and minor affairs, straightforwardness is the best policy. Loyalty always gets the better of astuteness, and the more so when the opponent is unprepared to meet it. Tricks can be well met by tricks, but tricks are impotent against truth and sincerity. But Mr. Seward, unhappily, has spent his life in various political tricks, and was surrounded by men whose intimacy must have necessarily lowered and unhealthily affected him. All his most intimates are unintellectual mediocrities or tricksters.

Seward is free from that infamous know-nothing-ism of which this Gen. Thomas is the great master (a man every few weeks accused of treason by the public opinion, and undoubtedly vibrating between loyalty here and sympathy with rebels).

All this must have unavoidably vitiated Mr. Sew-ard's better nature. In such way only can I see plainly why so many excellent qualities are marred in him. He at times can broadly comprehend things around him; he is good-natured when not stung, and he is devoted to his men.

As a patriot, he is American to the core — were only his domestic policy straight-forward and decided, and would he only stop meddling with the plans of the campaign, and let the War Department alone.

Since every part of his initiative with European cabinets failed, Seward very skilfully dispatches all the minor affairs with Europe — affairs generated by various maritime and international complications. Were his domestic policy as correct as is now his foreign policy, Seward would be the right man.

Statesmanship emerges from the collision of great principles with important interests. In the great Revolution, the thus called fathers of the nation were the offsprings of the exigencies of the time, and they were fully up to their task. They were vigorous and fresh; their intellect was not obstruct-ed by any political routine, or by tricky political praxis. Such men are now needed at the helm to carry this noble people throughout the most terrible tempest. So in these days one hears so much about constitutional formulas as safeguards of liberty. True liberty is not to be virtually secured by any framework of rules and limitations, devisable only by statecraft. The perennial existence of liberty depends not on the action of any definite and ascertainable machinery, but on continual accessions of fresh and vital influences. But perhaps such influences are among the noblest, and therefore among the rarest, attributes of man.

Abroad and here, traitors and some pedants on formulas make a noise concerning the violation of formulas. Of course it were better if such violations had been left undone. But all this is transient, and evoked by the direst necessity. The Constitution was made for a healthy, normal condition of the nation; the present condition is abnormal. Regular functions are suspended. When the human body is ruined or devoured by a violent disease, often very tonic remedies are used — remedies which would destroy the organism if administered when in a healthy, normal condition. A strong organism recovers from disease, and from its treatment. Human societies and institutions pass through a similar ordeal, and when they are unhinged, extraordinary and abnormal ways are required to maintain the endangered society and restore its equipoise.

Examining day after day the map of Virginia, it strikes one that a movement with half of the army could be made down from Mount Vernon by the two turnpike roads, and by water to Occoquan, and from there to Brentsville. The country there seems to be flat, and not much wooded. Manassas would be taken in the rear, and surrounded, provided the other half of the army would push on by the direct way from here to Manassas, and seriously attack the enemy, who thus would be broken, could not escape. This, or any plan, the map of Virginia ought to suggest to the staff of McClellan, were it a staff in the true meaning. Dybitsch and Toll, young colonels in the staff of Alexander I., 1813–'14, originated the march on Paris, so destructive to Napoleon. History bristles with evidences how with staffs originated many plans of battles and of campaigns; history explains the paramount influence of staffs on the conduct of a war. Of course Napoleon wanted not a suggestive, but only an executive staff; but McClellan is not a Napoleon, and has neither a suggestive nor an executive staff around him. A Marcy to suggest a plan of a campaign or of a battle, to watch over its execution!

I spoke to McDowell about the positions of Occoquan and Brentsville. He answered that perhaps something similar will be under consideration, and that McClellan must show his mettle and capacity. I pity McDowell's confidence.

Besides, the American army as it was and is educated, nursed, brought up by Gen. Scott,— the army has no idea what are the various and complicated duties of a staff. No school of staff at West Point; therefore the difficulty to find now genuine officers

of the staff.   If McClellan ever moves this army,
then the defectiveness of his staff may occasion losses
and even disasters.   It will be worse with his staff
than it was at Jena with the Prussian staff, who
were as conceited as the small West Point clique
here in Washington.

West Point instructs well in special branches, but
does not necessarily form generals and captains.
The great American Revolution was fought and
made victorious by men not from any military
schools, and to whom were opposed commanders
with as much military science as there was pos-
sessed and current in Europe.   Jackson, Taylor,
and even Scott, are not from the school.

I do not wish to judge or disparage the pupils
from West Point, but I am disgusted with the supercilious and ridiculous behavior of the clique here,
ready to form prætorians or anything else, and poisoning around them the public opinion.   Western
generals are West Point pupils, but I do not hear
them make so much fuss, and so contemptuously
look down on the volunteers.   These Western generals pine not after regulars, but make use of
such elements as they have under hand.   The best
and most patriotic generals and officers here, educated at West Point, are numerous.   Unhappily
a clique, composed of a few fools and fops, overshadows the others.

McClellan's speciality is engineering.   It is a speciality which does not form captains and generals
for the field, — at least such instances are very rare.

Of all Napoleon's marshals and eminent commanders, Berthier alone was educated as engineer, and his speciality and high capacity was that of a chief of the staff. Marescott or Todleben would never claim to be captains. The intellectual powers of an engineer are modeled, drilled, turned towards the defensive, — the engineer's brains concentrate upon selecting defensive positions, and combine how to strengthen them by art. So an engineer is rather disabled from embracing a whole battle-field, with its endless casualties and space. Engineers are the incarnation of a defensive warfare; all others, as artillerists, infantry, and cavalry, are for dashing into the unknown — into the space; and thus these specialities virtually represent the offensive warfare.

When will they begin to see through McClellan, and find out that he is not the man? Perhaps too late, and then the nation will sorely feel it.

Mr. Seward almost idolizes McClellan. Poor homage that; but it does mischief by reason of its influence on the public opinion.

DECEMBER, 1861.

McCLELLAN is now all-powerful, and refuses to divide the army into corps. Thus much for his brains and for his consistency.

The message — a disquisition upon labor and capital; hesitancy about slavery. The President wishes to be pushed on by public opinion. But public opinion is safe, and expects from the official leader a decided step onwards. The message gives no solution, suggests none, accounts not for the lost time — foreshadows not a vigorous, energetic effort to crush the rebellion; foreshadows not a vigorous, offensive war. The message is an honest paper, but says not much.

The question of emancipation is not clear even in the heads of the leading emancipationists; not one thinks to give freeholds to the emancipated. It is the only way to make them useful to themselves and to the community. Freedom without land is humbug, and the fools speak of exportation of the four millions of slaves, depriving thus the country of laborers, which a century of emigration cannot fill again. All these fools ought to be sent to a lunatic asylum.

To export the emancipated would be equivalent to devastation of the South, to its transformation into a wilderness. Small freeholds for the emancipated can be cut out of the plantations of . rebels, or out of the public lands of each State — lands forfeited by the rebellion.

State papers published. The instructions to the various diplomatic agents betray a beginner in the diplomatic career. By writing special instructions for each minister, Mr. Seward unnecessarily increased his task. The cause, reasons, etc., of the rebellion are one and the same for France or Russia, and a single explanatory circular for all the ministers would have done as well and spared a great deal of labor. Cavour wrote one circular to all cabinets, and so do all European statesmen. So, as they are, the State papers are a curious agglomeration of good patriotism and confusion. So the Minister to England is to avoid slavery ; the Minister to France has the contrary. All this is not smartness or diplomacy, but rather confusion, insincerity, and double-dealing. One must conclude that Lincoln and Seward have themselves no firm opinion. The instructions to Mexico would sound nobly-worded but for the confusion and the veil ordered to be thrown upon the cause of secession. That to Italy, above all to Austria, has a smack of a schoolmaster displaying his information before a gaping boy. It is offensive to the Minister going to Vienna. It may be suspected that some of these instructions were written to make capital at home, to astonish Mr. Lincoln with the knowledge of Europe and the familiarity with European affairs. All this display will prove to Europeans rather an ignorance of Europe. The correspondence on the Paris convention is splendid, although the initiative taken by Seward on this question was a mistake. But he argued well the case against the English and French reservations.

Never any government whatever treated so tenderly its worst and most dangerous enemies as does this government the Washington secessionists, spies for the enemy, and spreading false news here to frighten McClellan.

The old regular, but partly worn-out Republican leaders throttle and neutralize the new, fresh, vigorous accessions. So Curtis Noyes, one of the most eminent and devoted men, could not come into the Senate because Greeley wished to be elected.

No living man has rendered greater services to the people during the last twenty years than Greeley; but he ought to remain in his speciality. Greeley is no more fit for a Senator than to take the command of a regiment. Besides, the events already run over his head; Greeley is slowly breaking down.

McClellan is beset with all kinds of inventors, contractors, etc. He mostly endorses their suggestions, and on this authority the most extravagant orders are given by the War Department. All this ought to be investigated. Somebody back of Mc-Clellan may be found as being the real patron of these leeches.

If the genius or capacity of a commander consists not only in closely observing the movements of the enemy, but likewise in penetrating the enemy's plans and in modifying his own in proportion as they are deranged by an unexpected movement or a rapid march, then the generalship is altogether on the other side, and on ours not a sign, not a breath of it.

A civil war is mostly the purifying fire in a nation's existence. It is to be hoped that this great convulsion will purify the free States by sounding the death-knell of these small intriguing politicians. The American people at large will acquire earnestness, knowledge of men, and clear insight into its own affairs. Tricky politicians will be discarded, and true men backed by majorities.

The South has for its leaders the chiefs who for years organized the secession, who waged everything on its success, as life, honor, fortune, and who incite and carry with them the ignorant masses.

The reverse is in the North. Mr. Lincoln was not elected for suppressing the rebellion, nor did he make his Cabinet in view of a terrible national struggle for death or life. Neither Lincoln nor his Cabinet are the inciters or the inspiring leaders of the people, but only expressions — not *ad hoc* — of the national will. This is one reason why the administration is slower than the people, and why the rebel administration is quicker than ours.

The second reason, and generated by the first, is, that every rebel devotes his whole soul and energy to the success of the rebellion, forcibly forgetting his individuality. Our thus called leaders think first of their little selves, whose aggrandizement the public events are to secure, and the public cause is to square itself with their individual schemes.

Such is the policy of almost all those at the helm here. Not one among them is to be found deserving the name of a statesman, endowed with a great devotion, and with a great power, for the service of a great and noble aim. From the solemn hour that the fatherland honorably chains him to its service, the genuine statesman exists no more for himself, but for his country alone. If necessary, he ought to consider himself a victim to the public good, even were the public unjust towards him. He is to treat as enemies all the dirty, tricky, and mean passions and men. His enemies will hate, but the country, his enemies included, will esteem him. Such a man will be the genuine man of the American people, but he exists not in the official spheres.

It is for the first time in history that a young, insignificant man, without a past, without any reason, is put in such a lofty position as has been McClellan; he is to be literally kicked into greatness, and into showing eventually courage. All this is a psychological problem !

Kent's Commentary upon the qualifications of a President is the best criticism upon Lincoln.

These mosquitoes of public opinion, the sensation-seekers, the sentimental preachers, the lecturers, the amateurs of the thus called representative men, these oratorical falsifiers of history, but considered here as luminaries, are already at their pernicious, nay, accursed work.

They poison the judgment of the people. These hero-seekers for their sermons, lectures, and sensation productions, have already found all the criteria of a hero in McClellan, even in his chin, in the back of his horse, etc., etc., and now herald it all over the country. Curses be upon them.

No nation has ever raised idols with such facility as do the Americans. Nay, I do not suppose that there ever existed in history a nation with such a thirst for idols as this people. I may be a false prophet; but this new idol, McClellan, will cost them their life-blood.

The Blairs are now staunch supporters of McClellan. It is unpardonable. They ought to know, and they do know better. But Mr. Blair wishes to be Secretary of War in Cameron's place, and wishes to get it through McClellan.

And poor Lincoln! I pity him; but his advisers may make out of him something worse even than was Judas, in the curses of ages.

Polybius asserts that when the Greeks wrote about Rome they erred and lied, and when the Romans wrote of themselves they lied or boasted. The same the English do in relation to themselves, and to Americans. Above all, in this Trent affair, or excitement, all European writers for the press, professors, doctors, etc., pervert facts, reason, and international laws, forget the past, and lie or flatter, with a slight exception, as is Gasparin.

The Trent affair finished. We are a little humbled, but it was expedient to terminate it so. With another military leader than McClellan, we could march at the same time to Richmond, and invest Canada before any considerable English force could arrive there. But with such a hero at our head, better that it ends so. Europe will applaud us, and the relation with England will become clarified. Perhaps England would not have been so stiff in this Trent affair but for the fixed idea in Russell's, Newcastle's, Palmerston's, etc., heads that Seward wishes to pick a quarrel with England.

The first weeks of Seward's premiership pointed that way. Mr. Seward has the honors of the Trent affair. It is well as it is; the argument is smart, but a little too long, and not in a genuine diplomatic style. But Lincoln ought to have a little credit for it, as from the start he was for giving the traitors up.

The worst feature of the whole Trent affair is, that it brought back home from France this old mischief, General Scott. He will again resume his position as the first military authority in the country, confuse the judgment of Lincoln, of the press,

136 DIARY. [DECEMBER, 1861.

and of the people, and again push the country into
mire.

The Congress appointed a War Investigating
Committee, Senator Wade at the head. There is
hope that the committee will quickly find out what
a terrible mistake this McClellan is, and warn the
nation of him. But Lincoln, Seward, and the
Blairs, will not give up their idol.

Louis Napoleon said his word about the Trent
affair. All things considered, the conduct of the
Emperor cannot be complained of. The Thouvenel
paper is serious, severe, but intrinsically not unfriendly. Quite the contrary. Up to this time I
am right in my reliance on Louis Napoleon, on his
sound, cool, but broad comprehension.

Mr. Mercier behaves well, and he is to be relied
on, provided we show mettle and fight the traitors.
Now, as the European imbroglio is clarified, *at them,
at them!* But nothing to hope or expect from Mc-
Clellan. I daily preach, but in the wilderness.
Prince de Joinville made a very ridiculous fuss
about the Trent affair.

Americans believe that a statesman must be an
orator. Schoolboy-like, they judge on English precedents. In England, the Parliament is omnipotent;
it makes and unmakes administrations, therefore
oratory is a necessary corollary in a statesman; but
here the Cabinet acts without parliamentary wranglings, and a Jackson is the true type of an American statesman. Washington was not an orator, nor
was Alexander Hamilton.

JANUARY, 1862.

An ugly year ended in backing before England,
having, at least, relative right on our side. Further,
the ending year has revealed a certain incapacity in
the Republican party's leaders, at least its official
leaders, to administer the country and to grasp the
events. If the new year shall be only the continu-
ation of the faults, the mistakes, and the incapacities prevailing during 1861, then the worst is to
be expected.

The lowest in moral degradation is an European
defending slavery here or in Europe. Such Euro-

peans are far below the condemned criminals. Still lower are such Europeans who become defenders of slavery after having visited plantations, where, in the shape of wines and delicacies, they tasted human blood, and then, hyenas-like, smacked their lips and thirsted for more.

Always the same stories, lies, and humbugs concerning the hundreds of thousands of rebels in Manassas. These lies are spread here in Washington by the numerous secessionists — at large, by such ignoble sheets as the New York Herald and Times; and McClellan seems to willingly swallow these lies, as they justify his inaction and c——.

The city is more and more crowded with Jeremy Diddlers, with lecturers, with sensation-seekers, all of them in advance discounting their hero, and showing in broad light their gigantic stupidity. One of this motley finds in McClellan a Norman chin, the other muscle, the third a brow for laurels (of thistle I hope), another a square, military, heroic frame, another firmness in lips, another an unfathomed depth in the eye, etc., etc. Never I heard in Europe such balderdash. And the ladies — not the women and gentlewomen — are worse than the men in thus stupefying themselves and those around them.

The thus called arbitrary acts of the government prove how easily, on the plea of patriotic necessity, a people, nay, the public opinion, submits to arbitrary rule. All this, servility included, explains the facility with which, in former times, concentrated and concrete despotisms have been established. Here every such arbitrary action is submitted to, because it is so new, and because the people has the childish, naïve, but, to it, honorable confidence, that the power entrusted by the people is used in the interest and for the welfare of the people. But all the despots of all times and of all nations said the same. However, in justice to Mr. Lincoln, he is pure, and has no despotical longings, but he has around him some atomistic Torquemadas.

It will be very difficult to the coming generations to believe that a people, a generation, who for half a century was outrunning the time, who applied the steam and the electro-magnetic telegraph, that the same people, when overrun by a terrible crisis, moved slowly, waited patiently, and suffered from the mismanagement of its leaders. This is to be exclusively explained by the youthful self-consciousness of an internal, inexhaustible vital force, and by the child-like inexperience.

The Congress, that is, the majority, shows that it is aware of the urgency of the case, and of the dangerous position of the country. But still the best in Congress are chained, hampered by the formulas.

The good men in both the houses seem to be firmly decided not to quietly stand by and assist in the murder of the nation by the administrative and military incapacity. This was to be expected from such men as Wade, Grimes, Chandler, Hale, Wilson, Sumner (too classical), and other Republicans in the Senate, and from the numerous pure, radical Republicans in the House.

Burnside's expedition is a sign of life. But all these expeditions on the circumference, even if successful, will be fruitless if no bold, decided movement is at once made at the centre, at the heart of the rebellion. But McClellan, as his supporters say, matures his *strategical* plans. O God! General Scott lost *by strategy* three-fourths of the country's cause, and very probably by strategy McClellan will jeopardize what remains of it.

Will this McClellan ever advance? If he lingers, he may find only rats in Manassas. McClellan is ignorant of the great, unique rule for all affairs and undertakings, — it is to throw the whole man in one thing at one time. It is the same in the camp as in the study, for a captain as for a lawyer, the savant, and the scholar.

It is to be regretted that some of the men truly and thoroughly devoted to the cause of freedom and of humanity, mix with it such an enormous quantity of personal, almost childish vanity, as to puzzle many minds concerning the genuine nobleness of their devotion. It is to be regretted that those otherwise so self-sacrificing patriots discount even their martyrdom and persecutions, and credit them to their frivolous self-satisfaction.

Most of the thus-called well-informed Americans rather skim over than thoroughly study history. Above all, it applies to the general history of the Christian era, and of our great epoch (from the second half of the 18th century). Most of the Americans are only very superficially familiar with the

history of continental Europe, or know it only by
its contact with the history of England. Many of
them are more familiar with the classical wars of
Alexander, Hannibal, Cæsar, etc., than with those
of Gustavus, Frederick II., and even of Napoleon.
Were it otherwise, *strategy* would not to such an
extent have taken hold of their brains.

Mr. Adams was terribly unhorsed during the
Trent excitement in England ; he literally began to
pack up his trunks, and asked a personal advice
from Lord John Russell.

What a devoted patriot this Sandford in Belgium
is ; he has continual *itchings in his hand* to pay a
higher price for bad blankets that they may not fall
into the hands of secesh agents ; so with cloth, so
perhaps with arms. *Oh, disinterested patriot!*

Austria and Prussia whipped in by England and
France, and at the same time glad to have an occasion to take the airs of maritime powers. Austria
and Prussia sent their advice concerning the Trent
affair. The kick of asses at what they suppose to
be the dying lion.

Austria and Prussia! Great heavens! Ask the
prisons of both those champions of violated rights
how many better men than Slidell and Mason
groaned in them ; and the conduct of those powers
against the Poles in 1831! Was it neutral or honest ?

I am sure that Russia will behave well, and abstain from coming forward with uncalled-for and
humiliating advice. Russia is a true great power,

— a true friend, — and such noble behavior will be in harmony with the character of Alexander II., and with the friendliness and clear perception of events held by the Russian minister here. I hope that when the war is over the West Point nursery will be reformed, and a general military organization introduced, such a one as exists in Switzerland.

McClellan is a greater mistake than was even Scott. McClellan knows not the A B C of military history of any nation or war, or he would not keep this army so in camp. He would know that after recruits have been roughly instructed in the rudiments of a drill, the next best instructor is fighting. So it was in the thirty years' war; so in the American Revolution; so in the first French revolutionary wars. Strategians, martinets, lost the battles, or rather the campaigns, of Austerlitz, of Jena, etc. In 1813 German rough levies fought almost before they were drilled, and at Bautzen French recruits were victorious over Prussians, Russians, and Austrians. The secesh fight with fresh levies, etc.

Numerous political intriguers surrounding McClellan are busily laying tracks for him to the White House. What will Seward and Chase say to it, and even old Abe, who himself dreams of re-election, or at least his friends do it for him? All these candidates forget that the surest manner to reach the White House is not to think of it — to forget oneself and to act.

It is amusing to find in European papers all the various stories about Mr. Lincoln. There he is represented as a violent, blood-thirsty revolutionaire, dragging the people after him. In this manner, those European imbeciles are acquainted with American events, character, etc. They cannot find out that in decision, in clear-sightedness and soundness of judgment, the people are far ahead of Mr. Lincoln and of his spiritual or constitutional conscience-keepers. And the same imbeciles, if not *canailes*, speak of a mob-rule over the President, etc. Some one ought to enlighten those French and English supercilious ignorami that something like a mob only prevails in such cities as New York, Philadelphia, and Baltimore; and nine-tenths of such a mob are mostly yet unwashed, unrepublicanized Europeans. The ninety-nine one-hundredths of the freemen of the North are more orderly, more enlightened, more law-abiding, and more moral than are the English lordlings, somebodies, nobodies, and would-be somebodies. In the West, lynch-law, to be sure, is at times used against brothels, bar-rooms, gambling-houses, and thieves. It would be well to do the same in London, were it not that most of the lynch-lawed may not belong to the people. If the European scribblers were not past any honest impulse, they would know that the South is the generator and the congenial region for the mob, the fillibusters, the revolver and the bowie-knife rule. In the South the proportion of mobs to decency is the reverse of that prevailing in the free States. The *slavery gentleman* is a scarcely varnished savage, for whom the highest law is his reckless passion and will.

If Jeff. Davis succeeds, he will be the founder of a new and great slaveholding empire. His name will resound in after times; but history will record his name as that of a curse to humanity.

And so Davis is making history and Lincoln is telling stories. Beauregard gets inspired by the fumes of bivouacs; McClellan by the fumes of flatterers. Beauregard frightens us, McClellan rocks his baby. Beauregard shares the camp-fires of his soldiers; he sees them daily, knows them, as it is said, one by one; McClellan lives comfortably in the city, and appears only to the soldiers as the great Lama on special occasions. Camp-fellowship inspired all the great captains and established the magnetic current between the leader and the soldier.

McClellan organized a board of generals, arriving daily from the camps, to discuss some new fancy army equipment. And Lincoln, Seward, Blair, and all the tail of intriguers and imbeciles, still admire him. In no other country would such a futile man be kept in command of troops opposed to a deadly and skilful enemy.

For several weeks, McClellan and his chief of the staff (such as he is) are sick in bed, and no one is *ad interim* appointed to attend to the current affairs of our army of 600,000, having the enemy before their nose. Oh human imbecility! No satirist could invent such things; and if told, it would not be believed in Europe.

The McClellan-worship by the people at large is to be explained by the firm, ardent will of the people to crush the rebels, and by the general feeling of the necessity of a man for that purpose. Such is the case with the true, confiding people in the country ; but here, contractors, martinets, and intriguers are the blowers of that worship. Lincoln is as is the people at large ; but a Séward, a Blair, a Herald, a Times, and their respective and numerous tails, — as for their motives, they are the reverse of Lincoln and of the people.

Victories in Kentucky, beyond the circumference or the direct action from here ; they are obtained without strategy and by rough levies. But this voice of events is not understood by the McClellan tross.

Change in the Cabinet : Stanton, a new man, not from the parlor, and not from the hacks. His bulletin on the victory in Kentucky inaugurated a new era. It is a voice that nobody hitherto uttered in America. It is the awakening voice of the good genius of the people, almost as that which awoke Lazarus. This Stanton is the people ; I never saw him, but I hope he is the man for the events ; perhaps he may turn out to be *my* statesman.

I wish I could get convinced of the real superiority of Fremont. It is true that he was treated badly and had natural and artificial difficulties to over come ; it is true that to him belongs the credit of having started the construction of the mortar fleet ; but likewise it is true that he was, at the mildest, unsurpassingly reckless in contracts and expenditures, and I shall never believe him a general.

10

With all this, Fremont started a great initiative at a time when McClellan and three-fourths of the generals of his creation considered it a greater crime to strike at a *gentleman* slaveholder than to strike at the Union.

The courtesies and hospitalities paid to Thurlow Weed by English society are clamored here in various ways. These courtesies prove the high breeding and the good-will of a part, at least, of the English aristocracy and of English statesmen. I do not suppose that Thurlow Weed could ever have been admitted in such society if he were travelling on his own merits as the great lobbyist and politician. At the utmost, he would have been shown up as a *rara avis*. But introduced to English society as the master spirit of Mr. Seward, and as Seward's semi-official confidential agent, Thurlow Weed was admitted, and even petted. But it is another question if this palming of a Thurlow Weed upon the English high-toned statesmen increased their consideration for Mr. Seward. The Duke of Newcastle and others are not yet softened, and refuse to be humbugged.

Whoever has the slightest knowledge of how affairs are transacted, is well aware that the times of a personal diplomacy are almost gone. The exceptions are very rare, very few, and the persons must be of other might and intellectual mettle than a Sandford, Weed, or Hughes. Great affairs are not conducted or decided by conversations, but by great interests. Diplomatic agents, at the utmost,

serve to keep their respective governments informed
about the run of events. Mr. Mercier does it for
Louis Napoleon ; but Mr. Mercier's reports, however
friendly they may be, cannot much influence a man
of such depth as Louis Napoleon, and to imagine
that a Hughes will be able to do it! I am ashamed
of Mr. Seward ; he proves by this would-be-crotchety
policy how little he knows of events and of men,
and how he undervalues Louis Napoleon. Such
humbug missions are good to throw dirt in the eyes
of a Lincoln, a Chase, etc., but in Europe such
things are sent to Coventry. And Hughes to influence Spain ! Oh ! oh !

Dayton frets on account of the mission of Hughes.
Dayton is right. Generally Dayton shows a great
deal of good sense, of good comprehension, and a
noble and independent character. He is not a flatterer, not servile, and subservient to Mr. Seward, as
are others — Mr. Adams, Mr. Sandford, and some
few other diplomatic agents.

The active and acting abolitionists ought to concentrate all their efforts to organize thoroughly and
efficiently the district of Beaufort. The success of
a productive colony there would serve as a womb
for the emancipation at large.

Mr. Seward declares that he has given up meddling
with military affairs. For his own sake, and for
the sake of the country, I ardently wish it were so ;
but — I shall never believe it.

The Investigating Committee has made the most
thorough disclosures of the thorough incapacity of

McClellan; but the McClellan men, Seward, Blair, etc., neutralize, stifle all the good which could accrue to the country from these disclosures.   And Lincoln is in their clutches.   The administration by its in-fluence prevents the publication of the results of this investigation, prevents the truth from coming to the people.   Any hard name will be too soft for such a moral prevarication.

McClellan is either as feeble as a reed, or a bad man.   The disorder around here is nameless. Banks compares it to the time of the French Directory.   Banks has no guns, no cavalry, and is in the vanguard.   He begs almost on his knees, and cannot get anything.   And the country pays a chief of the staff, and head of the staffers.

The time must come, although it be now seem-ingly distant, that the people will awake from this lethargy; that it will perceive how much of the noblest blood of the people, how much time and money, have been worse than recklessly squandered. The people will find it out, and then they will ask those Cains at the wheel an account of the innocent blood of Abel, the country's son, the country's cause.

The defenders of, and the thus called moderate men on the question of slavery, utter about it the old rubbish composed of the most thorough ignorance and of disgusting fallacies, in relation to this pseudo science, or rather lie, about races.   More of it will come out in the course of the Congressional dis-cussions.   Not one of them is aware that independ-ent science, that comparative anatomy, physiology,

psychology, anthropology, that philosophy of history
altogether and thoroughly repudiate all these superficially asserted, or tried-to-be-established, intrinsic
diversities and peculiarities of races.   All these
would-be axioms, theories, are based on sand.   In
true science the question of race as represented
by the Southern school partisans of slavery, with
Agassiz, the so-called professor of Charleston by
European savans, at their head, — that question is
at the best an illusive element, and endangers the ·
accuracy of induction.   As it presents itself to the
unprejudiced investigator, race is nothing more than
the single manifestation of anterior stages of existence, the aggregate expression of the pre-historic
vicissitudes of a people.

If those would-be knowing arguers on slavery,
race, etc., were only aware of the fact that such
people as the primitive Greeks, or the ancestors of
classical Greeks, that the ancestors of the Latins,
that even the roving, robbing ancestors of the Anglo
Saxons, in some way or other, have been anthropoph-
agi, and worshipped fetishes; and even as thus called already civilized, they sacrificed men to gods, —
could our great pro-slavers know all this, they
would be more decent in their ignorant assertions,
and not, so self-satisfied, strut about in their dark
ignorance.

Those who are afraid that the freed negroes of the
South will run to the Northern free States, display ·
an ignorance still greater than the former.   When
the enslaved colored Americans in the South shall

be *all* thoroughly emancipated in that now cursed region, then they will remain in the, to them, congenial climate, and in the favorable economical conditions of labor and of existence.   Not only those emancipated will not run North, but the colored population from the free States, incited and stirred up by natural attractions, will leave the North for the South, as small streamlets and rivulets run into a large current or river.

The rebels extend on an immense bow, nearly one hundred miles, from the lower to the upper Potomac. Our army, two to one, is on the span of the arc, and we do nothing.   A French sergeant would be better inspired than is McClellan.

Drifting — The English blue book — Lord John could not act differently — Palmerston the great European fuss-maker — Mr. Seward's "two pickled rods" for England — Lord Lyons — His pathway strewn with broken glass — Gen. Stone arrested — Sumner's resolutions infuse a new spirit in the Constitution — Mr. Seward beyond salvation — He works to save slavery — Weed has ruined him — The New York press — "Poor Tribune" — The Evening Post — The Blairs — Illusions dispelled — "All quiet on the Potomac" — The London papers — Quill-heroes can be bought for a dinner — French opinion — Superhuman efforts to save slavery — It is doomed! — "All you worshippers of darkness cannot save it!" — The Hutchinsons — Corporal Adams — Victories in the West — Stanton the man! — Strategy (hear! hear!)

WE are obliged, one by one, to eat our official high-toned assertions and words, and day after day we drift towards putting the rebels on an equal footing with ourselves. We declared the privateers to be pirates (which they are), and now we proffer their exchange against our colonels and other honorable prisoners. So one radical evil generates numberless others. And from the beginning of the struggle this radical evil was and is the want of earnestness, of a firm purpose, and of a straight, vigorous policy by the administration. *Paullatim summa petuntur* may turn out true — but for the rebels.

The publication of the English blue book, or of official correspondence between Lord Lyons and Lord John Russell, throws a new light on the conduct of the English Cabinet; and, anglophobe as I am, I must confess that, all things considered, above all the unhappily-justified distrust of England in Mr. Seward's policy, — from the first day of our troubles Lord John Russell could not act differently from what he did. Lord John Russell had to reconcile the various and immense interests of England, jeopardized by the war, with his sincere love of human liberty. Therein Lord John Russell differs wholly from Lord Palmerston, this great European fuss-maker, who hates America. As far as it was possible, Lord J. Russell remained faithful to the noble (not hereditary, but philosophical) traditions of his blood. Lord John Russell's letter to Lord Lyons (No. 17), February 20, 1861, although full of distrust in the future policy of Mr. Lincoln's Cabinet towards England, is nevertheless an honorable document for his name.

Lord J. Russell was well aware that the original plan of Mr. Seward was to annoy and worry England. Everything is known in this world, and especially the incautious words and conversations of public men. Months before the inauguration, Mr. Seward talked to senators of both parties that he had in store "two pickled rods" for England. The one was to be Green (always drunken), the Senator from Missouri, on account of the colored man Anderson; the other Mr. Nesmith, the Senator from Oregon, and the San Juan boundaries. Undoubtedly the Southern senators did not keep secret the like inimical forebodings concerning Mr. Seward's inten-

tions towards England.   Undoubtedly all this must
have been known to Lord J. Russell when he wrote
the above-mentioned letter, No. 17.

More even than Lord John Russell's, Lord Lyons's
official correspondence since November, 1860, inspires the highest possible respect for his noble sentiments and character.   Above all, one who witnessed the difficulties of Lord Lyons's position here,
and how his pathway was strewn with broken glass,
and this by all kinds of hands, must feel for him
the highest and most sincere consideration.   From
the official correspondence, Lord Lyons comes out a
friend of humanity and of human liberty, — just the
reverse of what he generally was supposed to be.
And during the whole Trent affair, Lord Lyons's conduct was discreet, delicate, and generous.   Events
may transform Lord Lyons into an official enemy of
the Union; but a mind soured by human meanness
is soothingly impressioned by such true nobleness in
a diplomat and an Englishman.

Gen. Stone, of Ball's Bluff infamous massacre,
arrested.   Bravo!   At the best, Stone was one of
those conceited regulars who admired slavery, and
who would have wished to save the Union in their
own peculiar way.   I wish he may speak, as in all
probability he was not alone.

Sumner's resolutions infuse a new spirit in the
Constitution, and elevate it from the low ground of
a dead formula.   The resolutions close the epoch of
the Stories, of the Kents, of the Curtises, and inaugurate a higher comprehension of American con-

stitutionalism. During this session Charles Sumner triumphantly and nobly annihilated the aspersions of his enemies, representing him as a man of one hobby, but lacking any practical ideas. His speech on currency was among the best. Not so with his speech about the Trent affair. It is superficial, and contains misconceptions concerning treaties, and other blunders very strange in a would-be statesman.

Ardently devoted to the cause of justice and of human rights, Sumner weakens the influence which he ought to exercise, because he impresses many with the notion that he looks more to the outside effect produced by him than to the intrinsic value of the subject; he makes others suppose that he is too fond of such effect, and, above all, of the effect produced in Europe among the circle of his English and European acquaintances.

It is positively asserted that Lincoln agreed to take Mr. Seward in the Cabinet, because Weed and others urgently represented that Mr. Seward is the only man in the Republican party who is familiar with Europe, with her statesmen, and their policy. O Lord! O Lord! And where has Seward acquired all this information? Mr. Seward had not even the first A B C of it, or of anything else connected with it. And, besides, such a kind of special information is, at the utmost, of secondary necessity for an American statesman. Marcy had it not, and was a true, a genuine statesman. Undoubtedly, nature has endowed Seward with emi-

nent intellectual qualities, and with germs for an
eminent statesman.　But the intellectual qualities
became blunted by the long use of crotchets and
tricks of a politician, by the associations and influence of such as Weed, etc. ; thereby the better germs
became nipped, so to speak, in the bud.　Mr. Seward's acquired information by study, by instruction,
and by reading, is quite the reverse of what in
Europe is regarded as necessary for a statesman.
Often, very often, I sorrowfully analyze and observe
Mr. Seward, with feelings like those evoked in us by
the sight of a noble ruin, or of a once rich, natural
pánorama, but now marred by large black spots of
burned and dead vegetation, or by the ashes of a
volcano.

Now, Mr. Seward is beyond salvation — a " disappointed man," as he called himself in a conversation
with Judge Potter, M. C.; he changed aims, and
perhaps convictions.　For Mr. Seward, slavery is no
more the most hideous social disease ; he abandoned
that creed which elevated him in the confidence of
the people.　Now he works to preserve as much as
possible of the curse of slavery ; he does it on the
plea of Union and conservatism ; but in truth he
wishes to disorganize the pure Republican party,
which he hates since the Chicago Convention and
since the days of the formation of the Cabinet.
Under the advice of Weed, Mr. Seward attempts to
form a (thus called) Union and conservative party,
which at the next turn may carry him into the
White House.

Seward considers Weed his good genius; but in reality Weed has ruined Seward. Now Mr. Seward supports *strategy*, imbecility, and McClellan. The only explanation for me is, that Seward, participating in all military counsels and strategic plans, and not understanding any of them, finds it safer to back McClellan, and thus to deceive others about his own ignorance of military matters.

The press — the New York one —worse and worse; the majority wholly degraded to the standard of the Herald and of the Times. The *poor* Tribune, daily fading away, altogether losing that bold, lofty spirit of initiative to which for so many years the Tribune owed its all-powerful and unparalleled influence over the free masses. Now, at times, the Tribune is similar to an old, honest sexagenarian, attempting to draw a night-cap over his ears and eyes. The flames of the holy fire, so common once in the Tribune, flash now only at distant, very distant epochs. The Evening Post towers over all of them. If the Evening Post never at a jump went as far as once did the Tribune, the Evening Post never made or makes a retrograde step; but perhaps slowly, but steadily and boldly, moves on. The Evening Post is not a paper of politicians or of jobbers, but of enlightened, well-informed, and strong-hearted patriots and citizens.

Mr. Blair, after all, is only an ambitious politician. My illusion about both the brothers is wholly dispelled and gone. I regret it, but both sustain McClellan, both look askant on Stanton, and belong to the conditional emancipationists, colonizationists, and other RADICAL preservers of slavery. All such form a class of superficial politicians, of compromisers with their creed, and are corrupters of others.

How ardently I would prefer not to so often accuse others; but more than forty years of revolutionary and public life and experience have taught me to discriminate between deep convictions and assumed ones — to highly venerate the first, and to keep aloof from the second. Gold is gold, and pinchbeck is pinchbeck, in character as in metal.

McClellan acts as if he had taken the oath to some hidden and veiled deity or combination, by all means not to ascertain anything about the condition of the enemy. Any European if not American old woman in pants long ago would have pierced the veil by a strong reconnoissance on Centreville. Here "all quiet on the Potomac." And I hear generals, West Pointers, justifying this colossal offence against common sense, and against the rudiments of military tactics, and even science. Oh, noble, but awfully dealt with, American people!

At times Mr. Seward talks and acts as if he lacked altogether the perception of the terrible earnestness of the struggle, of the dangers and responsibilities of his political position, as well now before the people as hereafter before history. Often I can scarcely resist answering him, Beware, beware!

Lincoln belittles himself more and more. Whatever he does is done under the pressure of events, under the pressure of the public opinion. These agencies push Lincoln and slowly move him, notwithstanding his reluctant heaviness and his resistance. And he a standard-bearer of this noble people !

Those mercenary, ignorant, despicable scribblers of the London Times, of the Tory Herald, of the Saturday Review, and of the police papers in Paris, as the Constitutionnel, the Pays, the Patrie, all of them lie with unparalleled facility. Any one knows that those hungry quill-heroes can be got for a good dinner and a *douceur*.

I am sorry that the Americans ascribe to Louis Napoleon and to the French people the hostility to human rights as shown by those *echappes des bagnes de la literature*. Louis Napoleon and the French people have nothing in common with those literary blacklegs.

The *Journal des Debats*, the *Opinion Nationale*, the *Presse*, the *Siecle*, etc., constitute the true and honest organs of opinion in France. In the same way A. de Gasparin speaks for the French people with more authority than does Michel Chevalier, who knows much more about free trade, about canals and railroads, but is as ignorant of the character, of the spirit, and of the institutions of the American people, as he is ignorant concerning the man in the moon. So the lawyer Hautefeuille must have received a fee to show so much ill-will to the cause of humanity, and such gigantic ignorance.

Who began the civil war ? is repeatedly discussed

by those quill cut-throats and allies on the Thames and on the Seine.

Here some smaller diplomats (not Sweden, who is true to the core to the cause of liberty), and, above all, the would-be fashionable *galopins des legations*, are the cesspools of secession news, picked up by them in secesh society. Happily, the like *galopins* are the reverse of the opinions of their respective chiefs.

What superhuman efforts are made in Congress, and out of it, in the Cabinet, in the White House, by Union men, — Seward imagines he leads them, — by the weak-brained, and by traitors, to save slavery, if not all, at least a part of it. Every concession made by the President to the enemies of slavery has only one aim; it is to mollify their urgent demands by throwing to them small crumbs, as one tries to mollify a boisterous and hungry dog. By such a trick Lincoln and Seward try to save what can be saved of the peculiar institution, to gratify, and eventually to conciliate, the South. This is the policy of Lincoln, of Seward, and very likely of Mr. Blair. Such political *gobe-mouche* as Doolittle and many others, are, or will be, taken in by this manœuvre.

Scheme what you like, you schemers, wiseacres, politicians, and would-be statesmen, nevertheless slavery is doomed. Humanity will have the best against such pettifoggers as you. I know better. I have the honor to belong to that European generation who, during this half of our century, from

Tagus and Cadiz to the Wolga, has gored with its blood battle-fields and scaffolds; whose songs and aspirations were re-echoed by all the horrible dungeons; by dungeons of the blood-thirsty Spanish inquisition, then across Europe and Asia, to the mines of Nertschinsk, in the ever-frozen Altai. We lost all we had on earth; seemingly we were always beaten; but Portugal and Spain enjoy to-day a constitutional regime that is an improvement on absolutism. France has expelled forever the Bourbons, and universal suffrage, spelt now by the French people, is a progress, is a promise of a great democratic future. Germany has in part conquered free speech and free press. Italy is united, Romanism is falling to pieces, Austria is undermined and shaky, and broken are the chains on the body of the Russian serf. All this is the work of the spirit of the age, and our generation was the spirit's apostle and confessor. And so it will be with slavery, and all you worshippers of darkness cannot save it.

Not the one who strikes the first blow begins a civil war, but he who makes the striking of the blow imperative. The Southern robbers cannot claim exemption; they stole the arsenals, and struck the first blow at Sumpter. So much for the infamous quill-heroes of the London Times, the Herald, and *tutti quanti*.

The highest crime is treason in arms, and this crime is praised and defended by the English would-be high-toned press. But sooner or later it will come out how much apiece was paid to the London

Times, the Herald, and the Saturday Review for their venomous articles against the Union.

McClellan expelled from the army the Hutchinson family. It is mean and petty. Songs are the soul and life of the camp, and McClellan's *heroic deeds* have not yet found their minstrel.

After all, McClellan has organized — nothing! McDowell has, so to speak, formed the first skeletons of brigades, divisions, of parks of artillery, etc. The people uninterruptedly poured in men and treasures, and McClellan only continued what was commenced before him.

I positively know that already in December Mr. Lincoln began to be doubtful of McClellan's generalship. This doubtfulness is daily increasing, and nevertheless Mr. Lincoln keeps that incapacity in command because he does not wish *to hurt McClellan's feelings.* Better to ruin the noble people, the country! I begin to draw the conclusion that Mr. Lincoln's good qualities are rather negative than positive.

Mr. Adams complains that he is kept in the dark about the policy of the administration, and cannot answer questions made to him in London. But the administration, that is, Lincoln and Seward, are a little *a la* Micawber, expecting what may turn up. And, besides this, the great orator *de lana caprina* (Mr. Adams) deliberately degraded himself to the condition of a corporal under Mr. Seward's orders.

Victories in the West, results of the new spirit in the War Department. Stanton will be the man.

11

It is a curious fact that such commanders as Halleck, etc., sit in cities and fight through those under them; and there are ignoble flatterers trying to attribute these victories to McClellan, and to his *strategy*. As if battles could be commanded by telegraph at one thousand miles' distance. It is worse than imbecility, it is idiotism and *strategy*.

Stanton calls himself a man of one idea. How he overtops in the Cabinet those myrmidons with their many petty notions! One idea, but a great and noble one, makes the great men, or the men for great events. Would God that the people may understand Stanton, and that pettifoggers, imbeciles, and traitors may not push themselves between the people and Stanton, and neutralize the only man who has *the one idea* to break, to crush the rebellion.

Every day Mr. Lincoln shows his want of knowledge of men and of things; the total absence of *intuition* to spell, to see through, and to disentangle events.

If, since March, 1861, instead of being in the hands of pettifoggers, Mr. Lincoln had been in the hands of *a man of one idea* as is Stanton, ninetenths of the work would have been accomplished.

McClellan's flunkeys claim for him the victories in the West. It is impossible to settle which is more to be scorned in them, their flunkeyism or their stupidity.

Lock-jaw expedition. For any other government whatever, in one even of the most abject favoritism, such a humbug and silly conduct of the commander

and of his chief of the staff would open the eyes
even of a Pompadour or of a Dubarry. Here, *our
great rulers and ministers* shut the more closely
their mind's (?) eyes   *   *   *   *   *

For the first time in one of his dispatches Mr.
Corporal Adams *dares* to act against orders, and
mentions — but very slightly — slavery.   Mr. Adams observes to his chief that in England public
opinion is very sensitive; at last the old freesoiler
found it out.

How this public opinion in America is unable to
see the things as they naturally are.   Now the public fights to whom to ascribe the victories in the
West.   Common sense says, Ascribe them, 1st, to
the person who ordered the fight (Stanton); 2d,
exclusively to the generals who personally commanded the battles and the assaults of forts.   Even
Napoleon did not claim for himself the glory for
battles won by his generals when in his, Napoleon's,
absence.

For weeks McClellan and his thus called staff
diligently study international law, strategy (hear,
hear!), tactics, etc.   His aids translate for his use
French and German writers.   One cannot even
apply in this case the proverb, "Better late than
never," as the like hastily scraped and undigested
sham-knowledge unavoidably must obfuscate and
wholly confuse McClellan's — not Napoleonic —
brains.

The intriguers and imbeciles claim the Western
victories as the illustration of McClellan's great

strategy.   Why shows he not a little *strategy* under his nose here? Any old woman would surround and take the rebels in Manassas.

Now they dispute to Grant his deserved laurels. If he had failed at Donelson, the *strategians* would have washed their hands, and thrown on Grant the disaster.   So did Scott after Bull Run.

Mr. Lincoln, McClellan, Seward, Blair, etc., forget the terrible responsibility for thus recklessly squandering the best blood, the best men, the best generation of the people, and its treasures.   But sooner or later they will be taken to a terrible account even by the Congress, and at any rate by history.

It is by their policy, by their support of McClellan, that the war is so slow, and the longer it lasts the more human sacrifices it will devour, and the greater the costs of the devastation.   Stanton alone feels and acts differently, and it seems that the rats in the Cabinet already begin their nightly work against him.   These rats are so ignorant and conceited !

The celebrated Souvoroff was accused of cruelty because he always at once stormed fortresses instead of investing them and starving out the inhabitants and the garrisons.   The old hero showed by arithmetical calculations that his bloodiest assaults never occasioned so much loss of human life as did on both sides any long siege, digging, and approaches, and the starving out of those shut up in a fortress. This for McClellan and for the intriguing and ignorant RATS.

The Africo-Americans — Fremont — The Orleans — Confiscation — Amer · ican nepotism — The Merrimac — Wooden guns — Oh shame! — Gen. Wadsworth — The rats have the best of Stanton — McClellan goes to Fortress Monroe — Utter imbecility — The embarkation — McClellan a turtle — He will stick in the marshes — Louis Napoleon behaves nobly — So does Mr. Mercier — Queen Victoria for freedom — The great strategian — Senator Sumner and the French minister — Archbishop Hughes — His diplomatic activity not worth the postage on his correspondence — Alberoni-Seward — Love's labor lost.

MEN like this Davis, Wickliffe, and all the like *pecus*, roar against the African race. The more I see of this doomed people, the more I am convinced of their intrinsic superiority over all their white revilers, above all, over this slaveholding generation, rotten, as it is, to the core. When emancipated, the Africo-Americans in immense majority will at once make quiet, orderly, laborious, intelligent, and free cultivators, or, to use Européan language, an excellent peasantry; when ninety-nine one-hundredths of slaveholders, either rebels or thus called loyal, altogether considered, as human beings are shams, are shams as citizens, and constitute caricatures and monsters of civilization.

Civilization! It is the highest and noblest aim in human destinies when it makes the man moral and

165

true; but civilization invoked by, and in which strut traitors, slaveholders, and abettors of slavery, reminds one of De Maistre's assertion, that the devil created the red man of America as a counterfeit to man, God's creation in the Old World. This so-called civilization of the slaveholders is the devil's counterfeit of the genuine civilization.

The Africo-Americans are the true producers of the Southern wealth — cotton, rice, tobacco, etc. When emancipated and transformed into small farmers, these laborious men will increase and ameliorate the culture of the land; and they will produce by far more when the white shams and drones shall be taken out of their way. In the South, bristling with Africo-American villages, will almost disappear fillibusterism, murder, and the bowie knife, and other supreme manifestations of Southern *chivalrous high-breeding*.

Fremont's reports and defence show what a disorder and insanity prevailed under the rule of Scott. Fremont's military capacity perhaps is equal to zero; his vanity put him in the hands of wily flatterers; but the disasters in the West cannot be credited to him. Fremont initiated the construction of the mortar flotilla on the Mississippi (I positively know such is the fact), and he suggested the capture of various forts, but was not sustained at this sham, the head-quarters.

These Orleans have wholly espoused and share in the fallacious and mischievous notions of the McClellanites concerning the volunteers. Most probably with the authority of their name, they confirm McClellan's fallacious notions about the necessity of a great regular army. The Orleans are good, generous boys, but their judgment is not yet matured; they had better stayed at home.

Confiscation is the great word in Congress or out of it. The property of the rebels is confiscable by the ever observed rule of war, as consecrated by international laws. When two sovereigns make war, the victor confiscates the other's property, as represented by whole provinces, by public domains, by public taxes and revenues. In the present case the rebels are the sovereigns, and their property is therefore confiscable. But for the sake of equity, and to compensate the wastes of war, Congress ought to decree the confiscation of property of all those who, being at the helm, by their political incapacity or tricks contribute to protract the war and increase its expense.

Mr. Lincoln yields to the pressure of public opinion. A proof: his message to Congress about emancipation in the Border States. Crumb No. 1 thrown — reluctantly I am sure — to the noble appetite of freemen. I hope history will not credit Mr. Lincoln with being the initiator.

American nepotism puts to shame the one practised in Europe. All around here they keep offices in pairs, father and son. So McClellan has a father in-law as chief of the staff, a brother as aid, and then various relations, clerks, etc., etc., and the same in some other branches of the administration.

The Merrimac affair. Terrible evidence how active and daring are the rebels, and we sleepy, slow, and self-satisfied. By applying the formula of induction from effect to cause, the disaster occasioned by the Merrimac, and any further havoc to be made by this iron vessel, — all this is to be credited to McClellan.

If Norfolk had been taken months ago, then the rebels could not have constructed the Merrimac. Norfolk could have been easily taken any day during the last six months, *but for strategy* and the *maturing of great plans!* These are the sacramental words more current now than ever. Oh good-natured American people! how little is necessary to humbug thee!

Oh shame! oh malediction! The rebels left Centreville, — which turns out to be scarcely a breastwork, with wooden guns, — and they slipped off from Manassas.

When McClellan got the news of the evacuation, he gravely considered where to lean his right or left flanks, and after the consideration, two days after the enemy *wholly* completed the evacuation, McClellan moves at the head of 80,000 men — to storm the wooden guns of Centreville. Two hours after the news of the evacuation reached the head-quarters, Gen. Wadsworth asked permission to follow with his brigade, during the night, the retreating enemy. But it was not *strategy, not a matured plan.* If Gen. Wadsworth had been in command of the army, not one of the rats from Manassas would have escaped. The reasons are, that Gen. Wadsworth has a quick, clear, and wide-encompassing conception of events and things, a clear insight, and many other inborn qualities of mind and intellect.

The Congress has a large number of very respectable capacities, and altogether sufficient for the emergencies, and the Congress would do more good but for the impediments thrown in its way by the double-dealing policy prevailing in Mr. Lincoln's Cabinet and administration. The majority in Congress represent well the spirit of self-government. It is a pity that Congress cannot crush or purify the administration.

All that passes here is maddening, and I am very grateful to my father and mother for having endowed me with a frame which resists the blows.

The pursuit of the enemy abandoned, the basis of operations changed. The rats had the best of Stanton. *Utinam sim falsus propheta*, but if Stanton's influence is no more all-powerful, then there is an end to the short period of successes. Mr. Lincoln's council wanted to be animated by a pure and powerful spirit. Stanton was the man, but he is not a match for impure intriguers. Also McClellan goes to Fortress Monroe, to Yorktown, to the rivers. This plan reveals an utter military imbecility, and its plausibility can only catch ——.

1st. Common sense shows that the rebels ought to be cut off from their resources, that is, from railroads, and from communication with the revolted

States in the interior, and to be precipitated into the ocean. To accomplish it our troops ought to have marched by land to Richmond, and pushed the enemy towards the ocean. Now McClellan pushes the rebels from the extremity towards the centre, towards the focus of their basis, — exactly what they want.

I am sure that McClellan is allured to this strategy by the success of the gun-boats on the Mississippi. He wishes that the gun-boats may take Richmond, and he have the credit of it.

The Merrimac is still menacing in Hampton Roads, and may, some day or other, play havoc with the transports. The communications by land are always more preferable than those by water — above all for such a great army. A storm, etc., may do great mischief.

McClellan assures the President, and the other intriguers and fools constituting his supporters, that in a few days he will throw 55,000 men on Yorktown. He and his staff to do such a thing, which would be a masterpiece even for the French military leaders and their staffs! He, McClellan, never knew what it was to embark an army. Those who believe him are even greater imbeciles than I supposed them to be. Poor Stanton, to be hampered by imbecility and intrigue! I went to Alexandria to see the embarkation; it will last weeks, not days.

From Yorktown to Richmond, the country is marshy, very marshy; McClellan, a turtle, a *dasippus*, will not understand to move quick and to over-

come the impediments.   Faulty as it is to drive the
rebels from the sea towards their centre, this false
move would be corrected by rash and decisive movements.   But McClellan will stick in the marshes,
and may never reach Richmond by that road.

Any man with common sense would go directly
by land; if the army moves only three miles a day
it will reach Richmond sooner than by the other
way.   Such an army in a spell will construct turnpike roads and bridges, and if the rebels tear up
the railroads, they likewise could be easily repaired.
Progressing in the slowest, in the most genuine Mc-
Clellan manner, the army will reach Richmond with
less danger than by the Peninsula.

The future American historian ought to record in
gold and diamonds the names of those who in the
councils opposed McClellan's new strategy.   Oh !
Mr. Seward, Mr. Seward, why is your name to be
recorded among the most ardent supporters of this
strategy?

Jeff. Davis sneers at the immense amount of
money, etc., spent by Mr. Lincoln.   As he, Jeff.
Davis, is still quietly in Richmond, and his army
undestroyed, of course he is right to sneer at Mr.
Lincoln and McClellan, whom he, Jeff. Davis, kept
at bay with wooden guns.

Senator Sumner takes airs to defend or explain
McClellan.   The Senator is probably influenced by
Blair.   The Senator cannot be classed among trai-
tors and intriguers supporting the *great strategian.*

Perhaps likewise the Senator believes it to be *distingue* to side with *strategy*.

If the party and the people could have foreseen that civil war was inevitable, undoubtedly Mr. Lincoln would not have been elected. But as the cause of the North would have been totally ruined by the election of Lincoln's Chicago competitor, Mr. Lincoln is the lesser of the two evils.

A great nuisance is this competition for all kinds of news by the reporters hanging about the city, the government, and the army. Some of these reporters are men of sense, discernment, and character; but for the sake of competition and priority they fish up and pick up what they can, what comes in their way, even if such news is altogether beyond common sense, or beyond probability.

In this way the best among the newspapers have confused and misled the sound judgment of the people; so it is in relation to the overwhelming numbers of the rebels, and by spreading absurdities concerning relations with Europe. The reporters of the Herald and of the Times are peremptorily instructed to see the events through the perverted spectacles of their respective bosses.

Mr. Adams gets either frightened or warm. Mr. A. insists on the slavery question, speaks of the project of Mason and Slidell in London to offer certain moral concessions to English anti-slavery feeling,—such as the regulations of marriage, the repeal of laws against manumission, etc. Mr. Adams warns that these offers may make an impression in England.

When all around me I witness this revolting want of energy, — Stanton excepted, — this vacillation, these tricks and double-dealings in the governmental spheres, then I wish myself far off in Europe; but when I consider this great people outside of the governmental spheres, then I am proud to be one of the people, and shall stay and fall with them.

How meekly the people accept the disgrace of the wooden guns and of the evacuation of Manassas! It is true that the partisans of McClellan, the traitors, the intriguers, and the imbeciles are devotedly at work to confuse the judgment of the people at large.

Mr. Dayton's semi-official conversation with Louis Napoleon shows how well disposed the Emperor was and is. The Emperor, almost as a favor, asks for a decided military operation. And in face of such news from Europe, Lincoln, Seward, and Blair sustain the *do-nothing strategian!*

Until now Louis Napoleon behaves nobly, and not an atom of reproach can be made by the American people against his policy; and our policy many times justly could have soured him, as the acceptation of the Orleans, etc. No French vessels ran anywhere the blockade; secesh agents found very little if any credit among French speculators. Very little if any arms, munitions, etc., were bought in France. And in face of all these positive facts, the American wiseacres here and in Europe, all the bar-

room and street politicians here and there, all the
would-be statesmen, all the sham wise, are incessant
in their speculations concerning certain invisible,
deep, treacherous schemes of Louis Napoleon against
the Union. This herd is full of stories concerning
his deep hatred of the North; they are incessant in
their warnings against this dangerous and scheming
enemy. Some Englishmen in high position stir up
this distrust. On the authority of letters repeatedly received from England, Senator Sumner is
always in fits of distrust towards the policy of
France. The last discovery made by all these deep
statesmen here and in France is, that Louis Napoleon intends to take Mexico, to have then a basis for
coöperation with the rebels, and to destroy us.
But Mexico is not yet taken, and already the allies
look askance at each other. Those great Anglo-
American Talleyrands, Metternichs, etc., bring down
the clear and large intellect of Louis Napoleon to
the atomistic proportions of their own sham brains.
I do not mean to foretell Louis Napoleon's policy in
future. Unforeseen emergencies and complications
may change it. I speak of what was done up to
this day, and repeat, *not the slightest complaint can
be made against Louis Napoleon.* And in justice
to Mr. Mercier, the French minister here, it must
be recorded that he sincerely seconds the open policy
of his sovereign. Besides, Mr. Mercier now openly
declares that he never believed the Americans to be
such a great and energetic people as the events
have shown them to be. I am grateful to him for

this sense of justice, shared only by few of his diplomatic colleagues.

In one word, official and unofficial Europe, in its immense majority, is on our side. The exceptions, therefore, are few, and if they are noisy, they are not intrinsically influential and dangerous. The truest woman, Queen Victoria, is on the side of freedom, of right, and of justice. This ennobles even her, and likewise ennobles our cause. Not the bad wishes of certain Europeans are in our way, but our slowness, the McClellanism and its supporters.

Quidquid delirant reges, plectuntur achivi! The *achivi* is the people, and the McClellanists are the *reges*.

Mr. Seward, elated by victories, insinuates to foreign powers that they may stop the " recognition of belligerents." Oh imagination! Such things ought not even to be insinuated, as logic and common sense clearly show that the foreign cabinets cannot do it, and thus stultify themselves. Seward believes that his rhetoric is irresistible, and will move the cabinets of France and of England.　　＊　　＊　　＊
Not the " recognition of belligerents ; " let the rebels slip off from Manassas, etc. Mr. Seward would do better for himself and for the country to give up meddling with the operations of the war, and backing the bloodless campaigns of the *strategian*. But Mr. Seward, carried away by his imagination, believes that the cabinets will yield to his persuasive voice, and then, oh ! what a feather in his diplomatic

cap before the befogged Mr. Lincoln, and before the
people.   But *pia desideria.*

In all the wars, as well as in all the single campaigns and battles, every *captain* deserving this
name aimed at breaking his enemy in the centre or
at seizing his basis of operations, wherefrom the
enemy draws its resources and forces.   The great
strategian changed all this; he goes directly to the
circumference instead of aiming at the heart.

Mr. Seward, answering Mr. Dayton's dispatch concerning his, Dayton's, conversation with Louis Napoleon, points to Europe being likewise menaced by
revolutionists.   Unnecessary spread-eagleism, and
an awful want of any, even diplomatic, tact.   I hope
that Mr. Dayton, who has so much sound sense and
discernment, will keep to himself this freak of Mr.
Seward's untamable imagination.

Under the influence of insinuations received from
his English friends, Senator Sumner said to Mr.
Mercier (I was present) that with every steamer he
expects a joint letter of admonition directed by the
French and English to our government.   Mr. Mercier retorted, "How can you, sir, have such notions?
you are too great a nation to be treated in this way.
Such letters would do for Greece, etc., but not for
you."   I was sorry and glad for the lesson thus
given.

Archbishop Hughes was not over-successful in
France, and went off rather second-best in the opinion of the press, of the public, and of the Catholic,
even ultra-Montane clergy of France.   All this on

account of his conditional anti-slaverism and unconditional pro-slaverism. All this was easily to be
foreseen. His Eminence is in Rome, and from
Rome is to influence Spain in our favor.

Oh diplomacy! oh times of Capucine and Jesuit
fathers and of Abbes! We, the children of the
eighteenth century, we recall you to life. I do not
suppose that the whole diplomatic activity of his
Eminence is worth the postage of his correspondence.
But Uncle Sam is generous, and pays him well. So
it is with Thurlow Weed, who tries to be economical, is unsuccessful, and cries for more monish. A
schoolboy on a spree!

It seems that Weed loses not his time, and tries
with Sandford to turn *a penny* in Belgium. Oh disinterested saviors of the country, and patriots!

But for this violent development of our domestic
affairs, Mr. Seward would have appeared before the
world as the mediator between the Pope and the
insubordinate European nations, sovereigns, and
cabinets.

Oh, Alberoni! oh, imaginary! It beats any of
the wildest poets. In justice it must be recorded,
that this great scheme of mediation was dancing before Mr. Seward's imagination at the epoch when he
was sure that, once Secretary of State, his speeches
would be current and read all over the South; and
they, the speeches, would crush and extinguish secession. This Mr. Seward assured one of the patriotic members of Buchanan's expiring Cabinet.

Mr. Seward is now busy building up a conserva-

12

tive Union party North and South to preserve slavery, and to crush the rampant Sumnerism, as Thurlow Weed calls it, and advises Seward to do so.

Mr. Seward's unofficial agents, Thurlow Weed, his Eminence, and others, are untiring in the incense of their benefactor. Occasionally, Mr. Lincoln gets a small share of it.

Sandford in Paris and Brussels, Mr. Adams and Thurlow Weed in London, work hard to assuage and soften the harsh odor in which Mr. Seward is held, above all, among certain Englishmen of mark. It seems, however, that *love's labor is lost*, and Mr. Adams, scholar-like, explains the unsuccess of their efforts by the following philosophy: That in great convulsions and events it is always the most eminent men who become selected for violent and vituperative attacks. This is Mr. Seward's fate, but time will dispel the falsehoods, and render him justice. Well, be it so.

Weed tried hard to bring the Duke of Newcastle over to Mr. Seward; but the Duke seems perfectly unmoved by the blandishments, etc. To think that the strict and upright Duke, who knows Weed, could be shaken by the ubiquitous lobbyist! Rather the other way.

One not acquainted with Mr. Seward's ardent republicanism may suspect him of some dictatorial projects, to judge from the zeal with which some of the diplomatic agents in Europe, together with the unofficial ones there, extol to all the world Mr. Seward's transcendent superiority over all other

eminent men in America.   Are the European statesmen to be prepared beforehand, or are they to be befogged and prevented from judging for themselves ?
If so, again is *love's labor lost.*   European statesmen
can perfectly take Mr. Seward's measure from his
uninterrupted and never-fulfilled prophecies, and
from other diplomatic stumblings ; and one look
suffices European men of mark to measure a
Hughes, a Weed, a Sandford, and *tutti quanti.*

In Mr. Lincoln's councils, Mr. Stanton alone has
the vigor, the purity, and the simplicity of a man of
deep convictions.   Stanton alone unites the clear,
broad comprehension of the exigencies of the national question with unyielding action.   He is the
statesman so long searched for by me.   He, once a
friend of McClellan, was not deterred thereby from
condemning that do-nothing *strategy*, so ruinous
and so dishonorable.   Stanton is a Democrat, and
therefore not intrinsically, perhaps not even relative-
ly, an anti-slavery man, but he hesitates not now to
destroy slavery for the preservation of the Union.
I am sure that every day will make Stanton more
clear-sighted, and more radical in the question of
Union and rebellion.   And Seward and Blair, who
owe their position to their anti-slavery principles,
arcades ambo, try now to save something of slavery,
and turn against Stanton.

APRIL, 1862.

Immense power of the President — Mr. Seward's Egeria — Programme
of peace — The belligerent question — Roebucks and Gregories scums
— Running the blockade — Weed and Seward take clouds for camels
— Uncle Sam's pockets — Manhood, not money, the sinews of war —
Colonization schemes — Senator Doolittle — Coal mine speculation —
Washington too near the seat of war — Blair demands the return of a
fugitive slave woman — Slavery is Mr. Lincoln's " *mammy* " — He will
not destroy her — Victories in the West — The brave navy — McClellan subsides in mud before Yorktown — Telegraphs for more men —
God will be tired out ! — Great strength of the people — Emancipation in the District — Wade's speech — He is a monolith — Chase and
Seward — N. Y. Times — The Rothschilds — Army movements and
plans.

If the military conduct of McClellan, from the
first of January to the day of the embarkation of
the troops for Yorktown — if this conduct were
tried by French marshals, or by the French chief
staff, or by the military authorities and chief staffs
of Prussia, Russia, and even of Austria, McClellan
would be condemned as unfit to have any military
command whatever. I would stake my right hand
on such a verdict; and here the would-be strategians, the traitors, the intriguers, and the imbeciles
prize him sky-high.

Only by personal and close observation of the
inner working of the administrative machinery is it
possible to appreciate and to understand what an

180

immense power the Constitution locates in the hands
of a President.   Far more power has he than any
constitutional sovereign — more than is the power of
the English sovereign and of her Cabinet put together.   In the present emergencies, such a power
in the hands of a Wade or of a Stanton would have
long ago saved the country.

Mr. Seward looks to all sides of the compass for a
Union party in the South, which may rise politically
against the rebels.   That is the advice of Weed,
Mr. Seward's Egeria.   I doubt that he will find
many, or even any.   First kill the secesh, destroy
the rebel power, that is, the army, and then look
for the Union men in the South.   Mr. Seward, in
his generalizations, in his ardent expectations, etc.,
etc., forgets to consider — at least a little — human
nature, and, not to speak of history, this *terra incognita*.   Blood shed for the nationality makes it grow
and prosper ; a protracted struggle deepens its
roots, carries away the indifferent, and even those
who at the start opposed the move.   All such, perhaps, may again fall off from the current of rebellion, but that current must first be reduced to an
imperceptible rivulet ; and Mr. Seward, sustaining
the do-nothing strategian, acts against himself.

Mr. Seward's last programme is, after the capture
of Richmond and of New Orleans, to issue a proclamation — to offer terms to the rebels, to restore the
old Union in full, to protect slavery and all.   For
this reason he supports McClellan, as both have the
same plan.   Of such a character are the assurances

given by Mr. Seward to foreign diplomats and governments. He tries to make them sure that a large Union party will soon be forthcoming in the South, and again sounds his vaticinations of the sacramental ninety days. I am sorry for this his incurable passion to play the Pythoness. It is impossible that such repeated prophecies shall raise him high in the estimation of the European statesmen. Impossible! Impossible! whatever may be the contrary assertions of his adulators, such as an Adams, a Sandford, a Weed, a Bigelow, a Hughes, and others. When Mr. Seward proudly unveiled this his programme, a foreign diplomat suggested that the Congress may not accept it. Mr. Seward retorted that he cares not for Congress; that he will appeal to the people, who are totally indifferent to the abolition of slavery.

Why does Mr. Seward deliberately slander the American people, and this before foreign diplomats, whose duty it is to report all Mr. Seward's words to their respective governments? Such words uttered by Mr. Seward justify the assertions of Lord John Russell, of Gladstone, those true and high-minded friends of human liberty, that the North fights for empire and not for a principle. The people who will answer to Mr. Seward's appeal will be those whose creed is that of the New York Herald, the Boston Courier, the people of the Fernando and Ben Woods, of the Vallandighams, etc.

What is the use of urging on the foreign Cabinets — above all, England and France — to rescind the recognition of belligerents? They cannot do it. It does not much — nay, not any — harm, as the English speculators will risk to run the blockade if the rebels are belligerent or not. And besides, the English and French Cabinets may throw in Mr. Seward's face the decisions of our own prize courts, who, on the authority of Mr. Seward's blockade, in their judicial decisions, treat the rebels as belligerents. The European statesmen are more cautious and more consequential in their acts than is our Secretary.

As it stands now, the conduct of the English government is very correct, and not to be complained of. I do not speak of the infamous articles in the Times, Herald, etc., or of the Gregories and such scums as the Roebucks; but I am satisfied that Lord John Russell wishes us no harm, and that it is our own policy which confuses and makes suspicious such men as Russell, Gladstone, and others of the better stamp.

As for the armaments of secesh vessels in Liverpool and the Bahamas, it is so perfectly in harmony with the English mercantile character that it is impossible for the government to stop it.

The English merchant generally considers it as a lawful enterprise to run blockades; in the present case the premium is immense; it is so in a twofold manner. 1st, the immediate profits on the various cargoes exchanged against each other by a successful running of the blockade; such profits must equal several hundred per cent. 2d, the prospec-

tive profits from an eventual success of the rebellion
for such friends as are now supporting the rebels.
These prospects must be very alluring, and are
partly justified by our slow war, slow policy. I am
sure that the like armaments for the secessionists
are made by shares owned by various individuals;
the individual risk of each shareholder being comparatively insignificant when compared with the
prospective gains.

If Seward, McClellan, and Blair had not meddled
with Stanton, not weakened his decisions, nor befogged Mr. Lincoln, Richmond would be in our hands,
together with Charleston and Savannah; and all the
iron-clad vessels built in England for secesh would
be harmless.

Mr. Weed and Mr. Seward expect Jeff. Davis
to be overthrown by their imaginary Southern
Union party. O, wiseacres! if both of you had only
a little knowledge of human nature — not of that
one embodied in lobbyists — and of history, then
you would be aware that if Jeff. Davis is to be de-
posed it will be by one more violent than he, and
you would not speculate and take clouds for camels.
During the weeks of embarkation for Yorktown,
the thorough incapacity of McClellan's chief of the
staff was as brilliant as the cloudless sun. It makes
one shudder to think what it will be when the campaign will be decidedly and seriously going on.

It is astonishing, and psychologically altogether
incomprehensible, to see persons, justly deserving to
be considered as intelligent, deny the evidence of

their own senses; forbid, so to speak, their sound
judgment to act; to be befogged by thorough imbeciles; to consider incapacity as strategy, and to take
imbecility for deep, mysterious, great combinations
and plans. Even the Turks could not long be humbugged in such a way.

No sovereign in the world, not even Napoleon in
his palmiest days, could thus easily satisfy his military whims concerning the most costly and variegated material for an army, as does McClellan. He
changes his plans; every such change is gorgeously
satisfied and millions thrown away. Guns, mortars,
transports, spades, etc., appear at his order as if
by charm; and all this to veil his utter incapacity.
This Yorktown expedition uncovers Washington
and the North, and such a deep plan could have
been imagined only by a *strategian.*

What are doing in Europe all these various
agents of Mr. Seward, and paid by Uncle Sam? all
these Weeds, Sandfords, Hughes, Bigelows, and whoever else may be there? They cannot find means
in their brains to better direct, inform, or influence
the European press. Almost all the articles in our
favor are only defensive and explanatory; the offensive is altogether carried by the secesh press in England and in France. But to deal offensive blows, our
agents would be obliged to stand firm on human
principles, and show up all the dastardly corruption
of slavery, of slaveholders, and of rebels. Such a
warfare is forbidden by Mr. Seward's policy; and
perhaps if such a Weed should speak of corruption,

some English secesh may reprint Wilkeson's letter. In one word, our cause in Europe is very tamely represented and carried on. Members of the Chamber of Deputies in Paris complain that they can nowhere find necessary information concerning certain facts. There Seward's agents have not even been able to correct the fallacies about the epoch of the Morrill tariff, — fallacies so often invoked by the secesh press, — and many other similar statements. I shall not wonder if the public opinion in Europe by and by may fall off from our cause. Our defensive condition there justifies the assumptions of the secesh. As we dare not expose their crimes, the public in Europe must come to this conclusion, that secesh may be right, and may begin to consider the North as having no principle.

And to think that all these agents heavily phlebotomize Uncle Sam's pockets to obtain such contemptible results !

Many persons, some among them of influence and judgment, still speak and speculate upon what they call the starving of the rebellion. They calculate upon the comparative poverty of the rebels, repeating the fallacious adage, that money is the sinews of war. Money is so, but only in a limited degree, and more limited than is generally supposed ; more limited even now when war is a very expensive pastime.

This fallacy, first uttered by the aristocrat Thucydides, was repeated over and over again until it became a statesmanlike creed. But even Thucyd-

ides gave not to that *dictum* such a general sense,
and Macchiavelli scorned the fallacy and exposed it.
When poor, the Spartans have been the bravest.
The historical halo surrounding the name of Sparta
originated at that epoch when the use of money
and of gold had been almost forbidden. The wealth
of Athens began after the victories over the Per-
sians; but those victories were won when the Athe-
nians were comparatively poor. So it was with the
Romans until the subjugation of Carthage, and in
modern Europe the Swiss, etc., etc., etc.

Manhood in a people, and self-sacrifice, are the
genuine sinews of war; wealth alone saved no nation from disgrace and from death, nay, often accelerated the catastrophe.

The colonization of Africo-Americans is still discussed; very likely inspired by Seward and by his
Yucatan schemes. Senator Doolittle runs himself
down at a fearful rate. I regret Doolittle's mistake.
Those colonizers forget that if they should export
even 100,000 persons a year, an equal number will
be yearly born at home, not to speak of other im-
possibilities. If carried on on a small scale, this
scheme amounts to nothing; and on a grand scale
it is altogether impossible, besides being as stupid
as it is recklessly cruel. Only those persons insist
on colonization who hate or dread general emancipation.

When the slaves shall be emancipated, then the
owners of plantations will be forced to offer very
acceptable terms to the newly made free laborers to

have their plantations cultivated, which otherwise must become waste and useless lands, and the planters themselves poor starving wretches. With very little of governmental interference, the mutual relation between planter and laborer can be regulated, and the planter will be the first to oppose colonization.

Look from whatever side you like, a colonization schemer is a cruel deceiver, he is an enemy of emancipation, and if he claims to be an emancipator then he is an enemy of the planter and of the prosperity of the southern region.

Besides, the present scheme of colonization to Chiriqui is an infamous speculation to help some Ambrosio Thompson to work coal mines in that part of Central America. That individual has a grant for some lands in Chiriqui, and there these poor victims are to be exported. The grant itself is contested by the New Grenadian government. Those poor coolies will be the prey of speculators; there will arise claims against the Grenadian government — a rich mine for lobbyists and claimants. Infamy! and these fathers of the country are as blind as moles. Central America is always in convulsions, and of course the colonists will be robbed by every party of those semi-savages. The colonists being Methodists, etc., will be pointed out by the stupid Catholic clergy as being heretics and miscreants.

Washington's proximity to the theatre of war in

Virginia is the greatest impediment for rapid movements; it is the ruin of generals and of armies.

Being within reach of the seat of government
and of the material means, the generals are never
ready, but always have something to complete,
something to ask for, and so days after days elapse.
In all other countries and governments of the world
the commanders move on, and the objects of secondary necessity are sent after them.

In all other countries and wars the principal aim
of commanders is to become conspicuous by rapidity
of movements. The paramount glory is to have
achieved and obtained important results with comparatively limited means. Here, the greater the
slowness with which they move, the greater captains
they are; and the more expensive their operations,
the surer they are of the applause of the administration, and of a great many f——.

After all, the above is the result of pre-existing
causes. Slowness, indecision, and waste of money,
are the prominent features of this administration.

Stanton excepted, I again think of the dictum of
Professor Steffens, and every day believe it more.

Mr. Blair worse and worse; is more hot in support of McClellan, more determined to upset Stanton,
and I heard him demand the return of a poor fugitive slave woman to some of Blair's Maryland friends.

Every day I am confirmed in my creed that whoever had slavery for *mammy* is never serious in the
effort to destroy it. Whatever such men as Mr.
Lincoln and Mr. Blair will do against slavery, will

never be radical by their own choice or conviction, but will be done reluctantly, and when under the unavoidable pressure of events.

Mr. Seward restive and bitter against all who criticise. Mr. Seward assumes that everybody does his best, and ought therefore to be applauded. But Mr. Seward forgets the proverb about hell being paved with good intentions. In this terrible emergency the people want men who *really* do the best, and not those who only try and intend to do it.

McClellan had the full sway so long — appointed so many, perhaps more than sixty, brigadier generals — that it is not astonishing when those appointees prefer rather not to see for themselves, but blindly " hurrah " for their creator.

Victories in the West, triumphantly establishing the superiority of our soldiers in open battle-fields, and the superiority of all generals who are distant from any contact with Washington, as Pope, Grant, Curtis, Mitchell, Sigel, and others. The brave navy, — this pure democratic element which assures the greatest results, and makes the less laudatory noise. The navy is admirable; the navy is the purest and most glorious child of the people.

The destruction of the rebellion saves the future generations of the Southern whites. Secession would for centuries have bred and raised only formidable social hyenas.

McClellan subsided in mud before Yorktown. Any other, only even half-way, military capacity commanding such forces would have made a lunch of Yorktown. But our troops are to dig, perhaps their graves, to the full satisfaction of Mr. Lincoln, Mr. Seward, and Mr. Blair.

McClellan telegraphs for more men, and he has more already than he can put in action, and more than he has room for. He subsides in digging. The rebels will again fool him as they fooled him in Manassas. If McClellan could know anything, then he would know this — that nothing is so destructive to an army as sieges, as diggings, and camps, and nothing more disciplines and re-invigorates men, makes them true soldiers, than does marching and fighting. Poor Stanton! how he must suffer to be overruled by imbeciles and intriguers. McClellan telegraphing for reinforcements plainly shows how unmilitary are his brains. He and a great many here believe that the greater the mass of troops, the surer the victory. History mostly teaches the contrary; but speak to American wiseacres about history! He, McClellan, and others on his side, ignore the difficulty of handling or swinging an army of 100,000 men.

A good general, confident in his troops, will not hesitate to fight two to three. But McClellan feels at ease when he can, at the least, have two to one. In Manassas he had three to one, and conquered — wooden guns! We will see what he will conquer before Yorktown.

Louis Napoleon always well disposed, but of course he cannot swallow Mr. Seward's demand about belligerents. I am so glad and so proud that up to this day events justify my confidence in the French policy, although our policy may tire not only Louis Napoleon, but tire the God whom we worship and invoke. I should not wonder if God, tired by such McClellans, Lincolns, Sewards, Blairs, etc., finally gives us the cold shoulder. This demand concerning belligerents is a diplomatic and initiative step made by Mr. Seward; it is unsuccessful, as are all his initiatives, and no wonder.

Mr. Lincoln, incited by Mr. Seward and by Mr. Blair, overrules the opinion of the purest, the ablest, and the most patriotic men in Congress — that of Stanton, and of the few good generals unbefogged by McClellanism. Such a power as the Constitution gives to a President is the salvation of the people when in the hands of a Jackson, but when in the hands of a Lincoln, —— !

The muscular strength of the American people, and the strength of its backbone, beat all the Herculeses and Atlases supporting the globe. Any other people would have long ago broke down under the policy and the combined weight of Lincoln, Seward, and McClellan.

Mr. Lincoln is forced out again from one of his pro-slavery entrenchments; he was obliged to yield, and to sign the hard-fought bill for emancipation in the District of Columbia; but how reluctantly, with what bad grace he signed it! Good boy; he wishes not to strike his *mammy;* and to think that the friends of humanity in Europe will credit this emancipation not where it is due, not to the noble pressure exercised by the high-minded Northern masses, but to this Kentucky ——.

Senator Wade made a powerful speech in relation to the arrest of General Stone. It was powerful, patriotic, and rises to the skies over the Lilliputian oratory of the thus-called scholars, etc. Wade is a monolith, — he is cut out full in a rock.

It seems that the new law increasing the number of judges for the Supreme Court weakened many backbones. Congress ought to have added the clause that a senator can be nominated only after six years from the day of the promulgation.

Mr. Seward again chalked before the dazzled eyes of foreign powers certain future military operations; but again events have been so unpolite as to upturn Mr. Seward's prophecies.

The report of the Senate committee on the destruction of Norfolk speaks of the "insane delusion" of the administration. I am proud to have considered it in the same light about a year ago.

Mr. Thouvenel politely but logically refuses to acquiesce in Mr. Seward's demand concerning the belligerents. Thouvenel's reasons are plausible. The support given to strategy by Mr. Seward, — that support does more mischief to us than do all the pirates and all the violations of blockade. Let us take Richmond,—a thing impossible with McClellan, — and take by land Charleston, Savannah, etc.; then the pirates and belligerents are strangulated. And — as says Gen. Sherman — Savannah and Charleston could have been taken several months ago.

Orders from Washington forbade to do it; and it would be curious to ascertain how far Mr. Seward is innocent in the perpetration of these orders.

Chase and Seward dear-dearing each other! Amusing! Kilkenny cats! At this game Seward will have the best of Chase, who is not a match for tricks.

The New York Times attacks Capt. Dahlgren, of the Navy Yard. It is in the nature of the " little villain " to bespatter men of such devotion, patriotism, and eminent capacity as is Captain Dahlgren.

Thurlow Weed calls the Tribune " infernal," because it wishes a serious war, and thus prevents the raising of a Union party in the South, so flippantly looked for by him and Mr. Seward, his pupil. I see the time coming when all these *gentlemen* of the concessions, of the not-hurting policy, — when all these conservative seekers for the Union party will try, Pilatus-like, to wash their hands of the innocent blood; but you shall try, and not succeed, to whitewash your stained hands; you have less excuses on your side than had the Roman proconsul on his side.

When Mr. Mercier was in Richmond, some of the rebel leaders and generals told him that they believed not their senses on learning that McClellan was going to Yorktown; that he never could have selected a better place for them, and that they were sure of his destruction on the Peninsula.

Perhaps McClellan wished to try his hand and rehearse the siege of Sebastopol.

If McClellan's ignorance of military history were

not so well established, he would know that since
Archimedes, down to Todleben, more genius was
displayed in the defence than in the attack of any
place. The making of approaches, parallels, etc.,
is an affair of engineering school routine. Napoleon took Toulon rather as an artillerist, who, having,
calculated the reach of projectiles, put his battery
on a spot wherefrom he shelled Toulon. Napoleon
took Mantua by destroying the Austrian army which
hastened to the relief of the fortress. But the great
American strategian knows better, and satisfies (as
said above) the rebels.

The New York Herald, the New York Times, and
other staunch supporters of McClellan, again and
again trumpet that the rebels fear McClellan, that
they consider him to be the ablest general opposed
to them. The rebels are smart, and so is their ally,
the New York Herald. As for the Times, it is only
a flunkeying "little villain."

McDowell, Banks, Fremont have about 70,000
men; the last two are nearly at the head of the
Shenandoah valley; they could unite with McDowell, and march and take Richmond. They beg to
be ordered to do it, and so wishes Stanton; but,
fatally befogged by McClellan, by McClellan's clique
in the councils, or by strategians, Lincoln emphatically forbids any junction, any movement; the
President forbids McDowell to take Fredericksburg,
or to throw a bridge across the river. And thus
McClellan prevents any glorious military operation;
is losing in the mud a hundred men daily by disease,

and Mr. Lincoln — still infatuated. But infatuation is the disease of small and weak brains.

Rothschild in Paris, and very likely the Rothschilds in London, are for the North. But if the Rothschilds show that they well understand and respect the Old Testament, whose spirit is anti-slavery, they show they understand better the true Christian spirit than do the Christians. The Rothschilds show themselves more thoroughly of our century than are such Michel Chevaliers, or such impure Roebucks, and all the supporters of free trade in human flesh.

McClellan's supporters, and such strategians as Blair and Seward, assert that McClellan's plan was ruined by not sending McDowell to Gloucester; that then the whole rebel army would have been caught in a trap. That silly plan to go to the Peninsula is defended in a still more silly way.

By McDowell's going to Gloucester, Washington would have been wholly at the mercy of an army of thirty to forty thousand men; the celebrated defences of Washington, this result of the united wisdom of Scott and McClellan, facilitating to the rebel army a raid on Washington.

Further; McClellan, in concocting and *maturing* his thus called plans, probably believes that the rebels will do just the thing which, in his calculations, he wishes them to do; and such erroneous suppositions are the sole basis of his *plans*. But the rebels repeatedly showed themselves by far too smart for his *Napoleonic* brains; and besides, not much wit to the rebel generals was necessary to see through and through what the great Napoleon was about, by ordering McDowell to Gloucester. Of course, the rebel generals would not have had the politeness towards McClellan to sheepishly accede to his wishes, and go into the trap. The whole plan was worse than childish, and I am glad to learn that several generals showed brains to condemn it. The whole plan was up to the comprehension of Mc-Clellanites, of consummate strategians in McClellan's official tross, for those in the Cabinet and out of it.

Would God that all this ends not in disasters. If it ends well it will be the first time success has crowned such transcendent incapacity.

MAY, 1862.

THE capture of New Orleans. The undaunted
bravery of the Navy — this most beautiful leaf in
the American history. The Navy fights without
talk and *strategy*, because it does not look to win
the track to the White House. The capture of New
Orleans may lead the rebels to evacuate Yorktown
and to fool the great strategian.

It is a very threatening symptom, that no genuine
harmony — nay, no sympathy — exists between the
best, the purest, the most intelligent, the most energetic members of both the Houses of Congress and

198

the President, including the leading spirit of his
Cabinet. The New York Herald is the principal
supporter of Mr. Lincoln and Mr. Seward; in the
Congress their supporters are the Democrats, and
all those who wish to make concessions to the South,
who ardently wish to preserve slavery, and in any
way to patch up the quarrel.

In times as trying as are the present ones, such a
shameful and dangerous anomaly must, in the long
run, destroy either the government or the nation.
If it turns out differently here, the exclusive reason
thereof will be the great vitality of the people. All
the deep and dangerous wounds inflicted by the policy of the administration will be healed by the vigorous, vital energy of the people.

"For Heaven's sake finish quick your war!"
Such are the exclamations — nay, the prayers —
coming from the French statesmen, as Fould and
others, from our devoted friends, as Prince Napoleon, and from all the famishing, but nevertheless
nobly-behaving, operatives in England. And here
McClellan inaugurates before Yorktown a second
siege of Troy or of Sebastopol; Lincoln forbids the
junction of McDowell with Banks and Fremont, by
which Richmond could be easily taken from the
west side, where it ought to be attacked; and Mr.
Seward reads the like dispatches and backs McClellan; Mr. S. lights his lantern in search North and
South of the Union-saving party!

Speak to me of subserviency to power by European aristocrats, courtiers, etc.! What almost

every day I witness here of subserviency of influential men to the favored and office-distributing power, all things compared and considered, beats whatever I saw in Europe, even in Russia at the Nicolean epoch.

General Cameron, in his farewell speech, said that at the beginning of the civil war General Scott told him, Cameron, that he, Scott, never in his life was more pained than when a Virginian reminded him of his paramount duties to his State. I take note of this declaration, as it corroborates what a year ago I said in this diary concerning the disastrous hesitations of General Scott.

It is said that Turtschininoff is all in all in General Mitchell's command. Turtschininoff is a genuine and distinguished officer of the staff, and educated in that speciality so wholly unknown to West-Pointers. Several among the foreigners in the army are thoroughly educated officers of the staff, and would be of great use if employed in the proper place. But envy and know-nothingism are doubly in their way. Besides, the foreign officers have no tenderness for the Southern cause and Southern chivalry, and would be in the cause with their whole heart.

By the insinuations of an anonymous correspondent in the Tribune, Mr. Seward tries to re-establish his anti-slavery reputation. But how is it that foreign diplomats, that the purest of his former political friends, consider him to be now the savior of what he once persecuted in his speeches?

At every step this noble people vindicates and asserts the vitality of self-government, continually jeopardized by the inexhaustible errors of the policy followed by the master-spirits in the administration. European doctors, prophets, vindictive enemies like the London Times, the Saturday Review, etc., and the French journals of the police, all of them are daily — nay, hourly — baffled in their expectations — paper money and no bankruptcy, no inflation, bonds equal to gold, etc., etc.   And all this, not because there is any great or even small statesman or financier at the head of the administration, but because the people at large have confidence in themselves, in their own energies; because they have the determination to succeed, and not to be bankrupt; not to discredit their own decisions.   All these phenomena, so new in the history of nations, are incomprehensible to European wiseacres; they are too much for the hatred and dulness of the Europeans in France, England, and for that of the many Europeans here.

Yorktown evacuated! — under the nose of an army of 160,000 men, and within the distance of a rifle shot! — evacuated quietly, of course, during several days.   One cannot abstain from saying Bravo! to the rebel generals.   Their high capacity forces the mind to an involuntary applause.   Traitors, intriguers, and imbeciles applaud, extol the results of the bloodless strategy.   McClellan is used by the rebels only to be fooled by them.   It must be so.   It is one proof more of the transcendent capacity

of the strategian, and, above all, of the capacity and
efficiency of the chief of the staff of the great army.
Such an operation as that of Yorktown, anywhere
else, would be considered as the highest disgrace;
here, glorifications of strategy. McClellan's bulletins from Yorktown describe the rebel fortifications
as being almost impregnable. Of course impregnable! but only to him.

Battle at Williamsburg; and McClellan and his
so perfect staff altogether ignorant of the whole
bloody but honorable affair as fought against terrible
odds by Heintzelman and Hooker; but the great
Napoleon's bulletin mentions a *real* — Oh hear!
hear the great Mars! — *charge with the bayonet*,
made at the other extremity of Williamsburg, and
in which from twenty to forty men were killed!

Heintzelman's and Hooker's personal conduct,
and that of their troops, was heroic beyond name.
McClellan ignored the battle; ignored what was
going on, and, as it is said, gave orders to Sumner
not to support Heintzelman.

McClellan telegraphs that the enemy far outnum-
bers him (fears count doubly), but that he will
do his utmost and his best. This Napoleon of the
New York Herald's manufacture in everything is
the reverse of all the leaders and captains known
in history: all of them, when before the battle
they addressed their soldiers, represented the enemy
as inferior and contemptible; after the battle was
won, the enemy was extolled.

From the first of his addresses to this his last dis-

patch from Williamsburg, McClellan always speaks
of the terrible enemy whom he is to encounter ; and
in this last dispatch he tries to frighten not only his
army, but the whole country. During the night *the
terrible enemy* evacuated Williamsburg ; McClellan
breathes more free, takes fresh courage, and his bulletin estimates the enemy's forces at 50,000.

The track of truth begins to be lost. By compar-
ing dates, bulletins, and notes, it results that at the
precise minute when McClellan telegraphed his wail
concerning the large numbers of the enemy and the
formidable fortifications of Williamsburg, the rebels
were evacuating them, pressed and expelled therefrom by Hooker, Kearney, and Heintzelman. Oh
Napoleon ! Oh spirits not only of Berthier and of
Gneisenau, but of the most insignificant chiefs of
staffs, admire your caricature at the head of the
army commanded by this freshly-backed Napoleon !

A foreign diplomat was in McClellan's tent before
Yorktown, on the eve of the day when the rebels
wholly evacuated it. One of McClellan's aids suggested to the general that the comparative silence
of the rebel artillery might forebode evacuation.
"Impossible !" answered the New York Herald's
Napoleon. "I know everything that passes in their
camp, and I have them fast." (I have these details
from the above-mentioned diplomat.) In the same
minute, when the strategian spoke in this way, at
least half of the rebel army had already withdrawn
from Yorktown. Comments thereupon are super-
fluous.

Dayton, from Paris, very sensibly objects to the policy of insisting that England and France shall annul their decision concerning the belligerents. Dayton considers such a demand to be, for various reasons, out of season. I am sure that Dayton is respected by Louis Napoleon and by Thouvenel on account of his sound sense and rectitude, although he *parleys not* French. Dayton must impress everybody differently from that French parleying claims' prosecutor and itinerant agent of a sewing machine, who breakfasts in Brussels with Leopold, and the same day dines in Paris with Thouvenel, and may take his supper in h—l, so far as the interest of the cause is concerned. But Dayton seems not to be in favor with the department.

The admirers of McClellan assert that one parallel digged by him was sufficient to frighten the rebels and force them to evacuate. Good for what it is worth for such mighty ignorant brains. The mortars, the hundred-pounders, frightened the rebels; they break down not before parallels, strategy, or Napoleon, but before the intellectual superiority of the North, in the present case embodied in mortars and other armaments.

Following the retreating enemy, McClellan loses more prisoners than he makes from the enemy. A new and perfectly original, perfectly *sui generis* mode of warfare, but altogether in harmony with all the other martial performances of the pet of the New York Herald, of Messrs. Seward and Blair, and of the whole herd of intriguers and imbeciles.

People who approach him say that Mr. Lincoln's conceit groweth every day. I guess that Seward carefully nurses the weed as the easiest'way to dominate over and to handle a feeble mind.

Since Mr. Mercier judges by his own eyes, and not by those of former various Washington associations, his inborn soundness and perspicacity have the upper hand. He is impartial and just to both parties; he is not bound to have against the rebels feelings akin to mine, but he is well disposed, and wishes for the success of the Union.

The events are too grand and too rapid for Lincoln. It is impossible for him to grasp and to comprehend them. I do not know any past historical personality fully adequate to such a task. Happily in this occurrency, the many, the people at large, by its grasp and forwardness, supplies and neutralizes the inefficiency or the tergiversations, intrigues and double-dealings of the few, of the official leaders, advisers, etc.

I willingly concede to Mr. Lincoln all the best and most variegated mental and intellectual qualities, all the virtues as claimed for him by his eulogists and friends. I would wish to believe, as they do, Mr. Lincoln to be infallible and impeccable. But all those qualities and virtues represented to form the residue of his character, all shining when in private life, some way or other are transformed from positives into negatives, since Mr. Lincoln's contact with the pulsations and the hurricane of public life. Thus Mr. Lincoln's friends assert that all his efforts tend to conciliate parties and even individuals. This candor was beneficial and efficient in the court or bar-rooms, or around a supper table in Springfield. It was even more so, perhaps, when seasoned with stories more or less * * * But one who tries to conciliate between two antipodic principles, or between pure and impure characters, unavoidably must dodge the principal points at issue. Such is the stern law of logic. Who dodges, who biasses, unavoidably deviates from that straight and direct way at the end of which dwells truth. Further: feeble, expectative and vacillating minds, deprived of the faculty to embrace in all its depth and extension the task before them,— such minds cannot have a clear purpose, nor the firm perception of ways and means leading to the aim, and still less have they the sternness of conviction so necessary for men dealing with such mighty events, on which depend the life and death of a society. Such men hesitate, postpone, bias and deviate from the straight way. Such men believe themselves in the way to truth, when they are aside of it. It results therefrom, that when certain amiable qualities, such as conciliation, a little dodging, hesitation, etc., are practised in private life and in a very restrained area, their deviations from truth are altogether imperceptible, and they are then positive good qualities, nay, virtues. But such qualities, transported and put into daily friction with the tempestuous atmosphere of human events, lose their ingenuousness, their innocence, their good-na-

turedness; the imperceptibility of their intrinsic deviation becomes transparent and of gigantic dimen-
sions.

Mr. Lincoln's crystal-pure integrity prevented not
the most frightful dilapidation, nay, robbing of the
treasury by contractors, etc., etc. Nor has it kept
pure his official household. His friend Lamon and
the to-be-formed regiments; the splendid equipages
and *coupes* of his youthful secretaries, to be sure,
came not from Springfield, etc., etc., nor sees he
through the rascally scheme of the Chiriqui colonization.

Mr. Lincoln, his friends assert, does not wish to
hurt the feelings of any one with whom he has to
deal. Exceedingly amiable quality in a private individual, but at times turning almost to be a vice in
a man entrusted with the destinies of a nation. So
he never could decide to hurt the feelings of Mc-
Clellan, and this after all the numerous proofs of his
incapacity. But Mr. Lincoln hurts thereby, and in
the most sensible manner, the interests, nay, the
lives, of the twenty millions of people. I am sure
that McClellan may lose the whole army, and why
not if he continues as he began? and Mr. Lincoln
will support and keep him, as to act otherwise
would hurt McClellan's, Marcy's, Seward's, and perhaps Blair's feelings.

Finally, Mr. Lincoln, advised, they say, by Mr.
Seward, holds in contempt public opinion as manifested by the press, with the exception of the incense burnt to him by the New York Herald. If

this is true, Mr. Lincoln's mind is cunningly befogged.

It is very soothing for the quiet of private life
to ignore newspapers; but all over Europe men in
power, sovereigns and ministers, carefully and daily
study and watch the opinions of the newspapers,
and principally of those which oppose and criticise
them.

Such, Mr. Lincoln, is the wisdom of the truly experienced statesman. Better ask Louis Napoleon
than Seward.

I am astonished that concerning Mexico Louis
Napoleon was taken in by Almonte. Experience
ought to have fully made him familiar with the
general policy of political refugees. This policy
was, is, and will be always based on imaginary facts.

Political refugees befog themselves and befog
others. And this Mr. de Saligny must be a d——;
Louis Napoleon ought to expel him from the service.

Halleck likewise seems to lay the track to the
White House. Nothing has been done since he
took the command in person. Halleck, as does also
McClellan, tries to make all his measures so sure,
so perfect, that he misses his aim, and becomes
fooled by the enemy. In war, as in anything else,
after having quickly prepared and taken measures,
a man ought to act, and rely as much as possible on
fortune — that is, on his own acuteness — how to
cut the knot when he meets it in his path.

Halleck before Corinth, and McClellan before
Manassas and Yorktown, both spend by far more

time than it took Napoleon from Boulogne and Bre-
tagne to march into the heart of Germany, surround
and capture Mack at Ulm, and come in view of Vienna.

The French and English naval officers in the Mississippi assured our commanders that it was impossible to overcome the various defences erected by the
rebels.   Our men gave the lie to those envious forebodings.   McClellan, in a dispatch, assures the Secretary of War that he, McClellan, will take care of
the gunboats. *Risum teneatis.*

The most contemptible flunkeys on the face of the
earth are the wiseacres, and the thus-called framers
of public opinion.   Until yet McClellan, literally,
has not stood by when a cartridge was burned, and
they sing hosanna for him.

Ten thousand men have been disabled by diseases
before Yorktown ; add to it the several thousands
in a similar way disabled in the camp before Manassas, and it makes more than would have cost two
battles, fought between the Rappahannock and Richmond, — battles which must have settled the question.

Although ultra-Montane, the Bishop of Orleans
nobly condemns slavery.   The Bishop's pastoral is
an answer to H. E., Archbishop of New York.
The French bishop therein is true to the spirit of
the Catholic church.   The Irish archbishop, compared to him, appears a dabbler in Romanism.

During the administration of Pierce and of Buchanan, the Democratic senators ruled over the Pres-

14

rd, Mr. Blair, by the Republican senators, by men
like Wade, Wilson, Chandler, Grimes, Fessenden,
Hale, and others.

The retreat of the rebels was masterly conducted,
and their pursuit by McClellan has no name. Nowhere has this Napoleon got at them. The affair at
Williamsburg was bravely done by Heintzelman and
Hooker; but it was done without the knowledge of
McNapoleon, and contrary to his expectations and
strategy. This he confesses in one of his *masterly*
bulletins. Perhaps McNapoleon ignored Heintzelman's corps' heroic actions, because neither Heintzelman, nor Hooker, nor Kearney worship *strategy,
and the deep, well-matured plans of Mc.*

General Hunter's proclamation in South Carolina
is the greatest social act in the course of this war.
How pale and insignificant are Mr. Lincoln's disqui-
sitions aside of that proclamation, which is greeted
in heaven by angels and cherubim — provided they
are a reality.

Of course Mr. Lincoln overrules General Hunter's proclamation. It is too human, too noble, too
great, for the tall Kentuckian. Many say that Seward, Blair, Seaton from the Intelligencer, and other
Border State patriots, pressed upon Lincoln. I am
sure that it gave them very little trouble to put Mr.
Lincoln straight ——— with slaveocracy. Hence-

forth every Northern man dying in the South is to be credited to Mr. Lincoln !

Mr. Lincoln again publishes a disquisition, and points to the signs of the times. But does Mr. Lincoln perceive other, more awful, signs of the times? Does he see the bloody handwriting on the wall, condemning his unnatural, vacillating, dodging policy?

All things considered, it will not be astonishing in Europe if they lose patience and sneer at the North, when they learn that McClellan is continually doing strategy; when they will read his bulletins; when they will find out that from West Point to Richmond he pursued the enemy at the *enormous* speed of two miles a day, — and that of course nobody was hurt, — and finally, that, surrounded by a brilliant and costly staff, he was ignorant of the condition of the roads, and of the existence of marshes and swamps into which he plunged the army.

The President repeatedly speaks of his strong will to restore the Union. Very well; but why not use for it the best, the most decided, and the most thorough means and measures?

Continually I meet numbers and numbers of soldiers who are discharged because disabled in the camps during winter. Thus McClellan's bloodless strategy deprived several thousands of their health, without in the least hurting the enemy. And daily I meet numbers of able-bodied Africo-Americans, who would make excellent soldiers. I decided to

try to form a regiment of the Africo-Americans,
and, after whipping the F. F. V.'s, establish, beyond
doubt, the perfect equality of the thus called races.

McClellan subsides in mud, — digs, — and the
sick list of the army increases hourly at a fearful
ratio. And McClellan refuses to slaves admittance
within his lines. If, at least, McClellan was a fighting general ; but a mud-mole as he ——————.
Any other general in any other country, in Asia, in
Africa, etc., would use any elements whatever within
his grasp, by using which he could strengthen his
own and weaken the enemy's resources. McNapoleon knows better!

One of the best diplomatic documents by Mr.
Seward is that on Mexico ; and so is also the policy
pursued by him. Why does Mr. Seward dabble in
war and strategy at home?

McClellan digs, and by his wailings has disorganized the corps of McDowell, and of Banks, who retreats and is pressed by Jackson. The men who
advised, or the McClellan worshippers who prevented the union of McDowell with Banks and Fremont, are as criminal as any one can be in Mr.
Lincoln's councils.

Now Jackson is reorganized ; he penetrated between Fremont and Banks, who were sorely weakened by transferring continually divisions from one
to another army; and this between the Chickahominy and the lower Shenandoah.

New diplomatic initiative by Mr. Seward. France
and England are requested to declare to the rebels

that they have no support to expect from the above-
mentioned powers.

This initiative would be splendid if it could succeed; but it cannot, and for the same logical reasons as failed the recent initiative about belligerents.
Such unsuccessful initiatives are lowering the consideration of that statesman who makes them. Such
failures show a want of diplomatic and statesmanlike perspicacity.

The nation is assured by Mr. Lincoln and by Mr.
Seward that a perfect harmony prevails in the Cabinet. Beautiful if true.

General Banks attacked by Jackson and defeated;
but, although surrounded, makes a masterly retreat,
without even being considerably worsted. Bravo,
Banks! Such retreats do as much honor to a general as a won battle.

This bold raid of Jackson — a genuine general
— wholly disorganized that army which, if united
weeks ago, could have taken Richmond, and rendered Jackson's brilliant dash impossible. The military aulic council of the President is frightened out
of its senses, and asks the people for 100,000 defenders. General Wadsworth advised not to thus,
without any necessity, frighten the country.

On this occasion Governor Andrew, of Massachusetts, wrote a scorching letter to the administration
on account of General Hunter's proclamation. Governor Andrew always acts, speaks, and writes to the
point.

This alarming appeal, so promptly responded to,

has its good, as it will show to Europe the untired determination of the free States.

The President took it into his head to direct himself, by telegraph, the military operations from Fredericksburg to Shenandoah. The country sees with what results. The military advisers of the President seem no better than are his civil advisers — Seward, Blair, etc. If the President earnestly wishes to use his right as Commander-in-Chief, then he had better take in person the command of the army of the Potomac.

There McClellan's diggings and strategy neutralize the gallantry of the generals and of the troops. There action, not digging, is needed. I wrote to the President, suggesting to make Sigel his chief of the staff (Sigel has been educated for it), and then to let our generals fight under his, the President's, eyes.

Great injustice was and is done to Mr. Seward by the lying and very extensively spread rumor that he is often intoxicated. I am sure that it is not so, and I contradict it with all my might. At last I discovered the reason of the rumor. It is Mr. Seward's unhappy passion for generalizations. He goes off like a rocket. Most people hearing him become confused, understand nothing, are unable to follow him in his soarings, and believe him to be intoxicated. His devotees alone get in ecstacies when these rockets fly.

Every time after any success of our troops, that perfidious sheet, the London Times, puts on inno-

cent airs, and asks, "Why are the Americans so
bitter against England?" Why? At every disaster the Times pours upon the North the most mali-
cious, poisonous, and lacerating derisions; derisions
to pierce the skin of a rhinoceros. When in that
strain no feeling is respected by this lying paper.

Derision of the North was the Times's order of
the day even before the civil war really began.
People, who probably have it from the fountain itself, assert that in one of his hours of whiskey ex-
pansion the great Russell let the cat out, and confessed that the Times's firm purpose was, and is, to
definitely break the Union.

Until this hour that reptile's efforts have been unsuccessful; it could not even bring the Cabinet
over to its heinous purposes. A counterpoise and a
counter poison exist in England's higher spheres,
and I credit it to that noblest woman the queen, to
Earl Russell, and to some few others.

The would-be English *noblesse*, the Tories, and all
the like genuine nobodies, or *would-be* somebodies,
affect to side with the South. They are welcome
to such an alliance, and even parentage. *Similis
simili gaudet.* Nobody with his senses considers the
like *gentlemen* as representing the progressive, humane, and enlightened part of the English nation;
the American people may look down upon their
snobbish hostility. J. S. Mill — not to speak of his
followers — has declared for the cause of the North.
His intellectual support more than gorgeously compensates the cause of right and of freedom, even

for the loss or for the sneers of the whole aristocracy, and of snobdom, of somebodies and of would-be gentlemen of the whole Britannia Empire, including the Canadian beggarly manikins.

By their arrogance the Englishmen are offensive to all the nations of the world; but they are still more so by their ingrained snobbyism. (See about it Hugo Grotius.) Further : During the last thirty years the London Times and the Lord Fussmaker Palmerston have done more to make us hate England than even did the certain inborn and not over-amiable traits in the English character.

A part of the young foreign diplomacy here have a very strong secesh bend ; they consider the slave-holders to be aristocrats, and thus like to acquire an aristocratic perfume. But, aristocratically speaking, most of this promiscuous young Europa are parvenus, and the few titled among them have heraldically no noble blood in their veins. No wonder that here they mistake monstrosities for real noblesse. Enthusiastic is young Germany — that is, young Bremen.

Young European Spain here is remarkably discreet, as in the times of a Philip II., of an Alba.

Corinth evacuated under the nose of Halleck, as Manassas and Yorktown have been evacuated under the nose of McClellan. Nay, Halleck, equally strong as was the enemy, the first day of the evacuation ignores what became of Beauregard with between sixty and eighty thousand men. Oh generalship! Gen. Halleck is a gift from Gen. Scott. If Halleck makes not something better, it will turn out to be a very poor gift.   *Timeo Danaos*, etc., concerning the North and the gifts from " *the highest military authority in the land.*"

McDowell is grimly persecuted by bad luck.   Since March, twice he organized an excellent and strong corps, with which he could have marched on Richmond, and both times his corps was wholly disorganized — first by McClellan's wails for more, the second time by the President and his aulic council. And now all the ignorance and stupidity, together with all the McClellanites, accuse McDowell.   Pity that he was so near Washington ; otherwise his misfortune could not have so thoroughly occurred.

JUNE, 1862.

MR. SEWARD takes off from Mr. Adams the gag on the question of slavery. Perhaps even Mr. Adams might have been a little fretting. A long speculative dispatch, wherein, among some good things, one finds some generalizations and misstatements concerning the distress in Ireland, generated by want of potatoes (vide Parl. De.), and not from want of cotton, as says Mr. Seward — a confession that the government " covers the weakness of the insurgents " and " takes care of the welfare of the insurgents." What a tenderness, and what an ingratitude of the rebels to acknowledge it by blows!

218

Another confession, more precious, that the poor
slaves are the best and the only bravely devoted
Union men in the South, although occasionally shot
for their devotion by our generals, expelled from
the lines (vide Halleck's order No. 3), and deliv-
ered to the tender mercies of their masters. Finally,
immediate emancipation is held before the eyes
of the English statesmen rather as a Medusa head;
then a kind of story — perhaps to please Mr. Lincoln — or quotation from *some* writer, etc. So far
as I recollect, it is for the first time that diplomatic
circulars are seasoned by stories. But, *dit moi qui
tu hante je te dirai qui tu es.*

Mr. Seward repeatedly asserts, in writing and in
words, that he has no eventual views towards the
White House. Well, it may be so or not. But if
his friends may succeed in carrying his nomination,
then, of course, reluctantly, he will bend his head
to the people's will, and — accept. When in past
centuries abbots and bishops were elected, they
reluctantly accepted fat abbeys and bishoprics; the
investiture was given in the sacramental words,
accipe onus pro peccatis.

A battle by Richmond. McClellan telegraphs a
victory, and it comes out that we lost men, positions,
camps, and artillery. The President patiently bears
such humbugging, and the country — submits.

McClellan disgraces a part of the brave General
Casey's division. Whatever might have been the
conduct of the soldiers in detail, one thing is certain, that the division was composed of rough levies;

that they fought three hours, being almost surrounded by overwhelming forces; that they kept ground until reinforcements came; that the breaking of the division cannot be true, or was only partial, and that McClellan was not at all on the ground.

This battle of Fair Oaks is another evidence of the transcendent incapacity of the chief of the staff of the army of the Potomac, and of Gen. McClellan's veracity. In a subsequent bulletin the general confesses that he was misinformed concerning the conduct of Gen. Casey's division.

In any other army in the world, a chief of the staff who would assign to a division a post so advanced, so isolated, so cut off from the rest of the army, as was Gen. Casey's position, — such a chief of the staff would be at once dismissed. Here, oh here, nobody is hurt, nobody is to be hurt — only the bleeding people.

As to the conduct of the soldiers, they fought well; thorough veterans scarcely could have behaved better. McClellan turns out worse even than I expected.

The President's campaign against Jackson — very unsuccessful. Fremont came not up to the mark; disobeyed orders. No excuse whatever for such disobedience.

One is at a loss which is to be more admired, the ignorance or the impudence of such opinion-confusing and opinion-poisoning sheets as the New York Times, the World, the Herald, etc. They sing *ho-*

sanna for McClellan's victories.   In advance they praise the to-be-fought battles on selected fields of battle, and after the plans have been matured for weeks, nay for months.

A plan of a whole campaign, a general survey of it, may be prepared and matured long before the campaign begins.   But to mature for weeks a plan of a battle !   All the genuine great captains seldom had the selection of a field of battle, as they rapidly moved in search of or to meet their enemies, and fought them where they found them.   For the same reason, they scarcely had more than forty-eight hours to mature their plans.   Such is the history and the character of nine-tenths of the great battles fought in the world.

When Napoleon overthrew Prussia and Austria, he beforehand prepared those campaigns ; but neither Jena, Eylau, Friedland, Austerlitz or Wagram were the fields of battle of his special choice.   But Napoleon moved his armies as did all the great captains before him, and as must do all great captains after him.   Only American great captains sit down in the mud and dig.

At times in the West, Pope, Mitchell, Nelson, Grant moved their forces, and beat the enemy.   I am sure that these brave generals and the braves of the army of the Potomac most certainly are early risers.   A certain Napoleon never is visible before nine o'clock in the morning.   So I hear from a French officer who is not in the service, but follows the movements of the Potomac army.

In McClellan's army Heintzelman, Hooker, Kearney, Sumner, and many others, would move quick, would fight and beat; but a leaden weight presses, and solders them to the mud. I must write an article to the press concerning the rapidity of movements, — this golden rule for any conduct of a war.

Since he was in the field, McNapoleon neither planned nor assisted in person in any encounter. When are his great plans to burst out?

In one of his recently published dispatches, Mr. Seward makes an awful mistake in trying to establish the difference between a revolution and a civil war, as to their respective relations to foreign interference and support. A little knowledge of history, and a less presumption, would have spared to him such an exposure. A revolution in a nation can be effected, and generally is effected, without a foreign intervention, and without even an appeal to it. Most of the civil wars look to foreign help. So teaches history, whatever may be Mr. Seward's contrary generalizations.

Mr. Seward is unrelenting in his efforts to build up the Union-saving slavery party, and is sure, as he says, to be able to manage the Republicans, in and out of Congress. We shall see.

Senator Sumner very well discusses the tax-bill, and again shows the practical side of his intellect. Sumner proves that a laborious intellect can grasp and master the most complicated matters. If Sumner could only have more experience of men and things, he would not be so Germanly — *naïve*.

Mr. Seward triumphantly publishes the Turkish hatti, by which pirates are excluded from the Ottoman ports. Oh, Jemine! to be patronized by the Turks! Misfortune brings one with strange bedfellows.

On the occasion of the organization of slaves at Beaufort, Mr. Lincoln exclaimed, "Slavery is a big job, and will smother us!" It will, if dealt with in your way, Mr. President.

McClellan sends for mortars and hundred-pounders; these monsters are to fight, but not he. Well, even so, if possible.

The Southern leaders send to Europe officers of artillery to buy arms and ammunition, and are well served. Our good administration sends speculators, railroad engineers, agents of sewing machines, and the arms bought by them kill our own soldiers, and not the enemies.

English papers taunt the Americans that in one hundred years the country must become a monarchy. The Americans have now a foretaste of some among the features of monarchy, among others of favoritism. The Pompadours and the Dubarrys could not have sustained a McClellan at the cost of so many lives and so many millions. Then the dabbling in war, and other etc.'s, performed in the most approved Louis XIV.'s or Nicolean style.

Worse than the rebels, and by far more abject and degraded, are the defenders of slavery, of treason, and of rebellion in the Congress, in the press, and in the public opinion. No gallows high enough for them.

McClellan crowds the marshes with heavy artillery, and may easily lose them at the smallest disaster. His army is overburdened with artillery in a country where the moving of guns must be exceedingly difficult, nay, often impossible. And then the difficulty of having such a large number of men drilled for the service of guns. Scarcely any army in Europe possesses artillerists in such numbers as are now required here. Few guns well served make more execution than large numbers of them fired at random.

Instead of concentrating his army and attacking at once the rebels in Richmond, McClellan extends his army over nearly sixty miles! To keep such an extensive line more than 300,000 would be required. Oh, heavens! this man is more ignorant of warfare than his worst enemies have suspected him.

It is reported that at Corinth the rebels had not only wooden guns, but cotton manikins as sentries. God grant it may not be true, as it would make the slow, pedantic Halleck even below McClellan.

The future historian will be amazed, bewildered, nay, he may lose his senses, discovering the heaps of confusion and of ignorance which caused the disasters of Banks, the escape of Jackson, etc., etc.

It is impossible to resist the admiration inspired by the skill, the daring, the fertility of intellectual resources displayed by the rebels; all this is so thoroughly contrasted by what is done by our legal chiefs.

Pity that such manhood is shown in the defence of the most infamous cause ever known in the history of the world. To conquer an independence with the sole object to procreate, to breed, to traffic in, and to whip slaves !   .

The navy is glorious everywhere, and not fussy. The people can never sufficiently remunerate the navy, if patriotic services are to be remunerated. The same would be with the army but for the Napoleons !

The published correspondence between the rebels Rust and Hunter fully justifies my confidence in Louis Napoleon's sound judgment. That publication clearly establishes how the press here is wholly unable to conceive or to comprehend the policy of the great European nations. The press heaps outrages and nurses suspicions against Napoleon. The Sandfords and others knowingly stir up suspicions to make believe that their smartness averts the evil. Poor chaps ! When great interests are at stake, neither their fuss, nor any dispatch, however elaborate, can exercise a shadow of influence.

It seems that a Babylonian confusion prevails in the movements, in the distribution, and in the combination of the various parts of the army under McClellan. I should wonder if it were otherwise, with such a general and supported by such a chief of the staff.

Brave old Gideon Welles (Neptune) instructing

15

his sailors to fight, and not to calculate, and " not to deliver anybody against his personal wish."

These imbecile reporters and letter-writers for the press, and other sensationists, make me enraged with their sneers at the poverty of the rebels. If so, the more heroism. They forget the "beggars" of the Dutch insurrection against Philip II.

The cat is out, and I am sorry for it. The world is informed that the revolution is finished, and now the civil war begins. Oh generalizer! oh philosopher of history! oh prophet as to the speedy end of the civil *war!* Oh stop, oh stop! Not by digging will your pet McClellan bring the war to a speedy close.

I am often enraged against myself not to be able to admire Mr. Seward, and to be obliged to judge his whole policy in such, perhaps too severe, a manner. What can I do, what can I do? No one, not even Gen. Scott and Mr. Lincoln, since January, 1861, has exercised an influence equal to Mr. Seward's on the affairs of the country, and *amicus Plato, etc., sed magis amica veritas.*

Mr. Seward believes that July 4th will be celebrated by us in Richmond. He and McClellan spread this hope; Doolittle believes it. We could be in Richmond any day under any other general, not a Napoleon; we may never be there if led on by McClellan, inspired by Mr. Seward's policy.

The French amateur in McClellan's army is disgusted with McNapoleon, and speaks with contempt of the reckless waste of men, of material, etc. He calls it cruel, brainless, and uses a great many other exclamations.

The healthful activity of Stanton, his broad and clear perception of almost all exigencies of these critical times, are continually baffled and neutralized by the allied McClellan, Blair, Seward, New York Times and New York Herald. Such an alliance can easily confuse even the strongest brains.

The colonization again on the *tapis*, and all the wonted display of ignorance, stupidity, ill-will, and phariseeism towards genuine liberty.

Seward gave up his Yucatan scheme. Chiriqui has the lead. And finally, some foreign diplomats try to make conspicuous their little royalties. So Denmark tries to cultivate the barren rocks of St. Thomas with the poor captives. It will be a new kind of apprenticeship under cruel masters. I hear that Mr. Lincoln is caught in the trap, and that a convention *ad hoc* is soon to be concluded. This time, at least, Mr. Seward's name will remain outside.

I am uneasy, fearing we may commit some spread-eagleism towards France during this present Mexican imbroglio. I will do my utmost to explain to influential senators the truth concerning Louis Napoleon's political conduct towards the North, the absurdity of any hostile demonstration against France, and the dirt constituting the sub-stratum of the new Mexican treaty.

"French policy may change towards us," say the

anti-Napoleons; "Louis Napoleon will unmask his diplomatic batteries," etc., etc.

Well, Louis Napoleon may change when he finds that we are incorrigible imbeciles, and that the great interests, which to defend is his duty, are jeopardized; but not before. As for masked batteries, I considered worse than fools all those who believed in masked batteries at Manassas; and in the same light I consider all the believers in diplomatic masked batteries. I was not afraid of the one, and am not of the other.

Not one single French vessel has run, or attempted to run, the blockade; not one has left the ports of France, or of the French West Indies, loaded with arms or ammunition for the insurgents. As for the barking of French papers, or of some second or third rate saloons, barkings thus magnified by American letter-writers, I know too much of Paris and of society to take notice of it. I am sure that the whole rebel tross in Paris, male and female, have not yet been admitted into any single saloon of the *real* good or high society in Paris, and never will be. A thus called *highly accomplished and fashionable lady* from New Orleans, or from Washington, may easily be taken for a country dress-maker, or for a chamber-maid, not fit for first families of the genuine good and high society in Paris, and all over Europe.

Stanton, the true patriot, frets in despair at McClellan's keeping the army in the unhealthiest place of Virginia. Stanton's opponents, the rats, find all

right, even the deaths by disease. In the end Mc-
Clellan is to be all the better for it. Is there no
penitentiary for all this mob?

New regiments pour in, the people are sublime
in their devotion; only may these regiments not
become sacrificed to the Jaggernaut of imbecility.

Whatever may say its revilers, this Congress will
have a noble and pure page in American history.
I speak of the majority.

The Congress showed energy, clear and broad
comprehension and appreciation of the events and
of men. The Congress was ready for every sacrifice, and would have accelerated the crushing of the
rebellion but for the formulas, and for the inade-
quacy of the majority in the administration. If the
Congress had no great leaders, the better for it; it
had honest and energetic men, and their leader was
their purpose, their pure belief in the justice of
their cause and in the people. Such leaders elevate
higher any political body than could ever a Clay,
a Webster, etc., etc.

The Congress is palsied by the inefficiency of the
administration, and but for this, the Congress
would have done far more for the salvation of the
country. All the best men in Congress support
Stanton, and this alone speaks volumes. It is a
curse that the administration is so independent of
the Congress. Oh, why this Congress possesses not
the omnipotence of an English Parliament? Then
the Congress would have prevented all the evils
hitherto brought upon the country by the vacillating

military and general policy. Step by step this policy brings the country to the verge of an abyss, and
it will tax all the energy of the people not to be
precipitated in it.

Mr. Lincoln has gone to get inspiration and information from Gen. Scott. Good God! Can this
man never go out from this rotten tread-mill ? One
more advice from the " great ruin," and the country will also be a ruin.

Flatterers, sensation writers, and all this *magna
clientum caterva* extol to the skies Mr. Lincoln's
firmness and straight-forwardness. The firmness is
located, and is to be discovered in various places —
in the lips, in the chin, in the jaw, and God knows
where else. I cannot detect any firmness in his actions beyond that of sticking to McClellan, — of
whom he has the worst opinion, — and of resisting
the emancipation and the arming of Africo-Americans. He has firmness in letting the country be
ruined.

McClellan's bulletins constitute the most original
and strange collection of style in general, and of
military style in particular. Capt. Morin says that
the first thing is to teach McClellan how to write
military bulletins.

Mr. Seward's crew of politicians is busily at
work among congressmen, etc., to prepare a strong
party in support of the administration's eventual
concessions to slavery, in case Richmond is taken.
Ultra Democratic, half secession Senators are
sounded.

The more the events complicate, the more they require a powerful, all-embracing mind, but in the same proportion subside Mr. Lincoln, Mr. Seward, Mr. Weed, and all the rest of the great men. Alone the people and their true men subside not.

Poor McDowell suffers for the sins of others — above all, for those of Mr. Lincoln and of his aulic council. He is.internally broken down, but behaves nobly; not as does this poor Fremont, whose disappearance from the military scene cannot and must not be regretted. He is not a military capacity; he was again badly surrounded, and his last battle was fought at random, without any unity. I spoke about it with various foreign officers serving under him, and all agree in the incapacity of Fremont and of his staff.

Gen. Pope, a man for the circumstances, acted well in the West; at last a new man.

McClellan inaugurated new tactics. It is to approach the enemy's army by parallels and by trenches. He will not take or scare the enemy, but he will immortalize his name far above the immortality of all not great generals.

Night and day ambulances are conveying the sick and wounded here, and large numbers, thousands upon thousands, going north. One must cry tears of blood to witness such destruction, such a sacrifice of the noblest people on the shrine of utter military incapacity. And the traitors, the imbeciles, and the intriguers sing *hallelujah* to McClellan, and daily throw their slime at Stanton.

From time to time rumors and complaints are made concerning the ill-will or disloyalty of some of the *employés* in the Departments. The explanation thereof may be that some of the thus called old fogies, above all in the War Department, may be unfriendly to the war without being disloyal. Such venerables took root in comfortable situations; they slowly trod in the easy path of rusty and musty routine, and at once the war shook them to the bone, exposing the incapacity and the inefficiency of many; it forced upon them the horror of *cogitandi* about new matters, and an amount of daily duties to be performed in offices which formerly equalled sinecures. Further, these relics dread to be superseded by more active and intelligent men; and *inde iræ.*

JULY, 1862.

WHEN at epochs of great social convulsions events
and circumstances put certain individuals into an
eminent or elevated position, their names become in-
tertwined with the great epoch. In the eyes of the
masses and of the vulgar observers, such names acquire a high importance on account of the commonly made confusion between circumstances and
personal merit, and, moonlight-like, such names
reverberate not their own, but a borrowed splendor.
Thus much for the official pilots of this great people.

The usual paroxysm of the foreign intervention
fever. It ought to be so easy to understand, that
out of self-respect foreign powers will not risk any
intervention on paper; and to make an effective intervention a hundred thousand men will be necessary, as the first course. For such a service no

foreign power is prepared. Intervention is silly talk. McClellan and all kinds of his supporters do more for the South than could England and France united.

It was a poor trick to gather by telegraph the signatures of the governors for an offer of troops to the President. It was done for effect in Europe; but events seem to have a grudge against Mr. Seward; the same steamer carried over the Atlantic the news of our defeats in the Chickahominy swamps.

To attempt a change of such an extensive basis as was occupied by our army under the eyes of a daring, able, skilful enemy, in a country wooded and marshy, and without roads! This movement was perhaps necessary, and could not be avoided; but why at the start had such a basis been selected? Such a selection made disasters inevitable, and they followed.

All kinds of accounts pour in from these cursed fields of the Chickahominy. Foreign officers — whose veracity I can believe — speak enthusiastically of the undaunted bravery of the volunteers and of their generals; *but a general generalship* was not to be found during those titanic fightings. What I gathered from the *suite* of the Orleans is, that Gen. McClellan was totally confused, was totally ignorant of the condition of the corps, was never within distance to give or to be asked for orders, and was the first to reach the banks of the James and to sleep on board the gunboat Galena. At Winchester, Banks in person covered the retreat.

The Orleans left. I pity them ; they will be hooted in Europe. They shared some of McClellan's fallacious and petty notions, and very likely they have been gulled by the McClellan-Seward expectations of taking Richmond before July 4th.

Gen. Hunter's letter about fugitive slaves, and rebels fugitive from the flag of the Union, is the noblest contra distinction. No rhetor could have invented it. Hang yourselves, oh rhetors !

July 4th. — The gloomiest since the birth of this republic. Never was the country so low, and after such sacrifices of blood, of time, and of money ; and all this slaughtered to that Juggernaut of strategy, and to the ignoble motley of his supporters.

Oh you widows, bereaved mothers, sisters, and sweethearts, cry for vengeance ! Cry for vengeance, you shadows of the dead of the malaria, or fallen in the defence of your country's honor. Stupidity has stabbed in the back more deadly wounds than did the enemy in front. This is the 4th of July. Oh ! my old heart and my, not weak, mind are bursting with grief.

The people, the masses, sacrifice their blood, their time, their fortune. What sacrifice the official leaders and pilots? All is net gain for them. Thousands and thousands of families will be impoverished for life, nay, for generations. It is those nameless heroes on the fields of battle who alone uphold the honor of the American name, as it is the people at large who have the true statesmanship, and not the appointed guardsmen.

Rats, hounds, all the vermin, all the impure beasts, are after Stanton, for his not having sent reinforcements to McClellan; but none existed, and McClellan has exhausted and devoured all the reserves. Not reinforcements, but brains, were wanted, and brains are not transferable.

The people, sublime, runs again to the rescue, and Mr. Seward is so sacrilegious, so impious, as to say that the people is generally slow. He is fast on the road of confusion.

I am sure that the whole movement and attack of the rebels was made, as it could be made, at the utmost with 60,000 to 70,000 men, if even with such a number. The rebels never attacked our whole line, but always threw superior forces on some weak and isolated point. This the rebels did during the last battles. The rebels showed great generalship. Jackson is already the legendary hero, and deserves to be.

McClellan never attacked, but *always* was surprised and forced to fight, so the rebels were sure that he would not dare anything to counteract and counter-manœuvre their daring; so the rebel generals had perfect ease for the execution of their bold but skilful plans.

Lincoln sacrifices not Stanton, not even to Seward, to Blair, and to the slavocrats in Congress. That is something.

McClellan publishes a pompous order of the day for the 4th of July, and apes the phraseology of

Napoleon's bulletins from times when by a blow
Napoleon overthrew empires.

What I can gather from the accounts of the seven
days' fighting is, that during the battle at Gaines'
Mills (to speak technically), positively the whole
army was without any basis. But traitors, imbeciles and intriguers rend the air and the skies with
their praises of the great strategy and of the brilliant
generalship.

I am aware how difficult it will be to convince the
heroic army — that is, its rank and file — that their
disasters result from want of generalship, and not
from any inferiority in numbers. All over the world
incapable commanders raise the outcry of deficiency
in numbers to cover therewith their personal deficiency of brains. Similar events to McClellan's
wails, and the confusion they create in the armies
and in the people, are nothing new in the history of
wars.

A fleet of gunboats covers the army on the James
river. Once McClellan condescendingly boasted
that he would take care of the gunboats. The
worst is, that these gunboats could have done service against Charleston, Mobile, Savannah, etc.

After all, McClellan is not the greatest culprit. It
is not his fault that he is without military brains
and without military capacity. He tried to do the
best, according to his poor intellect. The great,
eternally-to-be-damned malefactors are those who
kept him in command after having had repeated proofs
of his incapacity; and still greater are those con-

stitutional advisers who supported McClellan against
the outcry of the best in the Cabinet and in the
nation. A time may come when the children of
those malefactors will be ashamed of their fathers'
names, and — curse them.

I have not scorn enough against the revilers and
accusers of Stanton. If Stanton could have had
his free will, far different would be the condition of
affairs. Stanton's first appearance put an end to
the prevailing lethargy, and marked a new and
glorious era. But, ah! how short! The rats and
the vermin were afraid of him, and took shelter behind the incarnated strategy. Stanton embraced
and embraces the *ensemble* of the task and of the
field before him. And this politician, Blair, to be
his critic! If Stanton had been left undisturbed in
the execution of his duties as the Secretary of War,
McClellan would have been obliged to march directly to Richmond, and the brainless strategy in the
Peninsula would have been crushed in the bud. If
Stanton had not been undermined, not only the people would have been saved from terrible disasters,
but McClellan, Lincoln, Seward, and Blair would
have been saved from reproaches and from malediction.

Stanton likewise shows himself to be a true statesman. A Democrat in politics, he very likely never
was such a violent and decided opponent of slavery
as the Sewards and Blairs professed to be throughout their whole lives. But now Stanton pierces the
fog, perceives the unavoidable exigencies, and is an

emancipationist, when the Sewards and the Blairs
try to compromise, nay, virtually to preserve slavery.

July 10*th*. — The rebels won time to increase and
gather their forces from the south. McClellan's
army may not prevent their turning against Pope,
who has too small a body to resist or to cover the
whole line from Fredericksburg to the Shenandoah.
If the rebels attack Pope he must retreat and concentrate before Washington ; and then again begins
the uphill work. The people generally pour in
blood, time and money ; but brains, brains are needed, and, without violating the formulas, the people
cannot inaugurate brains. Whatever the people
may do, the same quacks and bunglers will over
again commit the same blunders. Nothing can teach
a little foresight to the helmsman and to some of
his seconds. Rocked by his imagination, Mr. Seward never sees clearly the events before him and
what they generate.

The call for three hundred thousand men will be
responded to. The men will come ; but will statesmanship and generalship come with them ? I am
afraid that the rebels, operating with promptness
and energy, may give no time to the levies to be
fully organized ; the rebels will press on Washington.

McClellan reports to the President that he has
only 50,000 men left. The President goes to James
river, and finds 83,000 ready for action. Was it
ignorance in McClellan, or his inborn disrespect of
truth, or disrespect of the country, or something
worse, that made him make such a report ? And

all this passes, and Mr. Lincoln cannot hurt Mc. Clellan, although a gory shroud extends over the whole country.

A secretary of the French consul is here, and confirms my speculations concerning the numbers of the rebels in the last battles on the Chickahominy. The current and authoritative opinion in Richmond is, that from the Potomac to the Rio Grande the rebel force never exceeded 300,000 men. If so, the more glory; and it must be so, according to the rational analysis of statistics.

Mr. Seward writes a skilful dispatch to explain the battles on the Chickahominy. But no skill can succeed to bamboozle the cold, clear-sighted European statesmen.

No doubt Mr. Seward sincerely wished to save the Union in his own way and according to his peculiar conception, and, after having accomplished it, disappear from the political arena, surrounded by the halo of national gratitude.

But even for this aim of reconstruction of the Union as it was, Mr. Seward, at the start, took the wrong track, and took it because he is ignorant of history and of the logic in human affairs. To save the Union as it was, it was imperatively necessary to strike quick and crushing blows, and to do this in May, June, etc., 1861. Mr. Seward could have realized then what now is only a throttling nightmare — *the Union as it was*. But Mr. Seward sustained a policy of delays and not of blows; the struggle protracts, and, for reasons repeatedly mentioned, the suppression of rebellion becomes more and more difficult, and the reconstruction of the old Union as it was a *mirage* of his imagination.

But it is not Thurlow Weed, and others of that stamp, who could enlighten Mr. Seward on such subjects — far, far above their vulgar and mean politicianism. It is now useless to accuse and condemn Congress for its so-called violence, as does Mr. Seward, and to assert that but for Congress he, Mr. Seward, would have long ago patched up the quarrel. The Congress may be as tame as a lamb, and as subject as a foot-sole. Mr. Seward may on his knees proffer to the rebels a compromise and the most stringent safeguards for slavery; to-day the rebels will spurn all as they would have spurned it during the whole year. The rebels will act as Mason did when in the Senate hall Mr. Seward asked the traitor to be introduced to Mr. Lincoln.

The country is in more need of a man than of the many hundreds of thousands of new levies.

Some time ago Mr. Seward gathered around him his devotees in Congress (few in number), and unveiled to them that nobody can imagine what superhuman efforts it cost him to avert foreign intervention. Very unnecessary demonstration, as he knows it well himself, and, if it gets into the papers, may turn out to be offensive to the two cabinets, as they give to Mr. Seward no reason for making such statements. Should England and France ever decide upon any such step, then Mr. Seward may write as a Cicero, have all the learning of a Hugo Grotius, of a Vattel, and of all other publicists combined; he may send legions of Weeds and Sandfords to Europe, and all this will not weigh a feather with the cabinets of London and of Paris.

Further, no foreign powers occasioned our defeats *in the Chickahominy,* but those who were enraptured with the Peninsula strategy.

Mr. Seward's letter to the great meeting in New York shows that not his patriotism, but his confidence in success, is slightly notched.

Nobody doubts his patriotism; but Mr. Seward tried to shape mighty events into a mould after his not-over-gigantic mind, and now he frets because these events tear his sacrilegious hand.

After much opposition, vacillation, hesitation, and aversion, the President signed the confiscation and emancipation bill. A new evidence of how devotedly he wishes to avert any deadly blows from slavery, — this national shame.

The Congress adjourned after having done everything good, and what was in its power. It separated, leaving the country's cause in a worse condition than it was a year ago, after the Bull Run day. Many, nay, almost all the best members of both houses are fully aware in what hands they left the destinies of the nation. Many went away with despair in their hearts; but the constitutional formula makes it impossible for them to act, and to save what so badly needs a savior.

Intervention fever again. The worst intervention is perpetrated at home by imbeciles, by intriguers, by traitors, and by the — spades.

Mr. Dicey, an Englishman who travelled or travels in this country, — Mr. D. is the first among his countrymen who understands the events here, and who is just toward the true American people ; — Mr. D. truly says that the people fight without a general, and without a statesman, and are the more to be admired for it.

Mr. Seward tries to appear grand before the foreign diplomats, and talks about Cromwell, Louis Napoleon, *coup d' Etats* against the Congress, and about his regrets to be in the impossibility to imitate them. Only think, Cromwell, Napoleon I., Napoleon III., Seward ! Such dictatorial dreams may explain Mr. Seward's partiality for General McClellan, whom Seward may perhaps wish to use as Louis Napoleon used Gen. St. Arnoud.

Halleck is to be the American Carnot. But any change is an improvement. If Halleck extricates the army on the James river, and saves it from malaria, — this enemy more deadly than Jackson and McClellan combined, — then for this single action Halleck deserves well of the country, and his Corinth affair will, at least in part, be atoned for.

Mr. Lincoln makes a new effort to save his *mammy*, and tries to neutralize the confiscation bill. Mr. Lincoln will not make a step beyond what is called the Border-States' policy ; and it may prove too late when he will decide to honestly execute the

law of Congress. Mr. Seward gets into hysterics
at the hateful name of Congress. Similar spite he
showed to a delegation from the city of New York,
upbraiding some of its members, and assuring them
that delegations are not needed, — that the administration is fully up to the task. Yes, Stanton is, but
how about some others ?

Poor Mr. Lincoln ! he must stand all the mutual
puffs of Seward and Sandford, and some more in
store for him when the Weeds and Hughes will come
and give an account of their doings in Europe.

The report of the battle against Casey, as published by the rebel General Johnston, is a masterpiece of military style, and shows how skilfully the
attack was combined. The Southern leaders have
exclusively in view the triumph of their cause.
With many of our leaders, the people's cause is
made to square with their little selfishness.

Guerillas spread like locusts. Perhaps they are
the results of our Union-searching, slavery-saving
policy.

AUGUST, 1862.

Vulgatior fama est, that Mr. Lincoln was already raising his hand to sign a stirring proclamation on the question of emancipation ; that Stanton was upholding the President's arm that it might not grow weak in the performance of a sacred duty; that Chase, Bates, and Welles joined Stanton ; but that Messrs. Seward and Blair so firmly objected that the President's outstretched hand slowly began to fall back ; that to precipitate the mortification, Thurlow Weed was telegraphed ; that Thurlow Weed presented to Mr. Lincoln the Medusa-head of Irish riots in the North against the emancipation of slaves in the South ; that Mr. Lincoln's mind faltered (oh, Steffens) before such a Chinese shadow, and that thus once more slavery was saved. *Relata refero.*

General Wadsworth is the good genius of the poor and oppressed race. But for Wadsworth's noble soul and heart the Lamons and many other blood-hounds in Washington would have given about three-fourths of the fugitives over to the whip of the slavers.

Within the last four weeks 600,000 new levies are called to arms. With the 600,000 men levied previously, it is the heaviest draft ever made from a population. No emperor or despot ever did it in a similar lapse of time. The appreciation current here is, that the twenty millions of inhabitants can easily furnish such a quota; but the truth is that the draft, or the levy, or the volunteering, is made from about three millions of men between the ages of twenty and forty years. One million two hundred thousand in one year is equal to nearly 36-100, and this from the most vital, the most generative, and most productive part of the population.

The same analysis and percentage applied to the statistics of the population in the rebel States gives a little above 300,000 men under arms; however, the percentage of the drafts from the full-aged population in the South can be increased by some 15-100 over the percentage in the North. This increase is almost exclusively facilitated by the substratum of slavery, and our administration devotedly takes care *ne detrimentum capiat* that peculiar institution.

The last draft could be averted from the North if the four millions of loyal Africo-Americans were called to arms. But Mr. Lincoln, with the Sewards, the Blairs, and others, will rather see every Northern man shot than to touch the palladium of the rebels.

These new enormous masses will crush the rebellion, provided they are not marshalled by strategy; but nevertheless the painful confession must be made, that our putting in the field of three to one rebel may confuse a future historian, and contribute to root more firmly that stupid fallacy already asserted by the rebels, and by some among their European upholders, of the superiority of the Southern over the Northern thus called race. Such a stigma is inflicted upon the brave and heroic North by the strategy, and by the vacillating, slave-saving policy of the administration.

This is the more painful for me to record, as most of the foreign officers in our service, and who are experienced and good judges, most positively assert the superior fighting qualities of the Union volunteers over the rebels. Our troops are better fed, clad and armed, but over our army hovers the thick mist of strategy and indecision; the rebels are led not by anaconda strategians, but by fighting generals, desperate, and thus externally heroic; energy inspires their councils, their administration, and their military leaders.

If Stanton and Halleck succeed in extricating the army on the James river, then they will deserve the gratitude of the people. The malaria there must be more destructive than would be many battles.

Events triumphantly justify Stanton's opposition

to the Peninsula strategy and campaign. So ends this horrible sacrifice ; between fifty and sixty thousand killed or dead by diseases. The victims of this holocaust have fallen for their country's cause, but the responsibility for the slaughter is to be equally divided between McClellan, Lincoln, Seward and Blair. Even Sylla had not on his soul so much blood as has the above quatuor. When, after the victory over the allied Samnites and others, at the Colline gate of Rome, Sylla ordered the massacre of more than four thousand prisoners who laid down their arms ; when his lists of proscription filled with blood Rome and other cities of Italy, Sylla so firmly consolidated the supremacy of the *Urbs* over Italy and over the world, that after twenty centuries of the most manifold vicissitudes, transformations and tempests, this supremacy cannot yet be upturned. But the holocaust to strategy resulted in humiliating the North and in heaping glory on the Southern leaders.

If the newly called 600,000 men finish the rebellion before Congress meets, then slavery is saved. To save slavery and to avoid emancipation was perhaps the secret aim of Mr. Lincoln, Seward, and Blair ; who knows but that of Halleck, when the administration called for the additional 300,000 men ?

Persons who approach Halleck say that he is a thorough pro-slavery partisan. His order No. 3, the opinion of some officers of his staff, and his associations, make me believe in the truth of that report.

Mr. Seward says *sub rosa* to various persons, that slavery is an obsolete question, and he assures others that emancipation is a fixed fact, and is no more to be held back; that he is no more a conservative. How are we to understand this man? If Mr. Seward is sincere, then his last transformation may prove that he has given up the idea of finding a Union party in the South, or that he wishes to re-conquer — what he has lost — the confidence of the party. But this return on his part may prove *troppo tardi*.

The army of the Potomac is saved; the heroes, martyrs, and sufferers are extricated from the grasp of death. This epopee in the history of the civil war will immortalize the army, but the strategian's immortality will differ from that of the army.

England and France firm in their neutrality. Lord John Russell's speeches in Parliament are all that can be desired.

Will it ever be thoroughly investigated and eluci-dated why, after the evacuation of Corinth, the on-ward march of our everywhere-victorious Western armies came at once to a stand-still? The guerillas, the increase of forces in Richmond, and some event-ual diasters, may be directly traced to this inconceiv-able conduct on the part of the Western command-ers or of the Commander-in-chief. Was not some Union-searching at the bottom of that stoppage? When, months ago, a false rumor was spread about the evacuation of Memphis and Corinth, Mr. Seward was ready to start for the above-mentioned places, of course in search of the Union feeling. Perhaps others were drawn into this Union-searching, Union and slavery-restoring conspiracy.

I have most positive reasons to believe that Gen. Halleck wished to remove Gen. McClellan from the command of the army. The President opposed to it. Men of honor, of word, and of truth, and who are on intimate footing with Mr. Lincoln, repeatedly assured me that, in his conversation, the President judges and appreciates Gen. McClellan as he is judged and appreciated by those whom his crew call his enemies. With all this, Mr. Lincoln, through thin and thick, supports McClellan and maintains him in command. Such a double-dealing in the chief of a noble people! Seemingly Mr. Seward and Mr. Blair always exercise the most powerful influence. Both wished that the army remain in the malarias of the James river. Whatever be their reasons, one shudders in horror at the ease with which all those culprits look on this bloody affair. Oh you widowed wives, mothers, and sweethearts! oh you orphaned children! oh you crippled and disabled, you impoverished and ruined, by sacrificing to your country more than do all the Lincolns, McClellans, Blairs, and Sewards! Some day you will ask a terrible account, and if not the present day, posterity will avenge you.

It is very discouraging to witness that the President shows little or no energy in his dealings with incapacities, and what a mass of intrigues is used to excuse and justify incapacity when the nation's life-

blood runs in streams. Without the slightest hesitation any European government would dismiss an
incapable commander of an army, and the French
Convention, that type of revolutionary and nation-
saving energy, dealt even sharper with military and
other incapacities.

Regiments after regiments begin to pour in, to
make good the deadly mistakes of our rulers. The
people, as always, sublime, inexhaustible in its sacrifices! God grant that administrative incompetency
may become soon exhausted!

Mr. Seward told a diplomat that his (Seward's)
salary was $8,000, and he spends double the amount;
thus sacrificing to the country $8,000. When I hear
such reports about him, I feel ashamed and sorrow-
ful on his account. Such talk will not increase esteem for him among foreigners and strangers; and although I am sure that Mr. Seward intended to make
a joke, even as such it was worse than a poor one.

In his interview with a deputation composed of
Africo-Americans, Mr. Lincoln rehearsed all the
clap-trap concerning the races, the incompatibility
to live together, and other like *bosh*. Mr. Lincoln
promised to them an Eden — in Chiriqui. Mr. Lincoln promised them — what he ought to know is
utterly impossible and beyond his power — that
they will form an independent community in a country already governed by orderly and legally organized States, as are New Grenada and Costa Rica.
Happily even for Mr. Lincoln's name, the logic of
human events will save from exposure his ignorance

of international laws, and his too light and too quick assertions. I pity Mr. Lincoln; his honesty and unfamiliarity with human affairs, with history, with laws, and with other like etceteras, continually involve him in unnecessary scrapes.

The proclamation concerning the colonization is issued. It is a display of ignorance or of humbug, or perhaps of both. Some of the best among Americans do not utter their condemnation of this colonization scheme, because the President is to be allowed *to carry out his hobby.* The despots of the Old World will envy Mr. Lincoln. Those despots can no more *carry out their hobbies.* The *Roi s'amuse* had its time; but the *il bondo cani* of some here, at times, beats that of the *Italina in Algero.*

The two letters of Greeley to the President show that the old, indomitable lion begins to awake. As to Mr. Lincoln's answer, it reads badly, and as for all the rest, it is the eternal dodging of a vital question.

Mr. Lincoln's equanimity, although not so stoical, is unequalled. In the midst of the most stirring and exciting — nay, death-giving — news, Mr. Lincoln has always a story to tell. This is known and experienced by all who approach him. Months ago I was in Mr. Lincoln's presence when he received a telegram announcing the crossing of the Mississippi by Gen. Pope, at New Madrid. Scarcely had Mr. Lincoln finished the reading of the dispatch, when he cracked (that is the sacramental word) two not very washed stories.

When the history of this administration shall become well known, contemporary and future generations will wonder and be puzzled to know how the most intelligent and enlightened people in the world could produce such fruits and results of self-government.

The rebel chiefs take the offensive; they unfold a brilliancy in conception and rapidity in execution of which the best generals in any army might be proud. McClellan's army was to be prevented from uniting with Pope. But it seems that Pope manœuvres successfully, and approaches McClellan.

If only our domestic policy were more to the point, England and France could not be complained of. Mr. Mercier behaves here as loyally as can be wished, and carefully avoids evoking any misunderstandings whatever. So do Louis Napoleon, Mr. Thouvenel, Lord John Russell, notwithstanding Mr. Seward's all-confusing policy. Mr. Mercier never, never uttered in my presence anything whatever which in the slightest manner could irritate even the *thinnest-skinned* American.

As I expected, Louis Napoleon and Mr. Thouvenel highly esteem Mr. Dayton; and it will be a great mistake to supersede Mr. Dayton in Paris by the travelling agent of the sewing machine. It seems that such a change is contemplated in certain quarters, because the agent parleys poor French. Such a change will not be flattering, and will not be agreeable to the French court, to the French cabinet, and to the French good society.

On the continent of Europe sympathy begins to be unsettled, unsteady. As independence is to-day the watchword in Europe, so the cause of the rebels acquires a plausible justification. Various are the reasons of this new counter current. Prominent among them is the vacillating, and by Europeans considered to be INHUMAN, policy of Mr. Lincoln in regard to slavery, the opaqueness of our strategy, and the brilliancy of the tactics of the rebel generals, and, finally, the incapacity of our agents to enlighten European public opinion, and to explain the true and horrible character of the rebellion. Repeatedly I warned Mr. Seward, telling him that the tide of public opinion was rising against us in Europe, and I explained to him the causes; but of course it was useless, as his agents say the contrary, and say it for reasons easily to be understood.

McClellan's army landed, and he is to be in command of all the troops. I congratulate all therein concerned about this new victory. Bleed, oh bleed, American people! Mr. Lincoln and *consortes* insisted that McClellan remain in command. SISTE TANDEM CARNIFEX!

Mr. Roebuck, M. P., the gentleman! About thirty years ago, when entering his public career as a member for Bath, Mr. Roebuck was publicly slapped in the face during the going on of the election. A few years ago Mr. Roebuck went to Vienna in the interests of some lucrative railroad or Lloyd speculation, and returned to England a fervent and devoted admirer of the Hapsburgs, and a reviler of all that once was sacred to the disciple of Jeremy Bentham.

General Halleck may become the savior of the country. I hope and ardently wish that it may be so, although his qualifications for it are of a rather doubtful nature. Gen. Halleck wrote a book on military science, as he wrote one on international laws, and both are laborious compilations of other people's labors and ideas. But perhaps Halleck, if not inspired, may become a regular, methodical captain. Such was Moreau.

Also, Gen. Halleck is not to take the field in person. I am told that it was so decided by Mr. Lincoln, against Halleck's wish. What an anomalous position of a commander of armies, who is not to see a field of battle! Such a position is a genuine, new American invention, but it ought not to be patented, at least not for the use of other nations. It is impossible to understand it, and it will puzzle every one having sound common sense.

Gen. Butler commits a mistake in taunting and teasing the French population and the French consul in New Orleans. When Butler was going there, Mr. Seward ought to have instructed him concerning our friendly relations with Louis Napoleon, and concerning the character of the French consul in New Orleans, who was not partial to secesh. There may be some secesh French, but the bulk, if well managed, would never take a decided position against us as long as we were on friendly terms with Louis Napoleon.

The President is indefatigable in his efforts to —
save slavery, and to uphold the policy of the New
York Herald.

It is said that General Hunter is recalled, and so
was General Phelps from New Orleans; General
Phelps could not coolly witness the sacrilegious massacre of the slaves. The inconceivable partiality
of the President for McClellan may, after all, be
possibly explained by the fact that Mr. Lincoln and
Mr. Seward see in McClellan a — savior of slavery.

During two days' terrible fighting at Manassas, at
Bull Run, and all around, Pope cut his way through,
but the reinforcements from - McClellan's army in
Alexandria are *slow* in coming. McClellan and his
few pets among the generals may not object to see
Pope worsted. Such things happened in other armies, even almost under the eyes of Napoleon, as in
the campaign on the Elbe, in 1813. Any one worth
the name of a general, when he has no special position to guard, and hears the roar of cannon, by
forced marches runs to the field of battle. Not any
special orders, but the roar of cannon, attracted and
directed Desaix to Marengo, and Mac Mahon to
Magenta. The roar of cannon shook the air between Bull Run and Alexandria, and —— General McClellan and others had positive orders to run
to the rescue of Pope.

I should not wonder if the President, enthu-
siasmed by this new exploit of McClellan, were to
nominate him for his, the President's, eventual suc-
cessor ; Mr. Blair will back the nomination.

It is said that during these last weeks, Wallach, the editor of the unwashed *Evening Star*, is in continual intercourse with the President. *Arcades ambo.*

McClellan reduced in command ; only when the life of the nation was almost breathing its last. This concession was extorted from Mr. Lincoln ! What will Mr. Seward say to it ?

17

SEPTEMBER, 1862.

Consummatum est!—Will the outraged people avenge itself?—McClellan satisfies the President—After a year!—The truth will be throttled—Public opinion in Europe begins to abandon us—The country marching to its tomb—Hooker, Kearney, Heintzelman, Sigel, brave and true men—Supremacy of mind over matter—Stanton the last Roman—Inauguration of the pretorian regime—Pope accuses three generals—Investigation prevented by McClellan—McDowell sacrificed—The country inundated with lies—The demoralized army declares for McClellan—The pretorians will soon finish with liberty—Wilkes sent to the West Indian waters—Russia—Mediation—Invasion of Maryland—Strange story about Stanton—Richmond never invested—McClellan in search of the enemy—Thirty miles in six days—The telegrams—Wadsworth—Capitulation of Harper's Ferry—Five days' fighting—Brave Hooker wounded—No results—No reports from McClellan—Tactics of the Maryland campaign—Nobody hurt in the staff—Charmed lives—Wadsworth, Judge Conway, Wade, Boutwell, Andrew—This most intelligent people become the laughing-stock of the world!—The proclamation of emancipation—Seward to the Paisley Association—Future complications—If Hooker had not been wounded!—The military situation—Sigel persecuted by West Point—Three cheers for the carriage and six!—How the great captain was to catch the rebel army—Interview with the Chicago deputation—Winter quarters—The conspiracy against Sigel—Numbers of the rebel army—Letters of marque.

THE intrigues, the insubordination of McClellan's pets, have almost exclusively brought about the disasters at Manassas and at Bull Run, and brought the country to the verge of the grave. But the people are not to know the truth.

258

CONSUMMATUM EST ! The people's honor is stained
— the country's cause on the verge of the grave.
Will this outraged people avenge itself on the four
or five diggers ?

Old as I am, I feel a more rending pain now than
I felt thirty years ago when Poland was entombed.
Here are at stake the highest interests of humanity,
of progress, of civilization. I find no words to
utter my feelings; my mind staggers. It is filled
with darkness, pain, and blood.

Mr. Lincoln is the standard-bearer of the policy
of the New York Herald. So, before him, were
Pierce and Buchanan.

It is said that General McClellan fully satisfied
the President of his (the General's) complete innocence as to the delays which exclusively generated
the last disasters; also Gen. McClellan has justified
himself on military grounds. I wish the verdict of
innocence may be uttered by a court-martial of European generals. At any rate, the country was
thrown into an abyss.

After a year ! — One hundred thousand of the
best, bravest, the most devoted men slaughtered;
hundreds and hundreds of millions squandered; the
army again in the entrenchments of Washington;
everywhere the defensive and losses; the enemy on
the Potomac, perhaps to invade the free States; but
McClellan is in command, his headquarters as brilliant and as numerous as a year ago; the mean
flunkeys at their post; only the country's life-blood
pours in streams; but — that is of no account.

No acids are so dissolving and so corrosive as is the air of Washington on patriotism. How few resist its action! Among the few are Stanton, Chase (a passive patriot), Wadsworth, Dahlgreen, and those grouping around Stanton; so is Welles; likewise Fox; but they are powerless. Washington is likewise the greatest garroter of truth; and I am sure that the truth about the last battles will be throttled and never elucidated.

September 3: — The Cabinets of France and of England will have a very hard stand. to resist the pressure of public opinion, carried away by the skill and by the plausible heroism of the rebels. Public opinion will be clamorous that something be done in favor of the rebels. Happily, nothing else can be done but a war, and this saves us. But if the rebels succeed without Europe, the more glory for their chiefs, the more ignominy for ours. Public opinion begins to abandon us in Europe. Already I have explained some of the reasons for it.

The country is marching to its tomb, but the grave-diggers will not confess their crime and their utter incapacity to save it. This their stubbornness is even a greater crime. Will Halleck warn the country against McClellan's incapacity?

We have such generals as Hooker, Heintzelman, Kearney, etc., who fought continually, and with odds against them, and who never were worsted. Those three, among the best of the army, fought under Pope and mutineered not. In any other country such men would receive large, even the superior command ; here the palm belongs to the incapable, the *slow*, and to the flatterer. The same with Sigel. His corps is reduced to 6,000 men ; common sense shows that he ought to have at least 25,000 under him. Sigel begged the President to have more men ; the President sent him to Halleck and McClellan, who both snubbed him off. By my prayer Sigel, although disheartened, went to Stanton, who received him friendly and warmly, and promised to do his utmost. Stanton will keep his word, if only the West Point envy will not prevent him.

Hooker, Kearney, and Heintzelman were not in favor at the headquarters in the Peninsula, and their commands have been continually disorganized in favor of the pets of the Commander-in-Chief. The country knows what the three braves did since Yorktown down to the last day—the country knows that at the last disasters at Bull Run these heroic generals did their fullest duty. But not even their advice is asked at the double headquarters. Stanton alone cannot do everything. Rats may devour a Hercules.

It seems certain that the rebel generals have various foreign officers in their respective staffs. The rebels wish to assure the success of their cause ; here many have only in view their personal success.. The President, although not a Blucher, may make a Gneisenau out of Sigel, who has in view only the success of the cause, and no prospects towards the White House. Sigel would understand how to organize a genuine staff.

Most of the foreigners who came to serve here came with the intention to fight for the sacred principle of freedom, and without any further views whatever of career and aggrandizement. In this respect Americans are not just towards these foreigners, and the great men at headquarters will prefer to see all go to pieces than to use the capacity of foreigners, above all in the artillery and for the staff duties.

The mind—that is, Jeff. Davis, Jackson, Lee, etc. —has the best of the matter—that is, Lincoln, McClellan, Blair, and Seward; however, these positions are reversed when one considers the masses on both sides. But on our side the matter commands and presses down the mind; on the rebel side the mind of the chiefs vivifies, exalts, attracts, and directs the matter. And the results thereof are, that not the rebellion, but the North, is shaking.

As *a*, not only as *the* President, Mr. Lincoln represents nothing beyond the unavoidable constitutional formula. For all other purposes, as an acting, directing, inspiring, or combining power or agency, Mr. Lincoln becomes a myth. His reality is only manifested by preserving slavery, by sticking to McClellan, by distributing offices, by receiving inspirations from Mr. Seward, and by digging the country's grave. So it is from March 4, 1861, up to this, September 5th, 1862. What else Mr. Lincoln may eventually incarnate is not now perceptible.

Mr. Lincoln and Mr. Seward piloted the country

among breakers and rocks, from which to extricate the country requires a man who is to be the burning focus of the whole people's soul.

Other nations at times reached the bottom of an abyss, and they came up again when from the tempest rending them emerged such a savior. But here the formula may render impossible the appearance of such a savior. The formula is the nation's hearse. The formula has neutralized the best men in Congress, the best men in the Cabinet, as is Stanton.

The people have decided not, *propter vitam vivendi perdere causas;* but the various formulas, the schemers, the grave-diggers, and the aspirants for the White House, think differently.

The almost daily changes made by Mr. Lincoln in the command of the forces are the best evidences of his good-intentioned — debility.

Harmony belongs to the primordial laws of nature ; it is the same for human societies. But here no harmony exists between the purest, the noblest, and the most patriotic portion of the people, and the official exponent of the people's will, and of its higher and purer aspirations. So here all jars dissonantly ; all is confusion, because avenged must be every violation of nature's law.

I cannot believe that at this deadly crisis the salvation can come from Washington. The best man here has not his free action. And the rest of them are the country's curse. Mr. Lincoln, with McClellan, Seward, Blair, Halleck, and scores of such, are as able to cope with this crisis as to stop the revolution of our planet.

Up to this day, from among those foremost, the only man whose hands remain unstained with the country's, his mother's, and his brethren's blood, the last Roman, is Stanton.

September 7.—During last night troops marched to meet the enemy, saluting with deafening shouts and cheers the residence of McClellan; spit-lickers as a Kennedy, giving the sign by waving his hat. Such shouts would cheer up the mind but for the fact that they were mostly raised for the victory over those who demanded an investigation of the causes of *slowness* and insubordination,—those exclusive causes of the defeat of Pope's army. Those shouts were thrown out as defiance to justice, to truth, and to law. Those shouts marked the inauguration of the *pretorian regime*. General McClellan and other generals have forced the President to *postpone* the investigation into the conduct of the *slow* and of the insubordinate generals, all three special favorites of McClellan. General McClellan appeared before the soldiers surrounded by his *old identical staff*, by a tross of flatterers, and, Oh heavens! in the cortege Senator Wilson! Oh, *sancta* not *simplicitas*, but —— Oh, clear-sighted Republican!

Subsequently, I learned that Senator Wilson was present for a moment, and only by a pure accident, at that ovation.

Laeszt Dich dem Teufel bey'm Haare packen, so hat Er Dich bey'm Kopfe, says Lessing, and so it

may become here with this first success of the pretorians, or even worse than pretorians; these here
are Yanitschars of a Sultan.

Pope and his army accuse three generals of in-
subordination and mutiny on the field of battle.
McClellan prevents investigation; the brutal rule of
Yanitschars is inaugurated, thanks to you, Messrs.
Seward and Blair.

McDowell sacrificed to the Yanitschars; he is the
scapegoat and the victim to popular fallacy, to the
imbecility of the press, and, above all, to the intriguers and to the conspiracy of the mutinous pets
of McClellan. Weeks and weeks ago, I foretold to
McDowell that such would be his fate, and that only
in after-times history will be just towards him.

.The country begins to be inundated and opinion poisoned by all kinds of the most glaring lies,
invented and spread by the staffs, and the imbecile, blind partisans of McClellan. Here are some
from among the lies.

In January (oh hear, oh hear!) General McClellan
with 50,000 men intended to make a *flying* (oh
hear, oh hear!) expedition to Richmond, but Lincoln
and Stanton opposed it. This lie divides itself into
two points. 1st lie. In January, nobody opposed
General McClellan's will, and, besides, he was sick.
2d lie. If he was so pugnacious in January, why
has he not made with the same number of men a
flying expedition only to Centreville, right under his
nose?

Emanating from the staff, such a lie is sufficient

to show the military capacity of those who concocted it.

Second lie. That the expedition to Yorktown and the Peninsula strategy were forced upon McClellan. I hope that the Americans have enough memory left, and enough self-respect to recollect the truth.

Further, the above staff asserts that, when the truth will be known about the campaign, and the fightings in the Chickahominy, then justice will be done to McClellan.

Always and everywhere lost battles, bad and ignorant generalship, require explanations, justifications, and commentaries. Well-fought battles are justified on the spot, the same day, and by results. No one asks or makes comments upon the fighting of Jackson. Austerlitz, Jena, were commented on, explained, some of the chiefs were justified, but — by Austrian and Prussian commentators.

Until to-day French writers discuss, analyze, and comment upon the fatal battle of Waterloo. At Waterloo Napoleon was in the square of his heroic guards; but during the seven days' fighting on the Chickahominy, what regiment, not to say a square, saw in its midst the American Napoleon ?

A thousand others, similar to the above-mentioned lies, will be or are already circulated; the mass of the people will use its common sense, and the lies must perish.

On September 7th, Gen. McClellan gave his word to the President to start to the army at 12 o'clock, but started at 4 P. M. with a long train of well-packed wagons for himself and for his staff. To be sure, Lee, Jackson, and all the other rebel chiefs together, have not such a train ; if they had, they would not be to-day on the Potomac and in Maryland. Most certainly those quick-moving rebels start at least an hour earlier than they are expected to do.

September 9. — Up to this day Mr. Lincoln ought to have discovered whose advice transformed him into a standard-bearer of the policy of the New York Herald, and made him push the country to the verge of the grave ; and, nevertheless, Mr. Lincoln is deaf to the voice of all true and pure patriots who point out the malefactors.

Secondary events, as a lost battle, etc., depend upon material causes ; but such primordial events as is the thorough miscarriage of Mr. Lincoln's anti-rebellion policy, — such events are generated by moral causes.

Jefferson Davis, Lee, Jackson, and all the generals down to the last Southern bush-whacker, incarnate the violent and hideous passion of slavery, now all-powerful throughout the South. Here, Lincoln, Seward, McClellan, Blair, Halleck, etc., incarnate the negation of the purest and noblest aspirations of the North. Stanton alone is inspired by a national patriotic idea. No unity, no harmony between the people and the leaders ; this discord must generate disasters.

All over the country the lie is spread that the army demanded the reappointment of McClellan. First, the three mutinous generals did it ; but not a Kearney, the Bayard of America; very likely not Hooker and Heintzelman — all of them soldiers, patriots, and men of honor; nor very likely was it demanded by Keyes. I do not know positively what was the conduct of Gen. Sumner. Gen. Burnside owes what he is, glory and all, to McClellan. Burn. side's honest gratitude and honest want of judgment have contributed more than anything else to inaugurate the regime of the pretorians, to justify mutiny. Halleck's conduct in all this is veiled in mystery; it is so at least for the present; and as truth will be kept out of sight, the country may never know the truth about those shameful proceedings.

I learn that Heintzelman, against his own judgment, agreed in the McClellan movement. Well, if this is true, then, of course, the army, for a long time misled by uninterrupted intrigues, misled by papers such as the New York Herald and the Times, — the army or the soldiers mightily contributed to bring about this fatal crisis. An army composed of intelligent Americans, blinded, stultified by intriguers, declares for a general who never, up to this day, covered with glory his or the army's name. After this nothing more is to be expected, and no disaster on the field of battle, no dissolution of a national principle, can astonish my mind. Cursed be those who thus demoralized the sound judgment of the soldiers! Cursed be my personal experience of men and of things which makes me despair! But when an army or soldiers become intellectually brought down to such a standard, then the holiest cause will always be lost. Oh for a man to save the cause of humanity! But if even such a man should appear, these pretorians will turn against him.

The pretorians, with the New York Herald as their flag, will soon finish with liberty at home. McClellan, Barlow, the brothers Wood, and Bennett, may very soon be at the helm, with the 100,000 pretorians for support. *Similia similibus;* and here disgrace is to cure disgrace.

These helpless grave-diggers, above all, Seward, are on the way to pick a quarrel with England, sending a flying gunboat fleet under Wilkes into the West Indian waters. At this precise moment it were better to be very cautious, and rather watch strongly our coasts with the same gunboats.

September 11. — A military genius at once finds out the point where blows are to be struck, and strikes them with lightning-like speed. The rebels act in this manner; but what point was found out, what blows were ever dealt by McClellan?

Individuals similar to McClellan were idolized by the Roman pretorians, and this idolatry marks the epoch of the utmost demoralization and degradation of the Roman empire. Witnessing such a phenomenon in an army of American volunteers, one must give up in despair any confidence in manhood and in common sense.

The Journal of St. Petersburg of August 6th semi-officially refutes the insinuations that Russia intends to recognize the South, or to unite with

France and England for any such purpose, or for mediation. The language of the article is noble and friendly, as is all which up to this day has been done by Alexander II. Mr. Stoeckl, the Russian minister here, considerably contributes that such sound and friendly views on the condition of our affairs are entertained by the Russian Cabinet.

September 11. — Imbeciles agitate the question of mediation. European cabinets will not offer it now, and nobody, not even the rebels, would accept. No possible terms and basis exist for any mediation. A Solomon could not find them out. If Jackson and Lee were to shell Washington, then only the foreign ministers may be requested to step in and to settle the terms of a capitulation or of an evacuation. The foreign ministers here could act as mediators only if asked ; not otherwise. I am sure it will come out that the invasion of Maryland by the rebels is made under the pressure exercised in Richmond by the Maryland chivalry in the service of the rebellion. These runaways probably promised an insurrection in Maryland, provided a rebel force crosses the Potomac. (Wrote it to England.)

All around helplessness and confusion. Conscientiously I make all possible efforts to record what I believe to be true, and then truth will take care of herself.

After the study of the campaigns of Frederick II., above all, after the study of those marvellous campaigns, combinations, manœuvres of Napoleon, to witness every day the combinations of McClellan is more disgusting, more nauseous for the mind, than can be for the stomach the strongest dose of emetic.

The last catastrophe at Bull Run and at Manassas has a slight resemblance with the catastrophe at Waterloo. The conduct of the mutinous generals here is similar to the conduct of some of the French generals during the battle of Ligny and Quatre-Bras. But here was mutiny, and there demoralization produced by general and deeply rooted and fatally unavoidable causes. The demoralization of the French generals came at the end of a terrible epoch of struggles and sacrifices, of material exhaustion, when the faith in the destinies of Napoleon was extinct; here mutiny and demoralization seize upon the newly-born era.

September 13. — What a good-natured people are the Americans! A regiment of Pennsylvania infantry quartered for the night on the sidewalk of the streets; officers, of course, absent; the poor soldiers stretched on the stones, when so many empty large buildings, when the empty (intellectually and materially empty) White House could have given to the soldiers comfortable night quarters. It can give an idea how they treat the soldiers in the field, if here in Washington they care so little for them. But McClellan has forty wagons for his staff, and forty ambulances — no danger for the latter to be used. In European armies aristocratic officers would not dare to treat soldiers in this way — to throw them on the pavement without any necessity.

More than once in my life, after heavy fighting,

I laid down the knapsack for a cushion, snow for a mattrass and for a blanket; but by the side of the soldiers, the generals, the staffs, and the officers shared similar bedsteads.

I hear strange stories about Stanton, and about his having ruefully fallen in McClellan's lap. If so, then one more *man*, one more illusion, and one more creed in manhood gone overboard, drowned in meanness, in moral cowardice, and subserviency.

The worshippers of strategy and of Gen. McClellan try to make the public swallow, that the investment of Richmond by him was a magnificent display of science, and would have been a success but for 50,000 more men under his command.

To invest any place whatever is to cut that place from the principal, if not from all communications with the country around, and thus prevent, or make dangerous or difficult, the arrival of provisions, of support, etc.

Our gunboats, etc., in the York and the James rivers have virtually invested Richmond on the eastern side ; but that part of the Peninsula did not constitute the great source of life for the rebel army. The principal life-arteries for Richmond ran through four-fifths of a circle, beginning from the southern banks of the James river and running to the southern banks of the Rapidan and of the Rappahannock. Through that region men, material, provisions poured into Richmond from the whole South, and that whole region around Richmond was left perfectly open; but strategy concentrated its wisdom on the comparatively indifferent eastern side of the Chickahominy marshes, and cut off the rebels from — nothing at all.

September 13. — General McClellan, in search of the enemy, during the first six days makes thirty miles! Finds the enemy near Hagerstown. No more time for strategy.

September 14. — General McClellan telegraphs to General Halleck (*meliores ambo*) that he, McClellan, has "*the most reliable information that the enemy is* 190,000 *strong in Maryland and in Pennsylvania, besides* 70,000 *on the other side of the Potomac.*" (The same bosh about the numbers as in the Peninsula.)

The Generals Burnside, Hooker, Sumner, Reno, fought the battle at Hagerstown, and drove the enemy before them. General McClellan reports a victory, *but expects the enemy to renew the fighting next day in a considerable force* — (as at Williamsburg). McClellan telegraphs to Halleck, "*Look for an attack on Washington.*" The enemy retreats to recross the Potomac!

September 15. — General Wadsworth suggested to the President one of those bold movements by which campaigns are terminated by one blow: "To send Heintzelman and him, Wadsworth, with some 25,000 men, to Gordonsville (here and in Baltimore about 90,000 men), and thus cut off the enemy from Richmond, and prevent him from rallying his forces." But General Halleck opposes such a Murat's dash, on account of McClellan's "looked-for attack on Washington " — by his, McClellan's, imagination.

September 17. — When I wrote the above about Wadsworth and Heintzelman, I was under the impression that the victory announced by McClellan, Sept. 14, was more decisive ; that as he had fresh the whole corps of Fitz John Porter, and the greatest part of that of Franklin, and other supports sent him from Washington, he would give no respite to the enemy, and push him into the Potomac. It turned out differently.

The loss by capitulation of Harper's Ferry. It is a blow to us, and very likely a disgraceful affair, not for the soldiers, but for the commanders.

September 19. — Five days' fighting. Our brave Hooker wounded ; tremendous loss of life on both sides, and no decisive results. These last battles, and those on the Chickahominy, that of Shiloh, in one word all the fightings protracted throughout several consecutive days, are almost unexampled in history. These horrible episodes establish the bravery, the endurance of the soldiers, the bravery and the ability of some among the commanders of the corps, of the divisions, etc., and the absence of any *generalship in the commander.*

September 20. — Until this day Gen. McClellan has not published one single detailed report about any of his operations since the evacuation of Manassas in March. Thus much for the staff of the army of the Potomac. We shall see what detailed report he will publish of the campaign in

Maryland. McClellan's bulletins from Maryland are twins to his bulletins from the Peninsula; and there may be very little difference between the *gained* victories. To-day he is ignorant of the movements of the enemy, and has more than 30,-000 fresh troops in hand.

As in the Peninsula, so in Maryland. Although having nearly one-third more men than the enemy, General McClellan never forced the enemy to engage at once its whole force, never attacked the rebels on their whole line, and never had any positive notion about the number and the position of the opposing forces.

The rebels had the Potomac in their rear; our army pressed them in front, and — the rebels escaped.

I appeal to such military heroes as Hooker; I appeal to thousands of our brave soldiers, from generals down to the rank and file, and further I appeal to all women with hearts and brains here and in Europe.

September 20.— Gen. Mansfield killed at the head of his brigade. I ask his forgiveness for all the criticism made upon him in this diary. Last year, at the beginning of the war, Gen. Mansfield acted under the orders of Gen. Scott. This explains all.

As in the slaughters of the Chickahominy, so in the Maryland slaughters, *nobody hurt* in McClellan's numerous staff. Thank Heaven! Not only his life is charmed, but the charm extends over all who surround him, — men and beasts.

A malediction sticks to our cause. Hooker badly, very badly wounded. Hooker fought the greatest number of fights,— was never worsted in the Peninsula, nor in the August disasters, and he alone has the supreme honor of a nick-name, by the troopers' baptism : the *Fighting Joe*. Hooker, not McClellan, ought to command the army. But no pestilential Washington clique, none of the West-Pointers, back him, and the pets, the pretorians, may have refused to obey his orders.

After the escape of the rebels from Manassas in March, and after the evacuation of Yorktown, all the intriguers and traitors grouped around the New York Herald, and the imbeciles around the New York Times, prized high *the masterly strategy* and its bloodless victories. Now, in dead, by powder and disease, in crippled, etc., McClellan destroyed about 100,000 men, and the country's honor is bleeding, the country's cause is on the verge of a precipice.

How rare are men of civic heroism, of fearless civic courage ; men of the creed: *perisse mon nom mais que la patrie soit sauvée.*

General Wadsworth feels more deeply and more painfully the disasters, nay, the disgrace, of the country, than do almost all with whom I meet here. During the Congress, similar were the feelings of Senator Wade, Judge Potter, and of many other Congressmen in both the Houses. So feel Boutwell, Andrew, the Governor of Massachusetts, and I am sure many, many over the country.

But the sensation-men and preachers, lecturers, etc., alla re to be *   *   *   *

September 22. — By Mr. Seward's policy and by McClellan's strategy and war-bulletins the bravest and the most intelligent people became the laughing-stock of Europe and of the world.   And thus is witnessed the hitherto in history unexampled phenomenon of a devoted and brave people of twenty millions, mastering all the wealth and the resources of modern civilization, worsted and kept at bay by four to five million rebels, likewise brave, but almost beggared, and cut off from all external communications.

Sept. 23.   Proclamation *conditionally* abolishing slavery from 1863.   The *conditional* is the last desperate effort made by Mr. Lincoln and by Mr. Seward to save slavery.   Poor Mr. Lincoln was obliged to strike such a blow at his *mammy!*   The two statesmen found out that it was dangerous longer to resist the decided, authoritative will of the masses.   The words " resign," " depose," " impeach," were more and more distinct in the popular murmur, and the proclamation was issued.

Very little, if any, credit is due to Mr. Lincoln or to Mr. Seward for having thus late and reluctantly *legalized* the stern will of the immense majority of the American people.   For the sake of sacred-truth and justice I protest before civilization, humanity, and posterity, that Mr. Lincoln and Mr. Seward intrinsically are wholly innocent of this great satisfaction given to the right, and to national honor.   24

The absurdity of colonization is preserved in the proclamation.   How could it have been otherwise?

But if the rebellion is crushed before January 1st, 1863, what then?   If the rebels turn loyal before that term?   Then the people of the North will be cheated.   Happily for humanity and for national honor, Mr. Lincoln's and Mr. Seward's benevolent expectations will be baffled; the rebels will spurn the tenderly proffered leniency; these rebels are so ungrateful towards those who " cover the weakness of the insurgents," &c.   (See the celebrated, and by the American press much admired, despatch in May or June, 1862, Seward to Adams.)

The proclamation is written in the meanest and the most dry routine style; not a word to evoke a generous thrill, not a word reflecting the warm and lofty comprehension and feelings of the immense majority of the people on this question of emancipation.   Nothing for humanity, nothing to humanity. Whoever drew it, be he Mr. Lincoln or Mr. Seward, it is clear that the writer was not in it either with his heart or with his soul; it is clear that it was done under moral duress, under the throttling pressure of events.   How differently Stanton would have spoken !

General Wadsworth truly says, that never a noble subject was more belittled by the form in which it was uttered.   .

Brazilian m——s are much disturbed by the proclamation.

Sept. 23.   In his answer to the Paisley Parliamentary Reform Association, Mr. Seward complains that the sympathy of Europe turns now for secession.

O Mr. Seward, Mr. Seward, who is it that contributed to turn the current against the cause of right and of humanity? Months ago I and others warned you; the premonitory signs and the reasons of this change have been pointed out to you. Now you slander Europe, of which you know as little as of the inhabitants of the moon. The generous populations of the whole of Europe expected and waited for a positive, unhesitating, clear recognition of human rights; day after day the generous European minds expected to see some positive, authoritative fact confirm that lofty conception which, at the start of this rebellion, they had of the cause of the North. But the pure, generous tendencies of the American people became officially, authoritatively misrepresented; the public opinion in Europe became stuffed with empty generalizations, with official but unfulfilled prophecies, and with cold declamations. Those official generalizations, prophecies, and declamations, the supineness shown by the administration in the recognition of human rights, all this began to be considered in Europe as being sanctioned by the whole American people; and generous European hearts and minds began to avert in disgust from the *misrepresented* cause of the North.

Two issues are before history, before the philosophy of history, and before the social progress of our race. The first issue is the struggle between the pure democratic spirit embodied in the Free States, and the fetid remains of the worst part of humanity embodied in the South. The second issue is between the perennial vitality of the principle of self-government in the people, and the transient and accidental results of the self-government as manifested in Mr. Lincoln, in Mr. Seward, and their followers. I hope that this Diary will throw some light on the second issue, and vindicate the perennial against the transient and the accidental.

Sept. 24. If the events of this war should progress as they are foreshadowed in the proclamation of September 22, then the application of this proclamation may create inextricable complications. Not only in one and the same State, but in one and the same district, nay, even in the same township, after January 1st, 1863, may be found Africo-Americans, portions of whom are emancipated, the others in bondage. But the stern logic of events will- save the illogical, pusillanimous, confused half-measure, as it now is. (O Steffens !)

General McClellan confesses that if Hooker had not been wounded, then *the road*, by which the retreat of the rebels might have been cut off, would have been taken. Such a declaration is the most emphatic recognition of Hooker's superior military capacity. Seldom, however, has the loss of a general commanding only *en second*, or a wing, as did Hooker, decided the fortunes of the day. Why did not McClellan take *the road* himself, after Hooker was obliged to leave the field ? When Desaix, Bessières, and Lannes fell, Napoleon nevertheless won the respective battles.

Sept. 25. The military position of the rebels in Winchester seems to me one of the best they ever held in this war. Winchester is the centre of which Washington, Harper's Ferry, Williamsport, nay, even Wheeling, seem to be the circumference. Our army under McClellan is almost beyond the circle, crosses not the Potomac, and is now only to watch the enemy. So much for the great McClellan's victory. Truly, the enemy may be taken in the rear, its communications with Richmond, &c., cut off and destroyed; but *we are safe* on the Potomac, and this is sufficient. McClellan is *the man of large conceptions and rapid execution.* The best generals are *hors de combat;* as to Halleck, O, it is not to think, not to speak. Well, I may be mistaken, but I clearly see all this on the map of Virginia.

Sept. 25. The West Point spirit persecutes Sigel with the utmost rage. The West Point spirit seemingly wishes to have Sigel dishonored, defeated, even if the country be thereby destroyed. The Hallecks, &c., keep him in a subordinate position; *three days ago* his corps was a little over seven thousand, almost no cavalry, and most of the artillery without horses, and he in front.

The more I scrutinize the President's thus called emancipation proclamation, the more cunning and less good will and sincerity I find therein. I hope I am mistaken. But the proclamation is only an act of the military power, — is evoked by military

24 *

necessity, — and not a civil, social, humane act of justice and equity.

The only good to be derived from this proclamation is, that for the first time the word *freedom*, and a general comprehension of " emancipation," appear in an official act under the sanction of the formula, and are inaugurated into the official, the constitutional life of the nation. In itself it is therefore a great event for a people so strictly attached to legality and to formulas.

I do not recollect to have read in the history of any great, or even of a small captain, — above all of such a one when between thirty-four and thirty-six years old, — that he followed the army under his command in a travelling carriage and six, when the field of operations extended from fifty to seventy miles. Three cheers for McClellan, for his carriage and six !

HOW THE GREAT CAPTAIN WAS TO CATCH THE WHOLE REBEL ARMY IN MANASSAS, IN FEBRUARY AND MARCH, A. D. 1862.

It was to have been done by a brilliant and unsurpassable stroke of combined strategy, tactics, manœuvres, marches, and swimmings; also on land and water. (O, hear! O, hear!)

As every body knows, the rebels were encamped in the so *fearful* strongholds of Centreville and Manassas, all the time fooling the commander-in-chief of the federal army in relation to their *immense* numbers. To attack the rebels in front,

or to surround them by the Occoquan and Brentsville, would have been a too — simple operation;
by a special, an immense, space-embracing anaconda
strategy, the rebel army was to be cut off from the
whole of rebeldom, and forced to surrender *en masse*
to the inventor of (the not yet patented, I hope)
bloodless victories.   To accomplish such an immense result, a fleet of transports was already ordered to be gathered at Annapolis.   On them in
ten or fifteen days (O, hear!) an army of fifty to
sixty thousand, most·completely equipped, was to
be embarked, plus forty thousand in Washington,
all this to sail under the personal command of the
general-in-chief, and sail towards Richmond.   Richmond taken, the rebel army at Manassas would have
been cut off, and obliged to surrender on any terms.

The above splendid conception was, and still is,
peddled among the army and among the nation by
the admirers of, and the devotees of, anaconda
strategy.

The expedition was to land at the mouth of the
Tappahannock, a small port, or rather a creek, used
for shipping of a small quantity of tobacco.   As the
port or creek has only some small attempts at
wharves, the landing of such an enormous army, with
parks of artillery, with cavalry, pontoons, and material for constructing bridges, — the landing would
not have been executed in weeks, if in months; but
the projector of the plan, perfectly losing the notion
of time, calculated for ten days.   From that port
the *flying* expedition was to march directly on Rich-

mond through a country having only common field and dirt roads, and this in a season when all roads generally are in an impassable condition, through a country intersected by marshy streams, principal among them the Matapony and the Pamunkey — to march towards Richmond and the Chickahominy marshes. It seems that Chickahominy exercised an attractive, Armida-like charm on the great strategian. An army loaded with such immense trains would have sufficiently destroyed all the roads, and rendered them impassable for itself; and the *flying* expedition would at once have been transformed into an expedition sticking in the mud, similar to that subsequent in the peninsula. The enemy was in possession of Fredericksburg and of the railroad to Hanover Court House on one flank, and of all the best roads north of and through Chickahominy marshes on the other flank. The *flying* expedition would have had for base Tappahannock and a dirt road. O strategy! O stuff!

The much-persecuted General McDowell exposed the worse than crudity of the brilliant conception. By doing this, McDowell saved the country, the administration, and the strategian from immense losses and from a nameless shame. It is due to the people that the administration lay before the public the scheme and the refutation. A look on the map of Virginia must convince even the simplest mind of the brilliancy of this conception.

During all this time spent in such masterly operations, the rebel army in Manassas was to quietly

look on, to wait, and not move, not retreat on Richmond. Early in March, at once the rebel army,
always undisturbed, quietly disappeared from Manassas; and this is the best evidence of the depth
of that brilliant combination, peddled under the
name of the *flying expedition to Richmond*, pro-
jected for January, February, or March. I appeal
to the verdict of sound reason; the parties are,
common sense *versus* anaconda strategy and bloodless victories.

Sept. 27. The proclamation issued by the war
power of the President is not yet officially notified
to those who alone are to execute it — the armies
and their respective commanders. Who is to be
taken in? The papers publish a detailed account
of an interview between the President and an anti-
slavery deputation from Chicago. The deputation
asked for stringent measures in the spirit of the law
of Congress, which orders the emancipation of the
slaves held by the rebels. The President combated
the reasons alleged by the deputation, and tried to
establish the danger and the inefficiency of the
measure. A few days after the above-mentioned debate, the President issued the proclamation of September 22. Are his heart, his soul, and his convictions to be looked for in the debate, or in the proclamation?

The immense majority of the people, from the in-
most of its heart, greets the proclamation — a proof
how deeply and ardently was felt its necessity. The
gratitude shown to Mr. Lincoln for having thus exe-

cuted the will of his master, — this gratitude is the best evidence how this whole people is better, has a loftier comprehension of right and duty, than have its elected servants.

McClellan already speaks that the campaign is finished, and the army is to go into winter quarters. If the people, if the administration, and if the army will stand this, then they will justly deserve the scorn of the whole civilized and uncivilized world. But with such civil and military chiefs all is possible, all may be expected to be included in their programme of — vigorous operations.

Sept. 28.ʹ For some weeks I watch a conspiracy of the West Pointers, of the commanders-in-chief, of the staffs, and of the double know-nothing cliques united against Sigel. The aim seems to be to put Sigel and his purposely-reduced and disorganized forces in such a condition and position that he may be worsted or destroyed by the enemy. To avoid dishonoring the forces under him, to avoid exposing them to slaughter, and to avoid being thus himself dishonored, Sigel ought to resign, and make public the reasons of his resignation. A few days ago, I wrote and warned the Evening Post; but — but —

The Richmond papers confirm what I supposed concerning the motives which pushed the rebel army across the Potomac. As the Marylanders rose not in arms, and joined not the rebel army, the invaders had nothing else to do but to retreat and to recross the Potomac. McClellan ought to have thrown them into the river, which Hooker, if not wounded, would have done, or if he had the command of our army.

The rebels would have retreated into Virginia, even without being attacked by McClellan, even if he only followed them, say at one day's distance. Not having destroyed the rebels, McClellan, in reality, and from the military stand point, accomplished very little — near to nothing.   Hooker estimates the rebel force, at the utmost, at eighty thousand men, and that is all that they could have.   McClellan had about one hundred and twenty thousand. And — and he is to be considered the savior of Maryland and of Pennsylvania.   O, good American people!   The genuine Napoleon won all his great . battles against armies which considerably outnumbered his.

Mr. Seward menaces England with issuing *letters of marque* against the Southern privateers.   The menace is ridiculous, because it will not be carried out, and, if carried out, it will become still more ridiculous; it would be a very poor compliment to the navy to use the whole power of private enterprise against a few rovers, and it would be an official recognition of the rebels in the condition of belligerents.   *Quousque tandem* — O Seward — *abutere patientiam nostram ?*

Sept. 30.   Nearly three weeks after the battle of Antietam, General McClellan publishes what he and they call a report of his operations in Maryland; in all not twenty lines, and devoted principally to establish — on probabilities — the numerical losses of the enemy.   The report is a fit *pendant* to his bulletins; is excellent for bunkum, and to make other people justly laugh at us.

OCTOBER, 1862.

Costly Infatuation — The do-nothing strategy — Cavalry on lame horses
— Bayonet charges — Antietam —- Effect of the proclamation — Disas-
ters in the West — The abolitionists not originally hostile to McClellan —
Helplessness in the War Department — Devotedness of the people —
McClellan and the proclamation — Wilkes — Colonel Key — Routine engineers — Rebel raid into Pennsylvania — Stanton's sincerity — O, unfighting strategians! — The administration a success — *De gustibus* —
Stuart's raid — West Point — St. Domingo — The President's letter to
McClellan — Broad church — The elections — The Republican party
gone — The remedy at the polls — McClellan wants to be relieved —
Mediation — Compromise — The rhetors. — The optimists — The foreigners — Scott and Buchanan — Gladstone — Foreign opinion and action — Both the extremes to be put down — Spain — Fremont's campaign
against Jackson — Seward's circular — General Scott's gift — " O, could
I go to a camp!" — McClellan crosses the Potomac — Prays for rain —
Fevers decimate the regiments — Martindale and Fitz John Porter —
The political balance to be preserved — New regiments — O, poor
country!

WITH what a bloody sacrifice of men this people
pays for its infatuation in McClellan, for the moral
cowardice of its official leaders, and the intrigues and
the imbecility of the regulars, of some among the
West Pointers, of traitors led by the New York
Herald, by the World, and by certain Unionists on
the outside, and secessionists at heart! All these
combined nourish the infatuation. All things compared, Napoleon cost not so much to the French
people, and at least Napoleon paid it in glory. Mind

and heart sicken to witness all this here. The question to-day is, not to strengthen other generals, as Heintzelman and Sigel, and to take the enemy in the rear, but to give a *chance* to McClellan to win the ever-expected, and not yet by him won, *great battle*. McClellan continually calls for more men ; all the vital forces of the people are absorbed by him ; and when he has large numbers, he is incapable of using and handling them ; so it was at the Chickahominy, so it was at Antietam. In the way that McClellan acts now, he may use up all the available forces of the people, if nobody has the courage to speak out ; besides, any warning voice is drowned in the treacherous intrigues of the clique, in imbecility and infatuation.

At the meeting of the governors, at the various public conventions, in the thus called public resolutions — platforms, in one word — wherever, in any way, North, West, and East, the public life of the people has made its voice heard : *a vigorous prosecution of the war* was, and is, earnestly recommended to the administration. All this will be of no avail. By this time, by bloody and bitter experience, the American people ought to have learned it. With his civil and military aids and lieutenants, as the McClellans, the Hallecks, the Sewards, Mr. Lincoln has been at work ; and at the best, they have shown their utter incapacity, if not ill-will, to carry the war on vigorously and upon strictly military principles. Many persons in Washington know that Mr. Seward last winter firmly backed the *do-*

nothing strategy, in the firm belief that the rebels would be worried out, and submit without fighting. To those statesmen and Napoleons, Carnots, &c., it is as impossible to manœuvre with rapidity, to strike boldly and decidedly, as to dance on their *well-furnished* heads. Only such a good-natured people as the Americans can expect *something* from that whole *caterva*. To expect from Mr. Lincoln's Napoleons, Carnots, &c., vigorous and rapid military operations, is the same as to mount cavalry on thoroughly lame horses, and order it to charge *à fond de train*.

The worshippers of McClellan peddle that the Antietam victory became neutralized because the enemy fell back on its second and third line. Whatever may be in this falling back on lines, and accepting all as it is represented, one thing is certain, that when commanders win victories, generally they give no time to the enemy to fall back in order on its second and third lines. But every thing gets a new stamp under the new Napoleon. A few hours after the Antietam battle, General McClellan telegraphed that he "*knew not* if the enemy retreated into the interior or to the Potomac." O, O!

Many from among the European officers here have some experience of the manœuvring of large bodies — experience acquired on fields of battle, and on reviews, and those camp manœuvres annually practised all over Europe. In this way the European officers, more or less, have the *coup d'œil* for space and for the *terrain*, so necessary when an army is to be put in positions on a field of battle, and which *coup d'œil* few young American officers had the occasion to acquire. If judiciously selected for the duties of the staffs, such European officers would be of use and support to generals but for jealousy and the West Point cliques.

During this whole war I hear every body, but above all the West Point wiseacres and strategians, assert that charges with the bayonet and hand-to hand fighting are exceedingly rare occurrences in the course of any campaign. It is useless to speak to all those great judges of experience and of history.

In the account of the battles of Ligny and of Waterloo, Thiers mentions four charges with the bayonet and hand-to-hand fighting at Ligny, and nine at Waterloo, wherein one was made by the English, one was made by Prussians and by French, and one by the French with bayonet against English cavalry. In 1831 the Poles used the bayonet more than it was used in any one campaign known in history. O, West Point!

It deserves to be noticed that the conspirators against Pope and McDowell, and the pet pretorians of September 6 and 7, distinguished themselves not very much in the battle of Antietam. Hooker commanded McDowell's corps.

To the number of evils inflicted upon this country by the McClellan infatuation, must be added the fact that many young men, with otherwise sound intellects, have been taken in, stultified, poisoned beyond cure, by high-sounding words, as strategy, all-embracing scientific combinations, &c. — words identified with incapacity, defeats, and intrigue.

In all probability, Hooker alone, when he fought, had a fixed plan at the Antietam battle. As for a general plan, aiming either to throw the enemy into the river, or to cut him from the river, or to accomplish something final and decisive, seemingly no such plan existed. It looks as if they had ignored, at the headquarters, what kind of positions were occupied by the enemy; and the only purpose seems to have been to fight, but without having any preconceived plan. This, at least, is the conclusion from the manner in which the battle was fought. If any plan had existed, the brave army would have executed it; but the enemy retreated in order, and rather unmolested. *As always, so this time, the bravery of the army did every thing; and, as a matter of course, the generalship did—nothing.*

Oct. 4. The proclamation of September 22 may not produce in Europe the effect and the enthusiasm which it might have evoked if issued a year ago, as an act of justice and of self-conscientious force, as an utterance of the lofty, pure, and ardent aspirations and will of a high-minded people. Europe may see now in the proclamation an action of despair made in the duress of events; (and so it is in reality for Mr. Lincoln, Seward, and their squad.) And in this way, a noble deed, outpouring from the soul of the people, is reduced to pygmy and mean proportions by ——. The name is on every body's lips.

But it was impossible to issue this proclamation last year; at that time the master-spirit of Mr. Lincoln's administration emphatically assured the diplomats that the Union will be preserved, *were slavery — to rule in Boston.*

The continued disasters in the West can easily be explained by the fact, that those rotten skeletons, Crittenden, Davis, and Wickliffe control the operations of the generals.

Among the countless lies peddled by Mc Clellan's worshippers, the most enormous and the most impudent is that one by which they attempt to explain, what in their lingo they call, the hostility of the abolitionists towards Mc Clellan. Concerning this matter, I can speak with perfect knowledge of almost all the circumstances.

Not one abolitionist of whatever · hue, not one republican whatever, was in any way troubled or thought about the political convictions of General Mc Clellan at the time when he was put at the head of the army. All the abolitionists and republicans, who then earnestly wished, and now wish, to have the rebellion crushed, expected General Mc Clellan to do it by quick, decisive, soldier-like, military operations, manœuvres, and fights. Senators Wade, Chandler, Trumbull, &c., in October, 1861, principally aided Mc Clellan to become independent of General Scott. When, however, weeks and months elapsed without any soldier-like action, manifestation, or enterprise whatever, all those who were in earnest began to feel uneasy, began to murmur,

*not in reference to any political opinions, whatever,
held by General McClellan, but solely and exclusively on account of his military supineness. All
those who ardently wished, and wish, that neither
slaveholders nor slavery be hurt in any way, such
ones early grouped themselves around General
McClellan, believing to have found in him the
man after their own heart. . That cesspool of all
infamies, the New York Herald, became the mouth-
piece of all the like hypocrites. They and the Herald were the first to pervert and to misrepresent the
indignation-evoked by the do-nothing or nobody-hurt
strategy, and to call it the abolition outcry against
their fetish.*

Scarcely will it be believed what disorder, what
helplessness, and what incapacity rule paramount
in the expedition of any current business in the
strictly military part of the War Department. It
is worse than any imaginable red-tape and circum-
locution. And all this, being considered a speciality and a technicality, is in the exclusive hands
of the adjutant general, a master spirit among the
West Pointers. Generally, all relating to the thus
celebrated organization of the army is an exclusive
work of the West Point wisdom — is handled by
West Pointers; and, nevertheless, the general comprehension of all details in relation to an army,
how it is to be handled, all the military details of
responsibility, of higher discipline, &c., all this is
confusion, and strikes with horror any one either
familiar with such matters or using freely his sound

sense. A narrow routine which may have been
innocuous with an army of sixteen thousand with
General Scott and in peace, became highly mischievous when the army increased more than fifty
times, and the war raged furiously. All this confusion is specially produced by the wiseacres and doctors of routine. Undoubtedly it reacts on the army,
and shows of what use for the country is, and was,
that whole old nursery.

Wherever one turns his eyes, every where a deep
line separates the patriotic activity of the people
from the official activity. With the people all is
sacrifice, devotion, grandeur, and purity of purpose,
by great and small, by rich and poor, and with the
poor, if possible, even more than with the rich.
With the highest and higher officials it is either
weakness, or egotism, or coolness, or intrigue, or
ignorance, or helplessness. The exceptions are few,
and have been repeatedly pointed out. ·

Oct. 8. General McClellan's order to the army
concerning the President's proclamation shows up
the man. Not a word about the object in the
proclamation, but rather unveiled insinuations that
the army is dissatisfied with emancipation, and that
it may mutiny. The army ought to feel highly
honored by such insinuations in that lengthy disquisition about his ·(McClellan's) position and the
duties of the army. For the honor of the brave,
armed citizen-patriots it can be emphatically asserted that the patriotic volunteers better know
their duties than do those who preach to them.

Some suspect that Mr. Seward drew the paper for McClellan, but I am sure this cannot be. It may have been done by Bennett or some other of the Herald, or by Barlow. If this order is the result of Mr. Lincoln's visit to the camp, and of a transaction with Mac-Napoleon, then the President has not thereby increased the dignity of his presidential character.

Wilkes's Spirit of the Times incommensurably towers above the New York Press by its dauntless patriotism; by its clear, broad, and deep comprehension of the condition of the country.

Colonel Key's disclosures concerning the McClellan-Halleck programme, not to destroy the rebels and the rebellion until the next presidential election, are throttled by the dismissal of the colonel. But what he said, if put by the side of the words of the order to the army, that " the remedy for political errors, if any are committed, is to be found only in the action of the people at the polls," — all this ought to open even the most obtuse intellects.

Poor (Carlyle fashion) old Greeley hurrahs for McClellan and for the order No. 163 to the army. O for new and young men to swim among new and young events!

Oct. 11. Will any body in this country have the patriotic courage to reform the army? that is, to dismiss from the service the West Point clique in Washington and in the army of the Potomac. Such a proof of strong will cannot be expected from the

President; but perhaps Congress may show it. Those first and second scholars or graduates from West Point are all routine engineers; and who ever heard of whole armies commanded, moved, and manœuvred by engineers? American invention; but not to be patented for Europe.

Oct. 11.. The rebel raid into Pennsylvania, under the nose of McClellan. Is there any thing in the world capable of opening this people's eyes?

I doubt if at any time, and in the life of any great or small people, there existed such a galaxy of civil and military rulers, chiefs, and leaders, stripped of nobler manhood, as are the *great men* here. The blush of honor never burned their cheeks! O, the low politicians! Some persons doubt Stanton's sincerity in his dealings with individuals. I am not a judge thereof; but were it so, it can easily be forgiven if he only remains sincere and true to the cause.

One is amazed and even aghast at the impudence of the McClellan and West Point cliques. In their lingo, heroes like Kearney, like Hooker and Heintzelman, all such are superciliously mentioned as *only fighting generals.* O, unfighting strategians!

Stuart's brilliant raid. was executed the day of McClellan's bombastic proclamation about his having cleared Pennsylvania and Maryland of the the enemy. On the same day McClellan and other generals straggled about the country, visiting cities hundreds of miles distant from the camp. And such generals complain of straggling! Make the army fight! inspire with confidence the soldier — then he will not straggle.

The Evening Post, October 13, demonstrates that up to this day Mr. Lincoln's administration is " a grand and brilliant success." Well, *de gustibus non est disputandum.* Others may rightly think that the achievements enumerated by the Evening Post are exclusively due to the people ; that by the people they were forced upon the administration, (Stanton and the navy excepted ;) and that the numerous failures, the waste of human life, of money, and of time, are to be logically and directly traced to the administration. O, subserviency !

The McClellanites are indignant against the Pennsylvanians for not having caught Stuart and his three thousand horse. Bravo ! And what is the army for ? and, above all, what are the so expensive commander and his staff for ?

It is perhaps natural that many. from among the republican leaders attempt to prop up the reputation of Mr. Lincoln's administrative capacity, to kindle a halo around his name, and to sponge the waste of blood, of means, and of time, from the tracks of his Seward-Scott-Blair administration ; but stern historical justice shall not, and cannot, do it.

Whatever be the high *military and scientific prowess* shown by the first West Point graduates and scholars, all this in no way compensates for the *summum* of perverted notions which are reared there, and for the mock, sham, and clownish aris-

tocracy by which a high-toned West Pointer is
easily recognized. Of course many and many
are the exceptions; many West Point pupils are
animated by the noblest and purest American
spirit; but the genuine West Point spirit consists
in sneering and looking down with contempt at the
mother and nurse; that is, at the purely republican, purely democratic political institutions, at the
broad political and intellectual freedom to which
those clown-aristocrats owe their rearing, their little bit of information, and those shoulder-stripes by
which they are so mightily inflated.

What silly talk, to compare the St. Domingo
insurrection with the eventual results of emancipation in the South! In St. Domingo the slaves were
obliged to tear their liberty from the slaveholding
planter, and from a government siding with the
oppressor. Here the lawful government gives
liberty to a peaceful laborer, and the planter is an
outlawed traitor. But the genuine pro-slavery
democrat is stupidly obtuse.

Oct. 18. A few days ago the President wrote a
letter to McClellan, with ability and lucidity, exposing to view the military urgency of a movement on the enemy with an army of one hundred
and forty thousand men, as has now McClellan at
Harper's Ferry. But the letter ends by saying that
all that it contains is *not* to be considered by
McNapoleon as being an order. Of course Mac
obeys — the last injunction of the letter. Mr. Lincoln wishes not to hurt the great Napoleon's feel-

ings ; as for hurting the country, the people, the cause, this is of — no consequence ! Ah ! to witness all this is to be chained, and to die of thirst within the reach of the purest water.

Reverend Dr. Unitarian Sensation's broad church, admirer of the Southern gentleman, and a Jeremy Diddler.

Oct. 18. The elections in several of the States evidence the deep imprint upon the country · of Lincoln-Seward disorganizing, because from the first day vacillating, undecided, both-ways policy. The elections reverberate the moral, the political, and the belligerent condition in which the country is dragged and thrown by those two *master spirits*. No decided principle inspires them and their administration, and no principle leads and has a decided majority in the elections; neither the democrats nor the republicans prevail ; neither freedom nor submission is the watchword ; and finally, neither the North nor the South is decidedly the master on the fields of battle. All is confusion !

Scarcely one genuine republican was, or is, in the cabinet; the republican party is completely on the wane — and perhaps beyond redemption ; all this is a logical result, and was easily to be foreseen by any body, — only not by the wiseacres of the party, not by the republican papers in New York, as the Times, the Tribune, and the Evening Post, only not by the Sumners, Doolittles, and many of the like leaders, all of whom, when, about a year ago, warned against such a cataclysm, self-confidently smiled ; but who soon will cry more bitter tears than did the daughters of Judah over the ruins of Jerusalem.

And now likewise the phrase in McClellan's order No. 163, about "the remedy at the polls," the disclosures made by Colonel Key, receive their fullest, but ominous and cursed, signification.; and now the blind can see that it is policy, and not altogether incapacity, in McClellan to have made a war to preserve slavery and the rebels. And thus McClellan outwitted Mr. Lincoln.

In general, human nature is passionately attracted, nay, is subdued, by energy, above all by civic intrepidity. . It would have been so easy for Mr. Lincoln to carry the masses, and to avoid those disasters at the polls! But stubbornness is not energy.

From a very reliable source I learn that a few days after the battle of Antietam, General McClellan, or at least General or Colonel Marcy, of McClellan's staff, insinuated to the President that General McClellan would wish to be relieved from the command of the army, and be assigned to quiet duties in Washington — very likely to supersede Halleck. And the President seized not by the hairs the occasion to get rid of the nation's nightmare, together with the pets of the commander of the army of the Potomac. McClellan acted honestly in making the above insinuation; he is now, in part at least, irresponsible for any future disaster and blood.

Oct. 20. I have strong indications that European powers, as England and France, are very sanguine to mediate, but would do it only if, and when, *asked* by

26

our government. Those two governments, or some other half-friendly, may, semi-officially, insinuate to Mr. Seward to make such a demand. A few months ago, already Mr. Dayton wrote from Paris something about such a step. Mr. Seward is desperate, down-cast, and may believe he can serve his country by committing the cabinet to some such combination. I must warn Stanton and others.

In the Express and in the World the New York Herald found its masters in ignominy.

More or less mean, contemptible ambition among the helmsmen, but patriotism, patriotic ambition are below zero — here in Washington. For the sake and honor of human nature, I pray to destiny Stanton may not fail, and still count among the Wadsworths, the Wades, and the like pure patriots.

The democratic elections and majorities united to Mr. Seward may enforce a compromise, and God knows if Mr. Lincoln will oppose it to the last. Then the only seeming salvation of the north will be the indomitable decision of the rebels not to accept any terms except a full recognition.

Oct. 22. The incapacity of the military wise-acres borders on idiotism, if not on something worse. To do nothing McClellan absorbs every man, and keeps one hundred and forty thousand men on the Maryland side of the Potomac. Sigel has only a small command of twelve thousand men, in a position where, with one quarter of what is useless under McClellan, with his skill, his activity, and the *truly* patriotic devotion of his troops, of his officers, and of the commanders under him, Sigel would force the rebels to retreat from Winchester, and otherwise damage them far more than *will* or can do such McClellans, Hallecks, and all this c——e.

One of the greatest misfortunes for the American people is to have considered as statesmen the rhetors, the petty politicians, and the speech-makers. Now, those rhetors, petty politicians, and speech-makers are at the helm, are in the Senate, and — ruin the country.

The optimists and the subservients still console themselves and confuse the people by asserting that Mr. Lincoln will yet *come out* as a man and a statesman. Previous to such a happy change the country's honor and the country's political and material vitality will *run out*.

More than a year ago Mr. Seward said to the Prince Salm and to me, that this war ought to be fought out by foreigners; that the Americans fought the revolutionary war, but now they are devoted to peaceful pursuits; and that it is the duty of Europeans to save this refuge from the thraldoms in the old world.

Now, I see that Mr. Seward was right, although in a sense different from that in which he uttered the above sentence.

The Irish excepted, all the other 'foreign-born Americans, but preëminently the Germans, are more in communion with the lofty, pure, and humane element in the thus called American principle, are therefore more in communion with the creed of the

304 .   D I A R Y .   [October, 1862.

immense majority of Americans, than are they, the
present dabblers in politics, the would-be leaders,
(civil and military,) the would-be statesmen, all of
whom are eaten up by the admixture into what is
vital and perennial in the signification of America,
of all that in itself is local, muddy, petty, accidental, and transient.

Oct. 23. The recent publication of General
Scott's letter, and of a writing to President Buchanan, confirms my opinion that "the highest
military authority in the land" faltered after March
4, 1861, and inaugurated that defensive warfare
wherein we *stick* on the Potomac until this day.

Pseudo-liberal right-honorable Gladstone asserts
that Jeff. Davis "has made the South a nation;"
then Abraham Lincoln, with W. H. Seward and
G. B. McClellan, have destroyed a noble and generous nation.

England may now recognize the South, France
may join in it, but other great European powers, as
Russia, Spain, Prussia, Austria, will not follow in
such a wake. The recognition will not materially
improve the condition of the rebels, nor raise the
blockade. But as soon as recognized, Jeff. D. may
ask for a mediation, which the people — if not Mr.
Seward — will spurn. An armed mediation remains
to be applied, wherein, likewise, the other European powers will not concur. An armed mediation
between the two principles will be the *summum* of
infamy to which English aristocracy and English
mercantilism can degrade itself; if Louis Napoleon

joins therein, then his crown is not worth two years
lease, provided the Orleans have ——

If we should succumb under the united efforts of
imbecility, of pro-slavery treason, of Anglo-Franco-
European and of American perjury, then

Ultima cœlestis terram Astræa reliquit.

Oct. 25.   Only two or three days ago, in a conversation with a diplomat, Mr. Seward asserted that
both the extreme parties will be mastered — that
is, the secessionists and the abolitionists.   So Mr.
Seward confesses the *credo* and the gospel of the
New York Herald, the World, the Journal of Commerce, the National Intelligencer, and other similar
organs of secession.

Notwithstanding the numerous complications naturally generated by the vicinity of Cuba to Secessia, the Spanish government, Count Serrano, the
captain-general of Cuba, and Tassara, the Spanish
minister here, all have maintained the most loyal
relations towards the Federal government.   It were
to be very much regretted if a drunkard or a brute,
as in the affair of the Montgomery, should disturb
such relations.

Oct. 26.   McClellan-Blair-Seward tactics are
crowned with splendid success.   By his *simplicity*
Mr. Lincoln aided therein as much as he could.
The bad season is in; any successful campaign
impossible.   The rebels will be safe, and Gladstone
justified.

26 * .

It is so difficult to find out the truth concerning Fremont's campaign against Jackson, that some generalship may, after all, be credited to him. At any rate Fremont is a better general than McClellan and the pets in command under him, and Fremont is with his heart and soul in the cause, of which the McClellanites cannot be accused, all of them, their fetish included, having no heart and no soul.

Old Europe, and, above all, official Europe, and even the Gladstones, must be vindicated. Official Europe generally appreciates nations by their leaders. Europe demands from such leaders actions and proofs of statesmanship, of high capacity, if not of heroism. The attempt to astonish Europe by speeches, by oratory, and, still worse, by second-rate legal arguments, by what is called papers here, and in Europe diplomatic circulars and despatches, is the same as the attempt to eclipse bright sunlight with a burning candle. But our orators, and, above all, Mr Seward, flooded the European and the English statesmen with their, at the best, indifferent productions. Official Europe was favored with a shower of three various editions of *papers relating to foreign relations* in 1862, issued by the *State Department*, together with the Sanfords, the Weeds, the Hugheses, *et hoc genus omne.* Undoubtedly, the traitor Mason shows in England more of fire than does the cold, stiff, prickly, and dignified son and grandson of Presidents; and then the average of our press! O, Jemima!

In his circular, September 22, to our agents in Europe, Mr. Seward belies not himself. The emancipation is rather coldly announced, and it is visible that neither Mr. Seward's heart nor soul is in it.

The President has now the most reliable information that when Corinth was invested by Halleck, the rebel troops were wholly demoralized, and the enemy was astonished not to be attacked, as very little resistance would have been made. So much for General Scott's gift in Halleck.

The almost daily occurrences here long ago would have exasperated the hot-headed and warm-hearted nations in Europe, and treason would have become their watchword. O American people! thou art warm-hearted, but of *unparallelled endurance!*

No European nation, not even the Turks, would patiently bear such a condition of affairs. Every where the sovereign would have been forced to change, or to modify, the *personnel* of his ministers and advisers; and Mr. Lincoln is in the hands of Messrs. Seward and Blair, both worse even than McClellan, and — cannot shake them off.

Now, for the first time in my life, I realize why, during the last stages of the dissolution of the Roman empire, honest men escaped into monasteries, or why, at certain epochs of the great French revolution, the best men went to the army.

Ah! to witness here the meanest egotism, imbecility, and intrigue, coolly, one by one, destroy the honor and the future of this noble people. Curse

upon my old age! above all, curse upon my obes-
ity! Curse upon my poverty! What a cesspool!
what a mire! Only legal slaughterers all around!
O, could I go to a camp! but, of course, not to one
under McClellan. · Sigel's camp. Sigel's men are
not soulless; they fight for an idea, without an eye
to the White House.

The rhetors, the stump-speakers, the politicians,
and the intriguers hold the power, and — humanity and history shudder at the results.

Oct. 29. McClellan, with his wonted intrepidity
and rapidity, crossed the Potomac from all directions, pushes on Winchester, and — will find there
wherefrom every animal willingly discharges itself.

A foreign diplomat, one of the most eminent in
the whole *corps*, said yesterday, " No living being
so ardently prays for rain as does McClellan; rain
will prevent fighting, marching, &c." Such is the
estimation of our hero.

Fevers decimated many regiments at Harper's
Ferry. If McClellan would have marched only five
miles a day, fighting even such battles without
any generalship, as he did at Antietam, the army
would be healthier, and by this time would be in
Richmond.

The decision of the court of inquiry between a
patriot and the incarnation of West Point McClellanism, between Martindale and that Fitz-John
Porter, ought to open the eyes of any one, but —
not those of Mr. Lincoln.

Only two days ago Mr. Lincoln declared, that the

reason why McClellan and his pets are not removed is, not any confidence in McClellan's capacity, but to preserve the political balance between the republican and the democratic parties.

If there exist such spiritual creations as providence, genii, or angels watching over the destinies of nations, then, at the sight of Lincoln-Seward-Blair doings, providence, angels, genii avert their faces in despair.

Oct. 30. New regiments coming in. It cuts into the deepest of the heart to see such noble and devoted fellows going to be again wantonly slaughtered by the combined military and civic inefficiency of McClellan-Lincoln-Seward, and, above all, by their utter heartlessness.

When the rebels invaded Maryland, the *fighting* generals, as Heintzelman, advised to mass the troops between the rebels and the Potomac, cut them from their bases and communications, push them towards the North without a possibility of escape, instead of throwing them back on the Potomac. Harper's Ferry would have been saved. Every progress made by the rebels in a Northern direction would have assured their ruin; soon their ammunition would have been exhausted, and surrender was inevitable. But this bold plan of a *fighting* general could not be comprehended by pets and pretorians. Since, daily and daily occasions occur to destroy the rebels; but that is not the game. Instead of cutting the rebels from Gordonsville and Richmond, which could have been done any time during the last five weeks if Heintzelman and Sigel were not so thoroughly weakened by an ignorant, or worse, distribution of troops, McClellan with all his might pushes the rebels back to Richmond, back on their bases and their resources.   O, poor country!

Even I feel humiliated to continually ascertain, by various direct and indirect sources from Europe, in what little estimation— if not worse — is held our administration by the principal statesmen and governments of the old world.

NOVEMBER, 1862.

Empty rhetoric — The future dark and terrible — Wadsworth defeated —
The official bunglers blast every thing they touch — Great and holy
day! McClellan gone overboard! — The planters — Burnside — McClellan nominated for President — Awful events approaching — Dictatorship dawns on the horizon — The catastrophe.

O GOD, O God! to witness how, by the hands
of Lincoln-Seward-McClellan, this noblest human
structure is crumbled — and, perhaps, soon

> Pulvere vix tactæ poterunt monstrare ruinæ.

May God preserve this people — those noble patriots, of which Wadsworth, Wade, Potter of Wis-
consin, Stanton, Governor Andrew, and many others
are the types, when the country will be ruined and
rended by the firm, Lincoln-Seward-McClellan, to
realize the pang, —

> Nessun maggior' dolor' che ricordarsi dell tempo felice
> Nella miseria.

O, I know what it is!

Mr. Seward's letter, October 28, to Messrs. Con-
nover and Palmer, is a display of that empty rhetoric whose dust he is wont to throw into the eyes
of the good-natured masses. His plea for united
action — of course with him — is the most bitter
irony on himself. Mr. Seward's policy and action

are at the helm, and he piloted "our noble ship of state" on worse breakers than those "of eighteen months ago."

Mr. Seward's letter is dumb on the object of the Cooper meeting. Of course, Mr. Seward would rather swallow a viper than applaud the abolition of slavery.

Nov. 5. Lincoln-Seward politically slaughtered the republican party, and with it the country's honor. The future looks dark and terrible. I shudder. Dishonor on all sides. Lincoln will not understand to use the lease of power left to him — or to fall as a man. But to be candid, most of the thus called leaders prepared this defeat, and most of them at the last moment may lack decision and dignity. How repeatedly I warned the Sumners, Wilsons, and other wiseacres, that such will be the end, that the people at large will become exasperated by Lincoln's administration!

The issue brought before the people was all but dignified. It would have been better to make a straightforward issue against the incapacity and the democratic ill-will of McClellan, than to dodge the question, and force honest and noble men to speak against their convictions. The issue, as made, was concocted by journalists, by politicians; but not by statesmen, not by genuine great leaders.

Seward triumphs. His insincerity preëminently contributed to defeat Wadsworth. Mephisto-like, he rejoices in thus having humbled the pure and radical patriots.

At any rate, I shall try to expose Seward. *Arrive que pourra.* But for him the sacred cause would have been victorious, and now — horror! horror!

The pro-Romanist clergy is more furiously and savagely pro-slavery than are the Rhetts, the Yanceys, in the South ; the poor Africo-Americans are, if not the truest Christians in this country, at any rate their Christianity is sublime when compared with the pro-Romanism.

O, for civic intrepidity, or all is lost! High-minded, intrepid, self-forgetful civism and abnegation alone can avert the catastrophe. Such is the mass of the people — but its leaders!

Nov. 8. Hooker has the military instinct in him which lights the fire, and the inspiration of the god of battles ; as Halleck has nothing of the one and of the other, and as Mr Lincoln is — Mr. Lincoln, so Hooker is not to be put in command of the army. Lincoln and Halleck will find out their man. *Similis simili gaudet*, or, *przywitala sie dupa z wiechciem.*

Nov. 9. The official bunglers have blasted every thing they touched : the people's virgin enthusiasm and unparalleled devotion ; they have endangered the country's safety. It is to hope for a miracle to expect any thing for the better at the hands of the bunglers. Will the shallow rhetors, will the would-be leaders in the Congress, be as subservient to the bunglers as they have been up to this hour ?

Nov. 9. Great and holy day! McClellan gone overboard! Better late than never. But this be-lated act of justice to the country cannot atone for

. 27

all the deadly disasters, will not remove the fearful responsibility from Lincoln-Seward-Blair, for having so long sustained this horrible vampire. Now is Seward's turn to jump.

It must be acknowledged, in justice to the average of the better class of planters, that the superficial, sociable intercourse with them is more easy, and what is commonly considered more European, than is similar intercourse with any corresponding class in the North. Therein consists the whole attraction exercised by the Southerners on Europeans visiting America — the diplomats included. I, for one, am always uneasy, anxious, as if touching hot iron, when in intercourse here with men with whom I am very intimate, (on the outside,) and who now are in power. I never felt so out of the track when — once — in intercourse with sovereigns, and with eminent men in Europe.

Nov. 11. General Burnside succeeds to McClellan — gives a military ovation to his predecessor. In his order of the day, Burnside pays homage to McClellan, and thus implicitly condemns the government. Burnside permits McClellan to issue such a parting word as must shake the army and the country.

Nov. 12. The democrats nominate McClellan for the next presidency. Thus Mr. Lincoln's helplessness, Seward's hatred of the republican creed, the treason, the imbecility, the intrigues of various others, the lack of civic energy in the New York republican press and in the republican politicians, except some repeatedly mentioned in this Diary, — all this combined has built up a pedestal for such a McClellan !

Strange and awful events may occur even before the end of Mr. Lincoln's administration. The democratic leaders are perverse, unprincipled, reckless, daring beyond conception ; success is their creed, and no conscience, no honor restrain them ; and in the management of the public opinion and of their party the democrats have evidenced a skill far above that of the republican leaders ; further, the democrats evoke the vilest, the most brutish passions dormant in the masses ; the democrats are supported by all that is brutal, savage, ignorant, and sordid ; and, to crown and strengthen all, the democrats, united to Romanist priesthood, rule over the Irishry.

And thus the relentless hatred with which the democrats persecute any elevated, noble, humane aspiration ; the helplessness, the incapacity of the official and unofficial leaders of the republican party : both these agencies combined may deal such a blow to the pure and humane republican creed that it may not recover therefrom during the next twenty-- five years.

To sum up, —

Dictatorship with Mc Clellan seems to dawn upon the horizon ; the smallest disaster — Burnside, ah ! — will precipitate the catastrophe. I pray to God (and for the first time) that I may be mistaken.